THIS IS A WORK OF FICTION AND ANY RESEMBLANCE OF CHARACTERS TO
PERSONS LIVING OR DEAD IS PURELY COINCIDENTAL.

KIDS CAN PRESS ACKNOWLEDGES THE FINANCIAL SUPPORT OF THE
GOVERNMENT OF ONTARIO, THROUGH THE ONTARIO MEDIA DEVELOPMENT
CORPORATION'S ONTARIO BOOK INITIATIVE; THE ONTARIO ARTS COUNCIL;
THE CANADA COUNCIL FOR THE ARTS; AND THE GOVERNMENT OF CANADA,
THROUGH THE BPIDP, FOR OUR PUBLISHING ACTIVITY.

PUBLISHED IN CANADA BY   PUBLISHED IN THE U.S. BY
KIDS CAN PRESS LTD.   KIDS CAN PRESS LTD.
25 DOCKSIDE DRIVE   2250 MILITARY ROAD
TORONTO, ON   M5A 0B5   TONAWANDA, NY 14150

WWW.KIDSCANPRESS.COM

EDITED BY KAREN LI
DESIGNED BY RACHEL DI SALLE

THE HARDCOVER EDITION OF THIS BOOK IS SMYTH SEWN CASEBOUND.
THE PAPERBACK EDITION OF THIS BOOK IS LIMP SEWN WITH A DRAWN-ON
COVER.

MANUFACTURED IN SHEN ZHEN, GUANG DONG, P.R. CHINA, IN 4/2012 BY
PRINTPLUS LIMITED

CM 12 0 9 8 7 6 5 4 3 2 1
CM PA 12 0 9 8 7 6 5 4 3 2 1

LIBRARY AND ARCHIVES CANADA CATALOGUING IN PUBLICATION

RIOUX, JO-ANNE
      THE GOLDEN TWINE / JO RIOUX.

(CAT'S CRADLE)
ISBN 978-1-55453-636-8 (BOUND)   ISBN 978-1-55453-637-5 (PBK.)

I. TITLE. II. SERIES: RIOUX, JO-ANNE. CAT'S CRADLE.

PN6733.R56G65 2012   J741.5'971   C2012-900814-1

Kids Can Press is a Corus™ Entertainment company

CAT'S CRADLE

Book 1 · The Golden Twine

JO RIOUX

KIDS CAN PRESS

To Keith, for always believing in me.

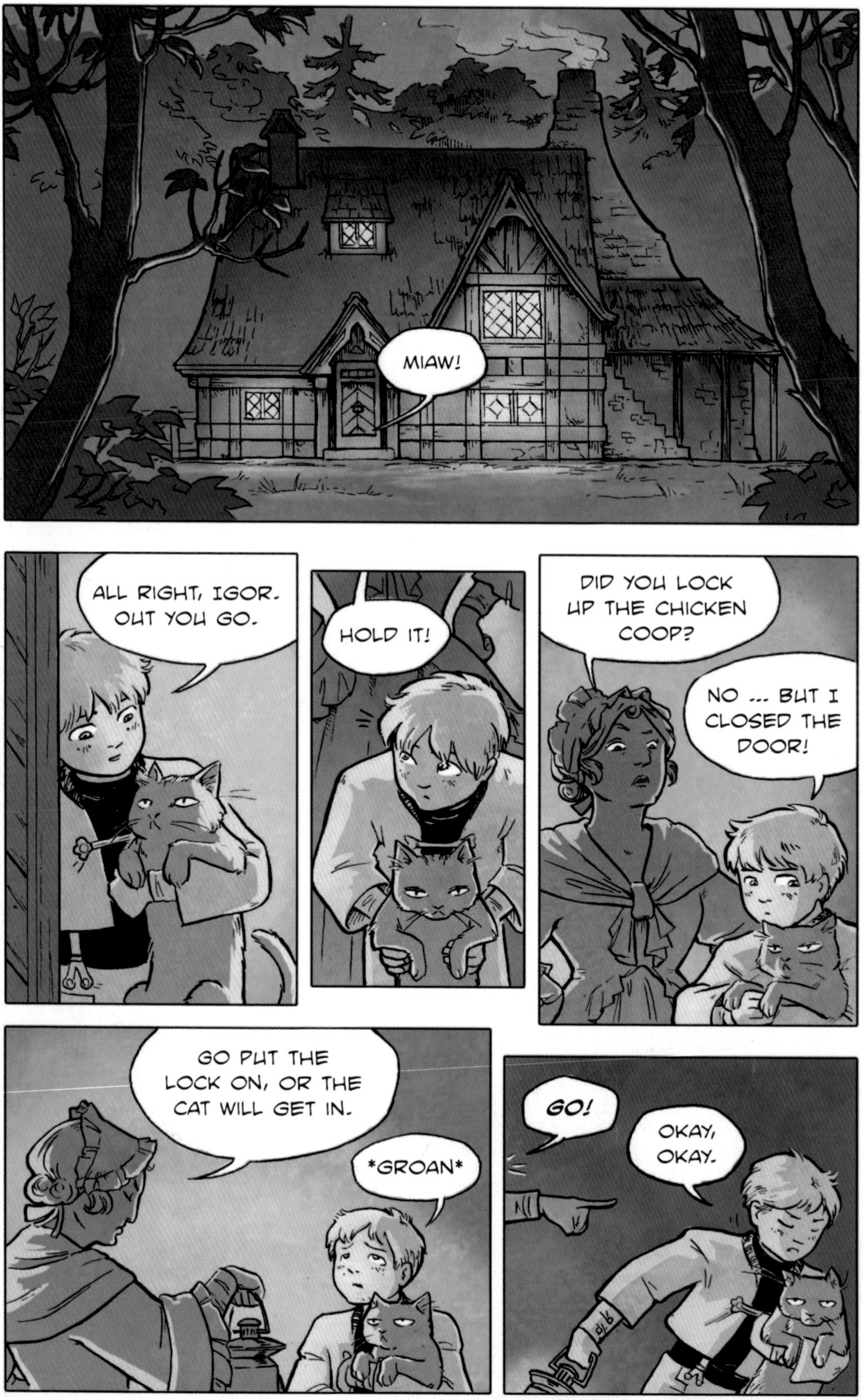
MIAW!
ALL RIGHT, IGOR. OUT YOU GO.
HOLD IT!
DID YOU LOCK UP THE CHICKEN COOP?
NO ... BUT I CLOSED THE DOOR!
GO PUT THE LOCK ON, OR THE CAT WILL GET IN.
GROAN
GO!
OKAY, OKAY.

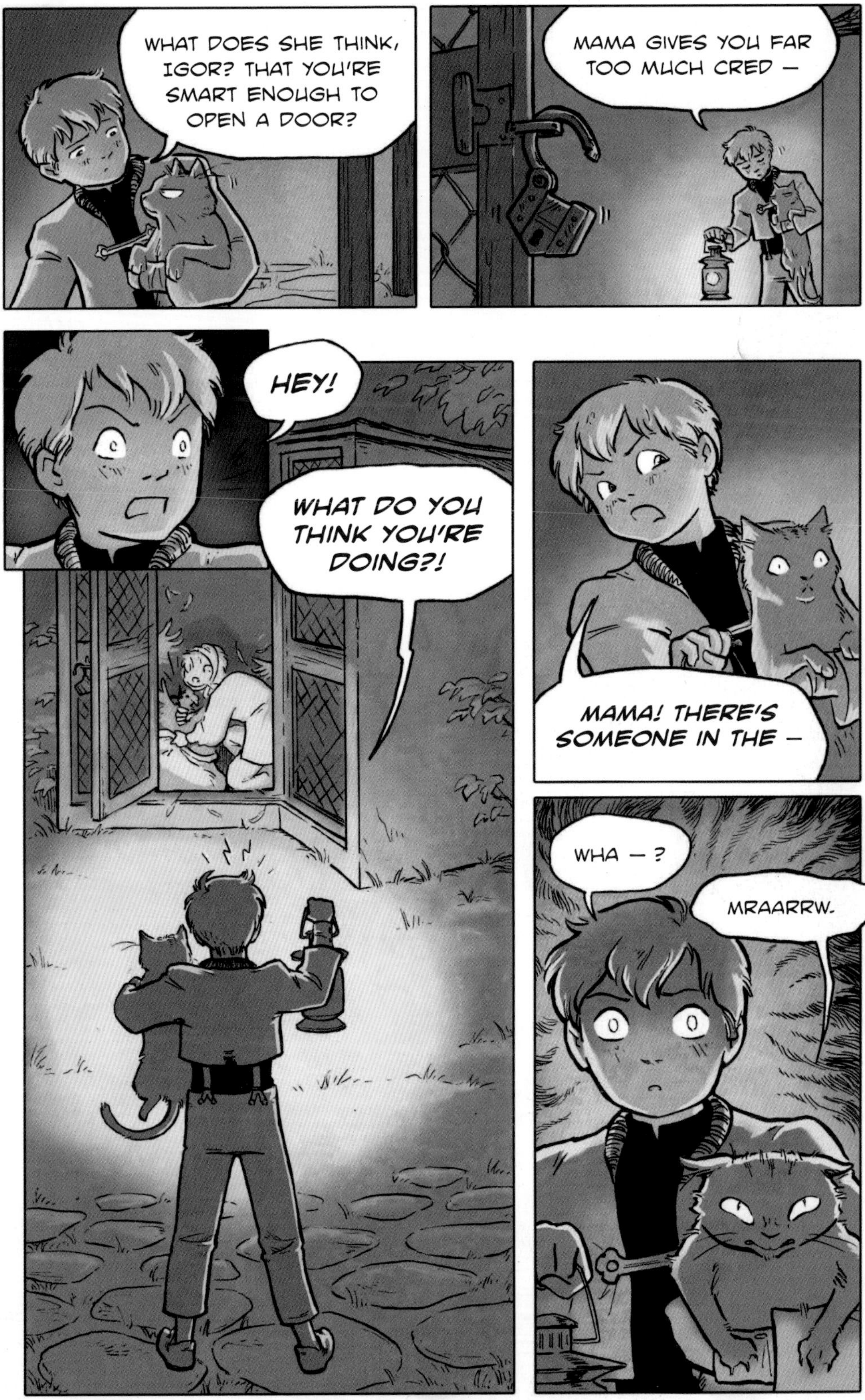
WHAT DOES SHE THINK, IGOR? THAT YOU'RE SMART ENOUGH TO OPEN A DOOR?
MAMA GIVES YOU FAR TOO MUCH CRED —
HEY!
WHAT DO YOU THINK YOU'RE DOING?!
MAMA! THERE'S SOMEONE IN THE —
WHA — ?
MRAARRW.

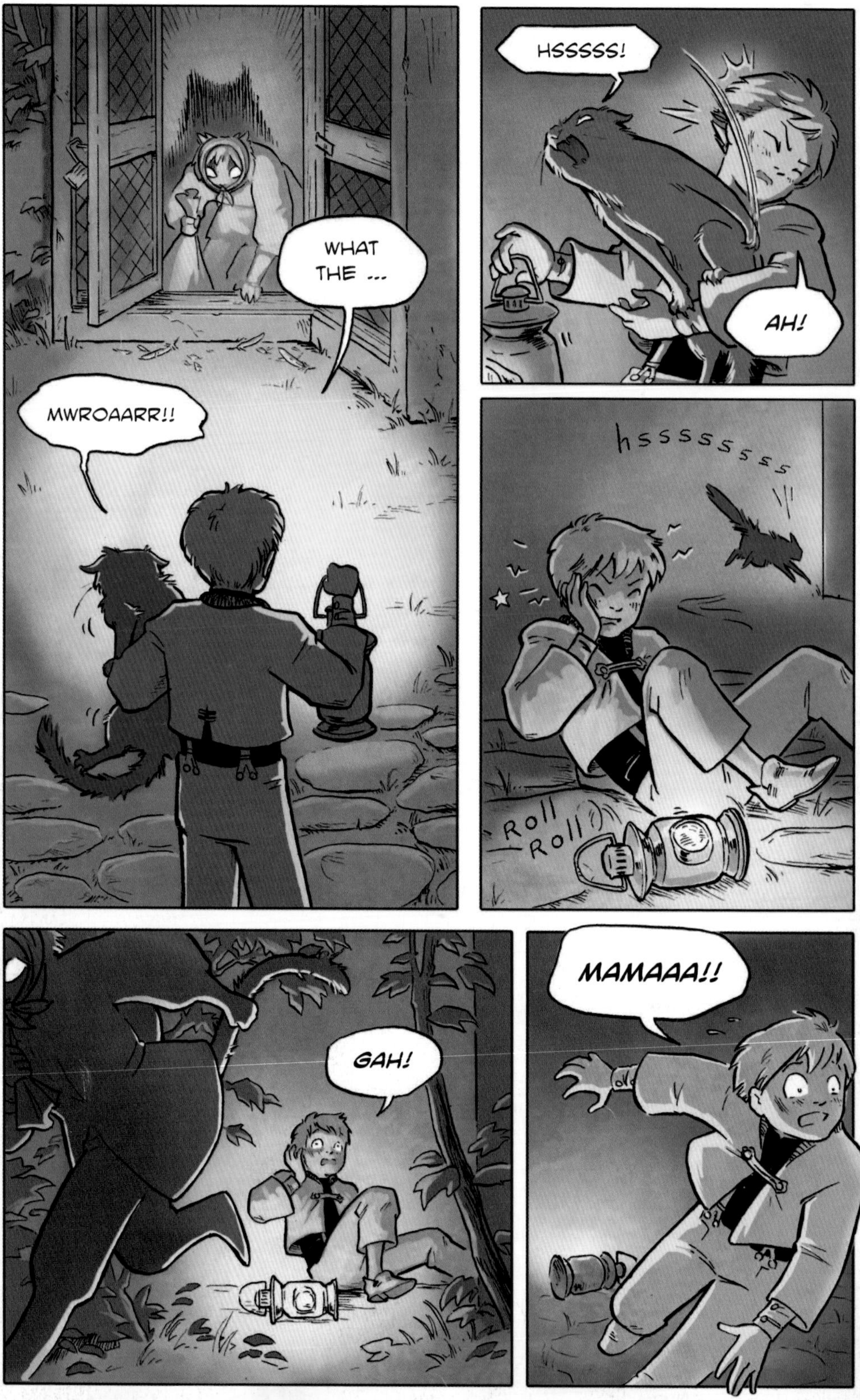
WHAT THE ...
MWROAARR!!
HSSSSS!
AH!
hsssssss
Roll Roll
GAH!
MAMAAA!!

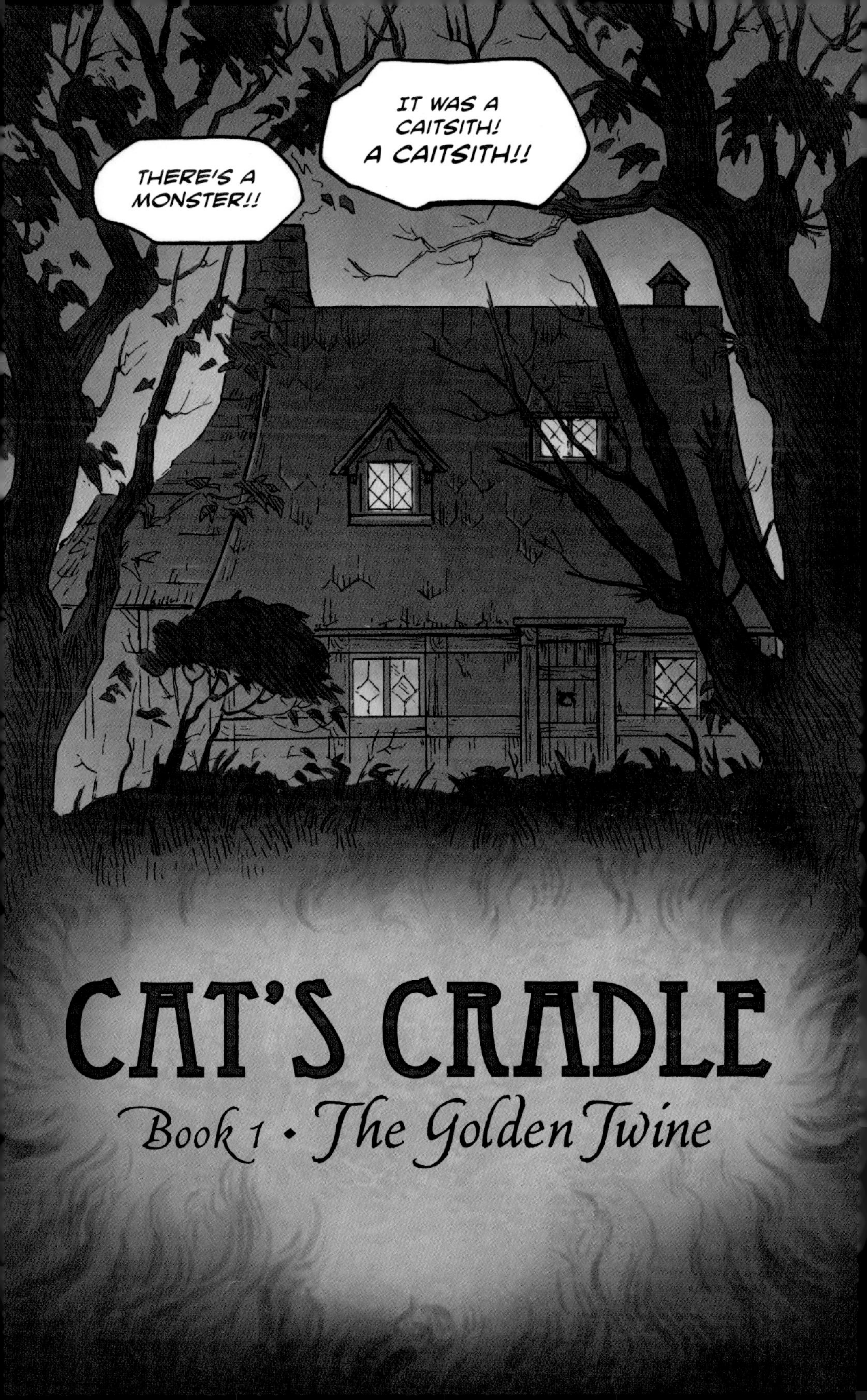
THERE'S A MONSTER!!
IT WAS A CAITSITH! A CAITSITH!!
CAT'S CRADLE
Book 1 • The Golden Twine

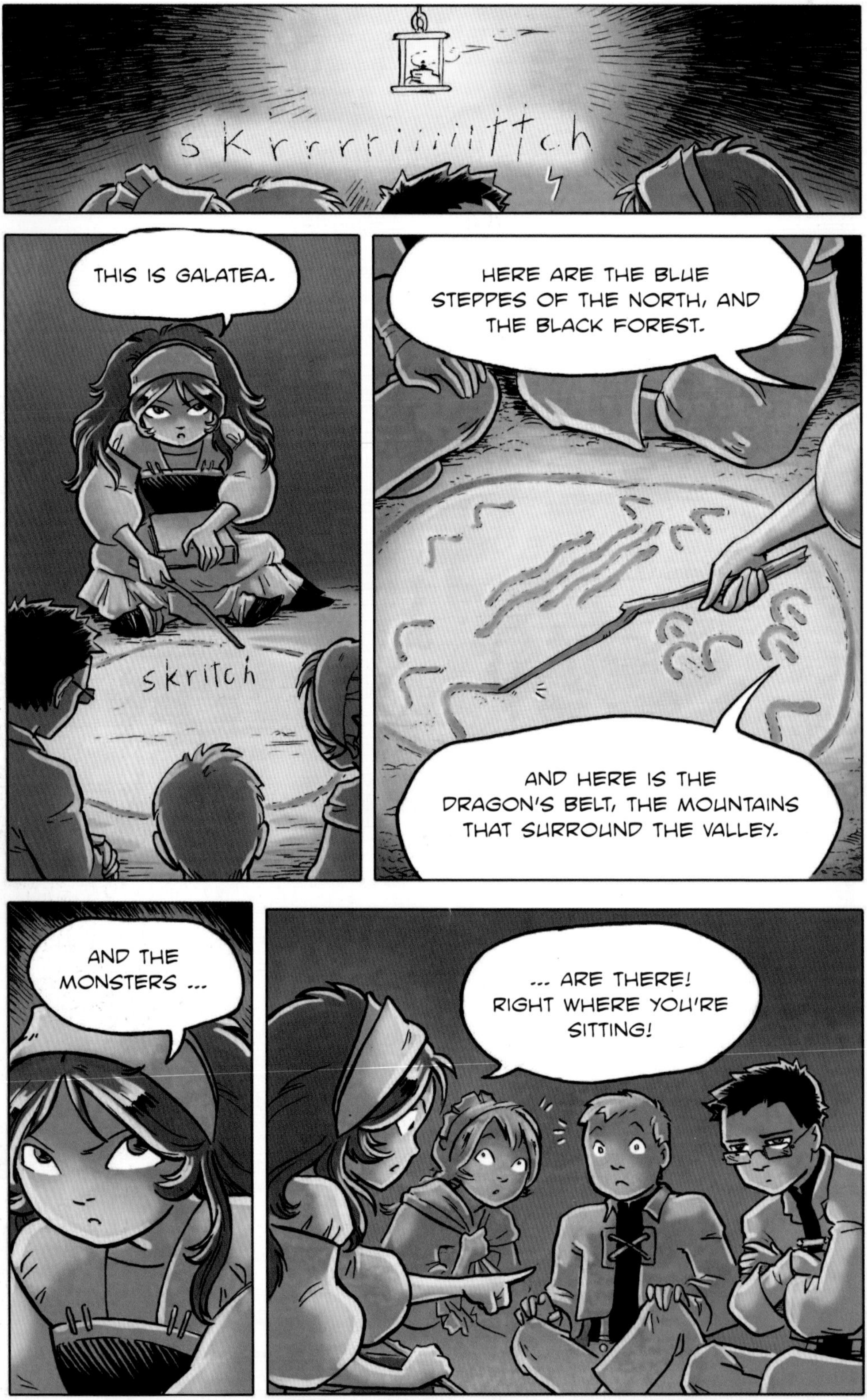
sKrrrriiiiittch
THIS IS GALATEA.
skritch
HERE ARE THE BLUE STEPPES OF THE NORTH, AND THE BLACK FOREST.
AND HERE IS THE DRAGON'S BELT, THE MOUNTAINS THAT SURROUND THE VALLEY.
AND THE MONSTERS ...
... ARE THERE! RIGHT WHERE YOU'RE SITTING!

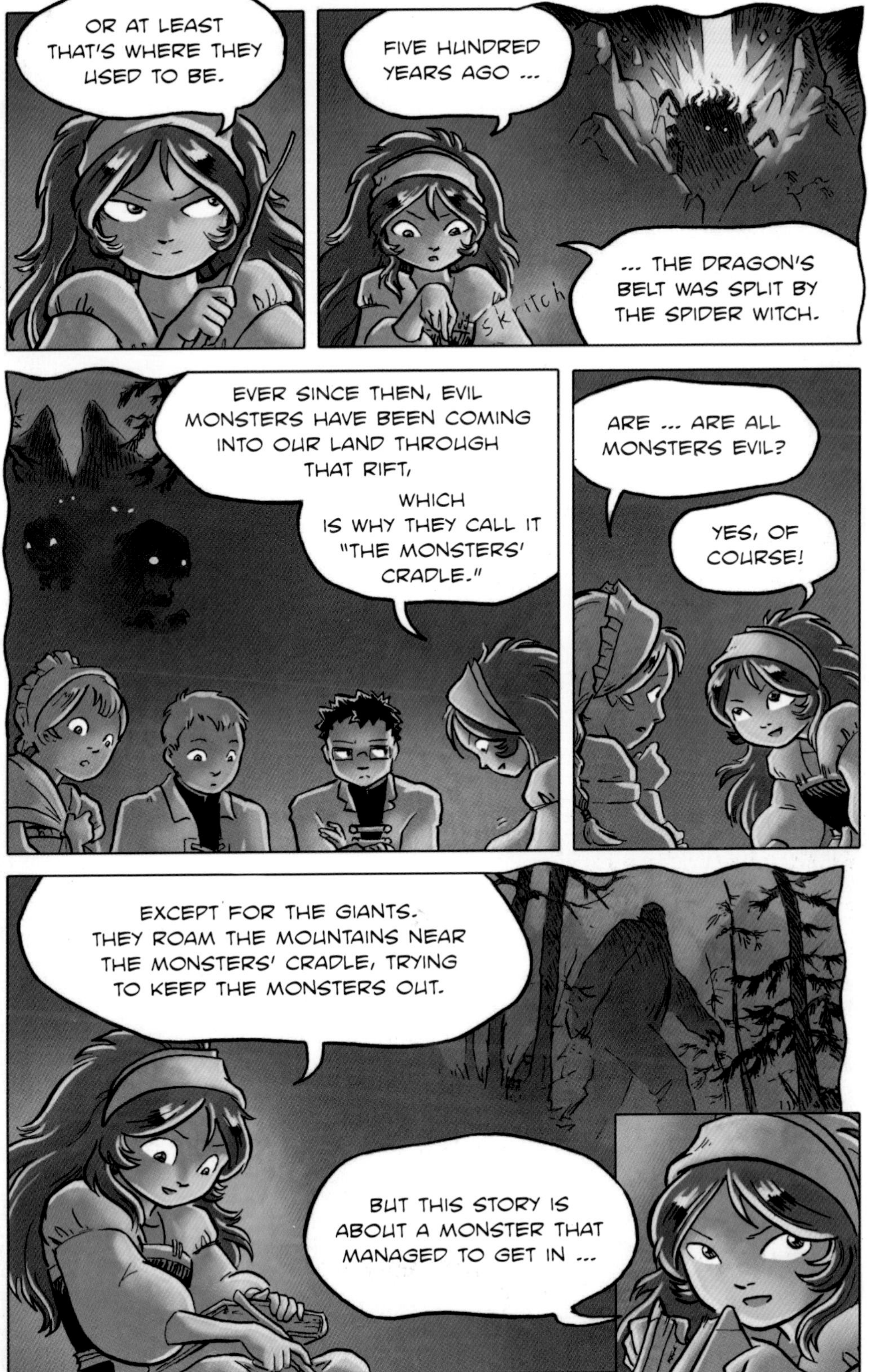
OR AT LEAST THAT'S WHERE THEY USED TO BE.
FIVE HUNDRED YEARS AGO ...
... THE DRAGON'S BELT WAS SPLIT BY THE SPIDER WITCH.
skritch
EVER SINCE THEN, EVIL MONSTERS HAVE BEEN COMING INTO OUR LAND THROUGH THAT RIFT,
WHICH IS WHY THEY CALL IT "THE MONSTERS' CRADLE."
ARE ... ARE ALL MONSTERS EVIL?
YES, OF COURSE!
EXCEPT FOR THE GIANTS. THEY ROAM THE MOUNTAINS NEAR THE MONSTERS' CRADLE, TRYING TO KEEP THE MONSTERS OUT.
BUT THIS STORY IS ABOUT A MONSTER THAT MANAGED TO GET IN ...

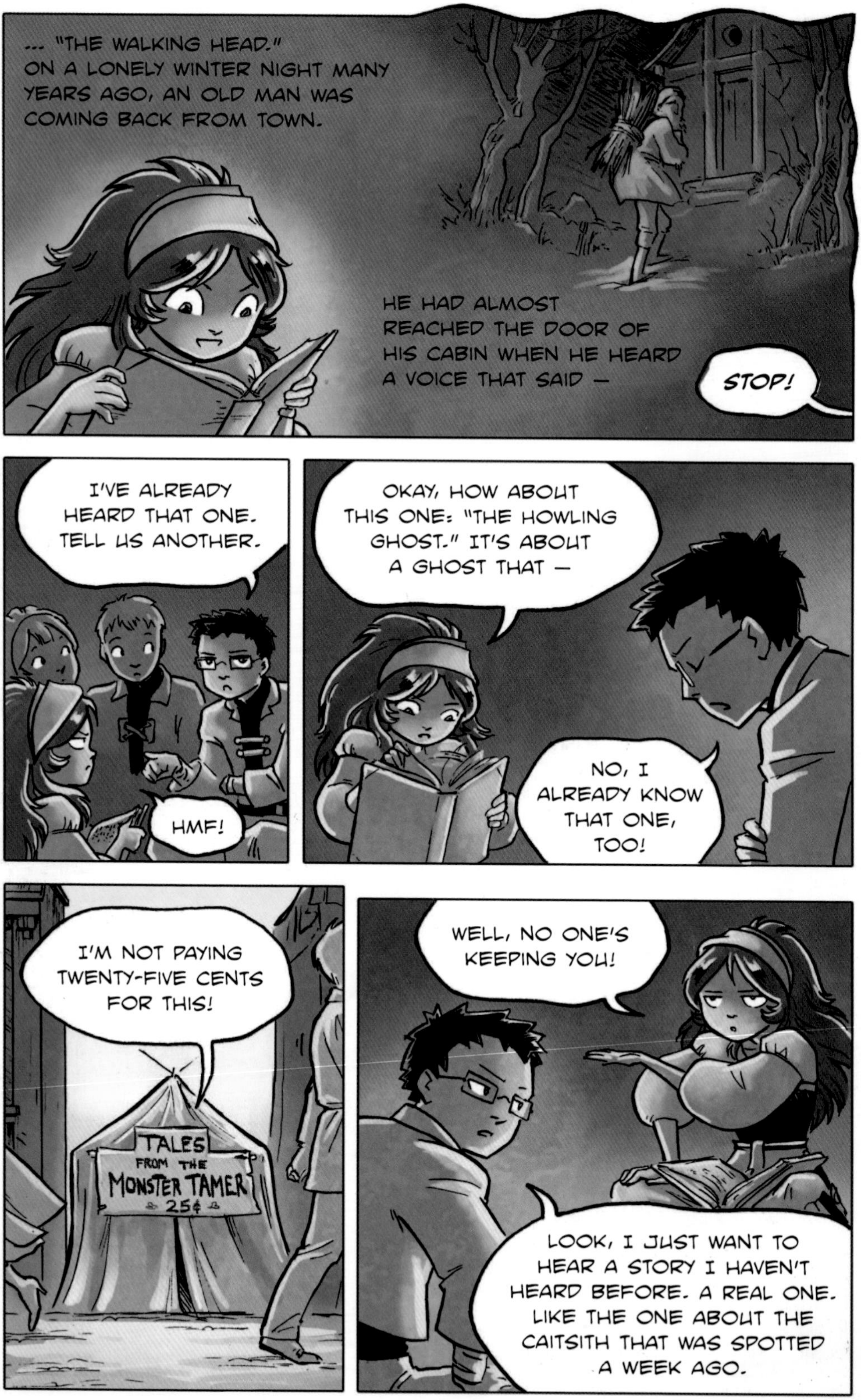
... "THE WALKING HEAD."
ON A LONELY WINTER NIGHT MANY YEARS AGO, AN OLD MAN WAS COMING BACK FROM TOWN.
HE HAD ALMOST REACHED THE DOOR OF HIS CABIN WHEN HE HEARD A VOICE THAT SAID —
STOP!
I'VE ALREADY HEARD THAT ONE. TELL US ANOTHER.
HMF!
OKAY, HOW ABOUT THIS ONE: "THE HOWLING GHOST." IT'S ABOUT A GHOST THAT —
NO, I ALREADY KNOW THAT ONE, TOO!
I'M NOT PAYING TWENTY-FIVE CENTS FOR THIS!
TALES FROM THE MONSTER TAMER 25¢
WELL, NO ONE'S KEEPING YOU!
LOOK, I JUST WANT TO HEAR A STORY I HAVEN'T HEARD BEFORE. A REAL ONE. LIKE THE ONE ABOUT THE CAITSITH THAT WAS SPOTTED A WEEK AGO.

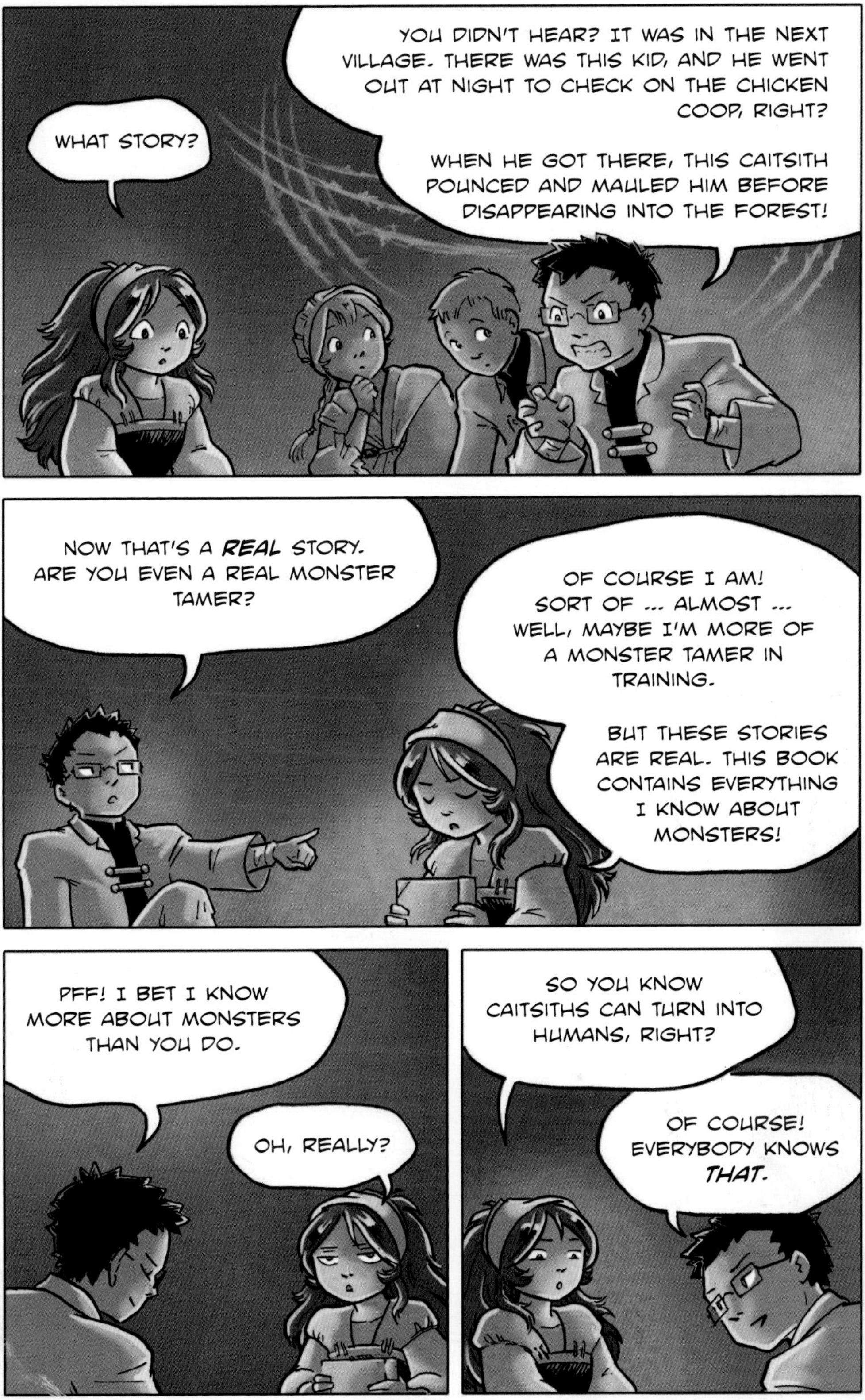
WHAT STORY?
YOU DIDN'T HEAR? IT WAS IN THE NEXT VILLAGE. THERE WAS THIS KID, AND HE WENT OUT AT NIGHT TO CHECK ON THE CHICKEN COOP, RIGHT?
WHEN HE GOT THERE, THIS CAITSITH POUNCED AND MAULED HIM BEFORE DISAPPEARING INTO THE FOREST!
NOW THAT'S A ***REAL*** STORY. ARE YOU EVEN A REAL MONSTER TAMER?
OF COURSE I AM! SORT OF ... ALMOST ... WELL, MAYBE I'M MORE OF A MONSTER TAMER IN TRAINING.
BUT THESE STORIES ARE REAL. THIS BOOK CONTAINS EVERYTHING I KNOW ABOUT MONSTERS!
PFF! I BET I KNOW MORE ABOUT MONSTERS THAN YOU DO.
OH, REALLY?
SO YOU KNOW CAITSITHS CAN TURN INTO HUMANS, RIGHT?
OF COURSE! EVERYBODY KNOWS *THAT*.

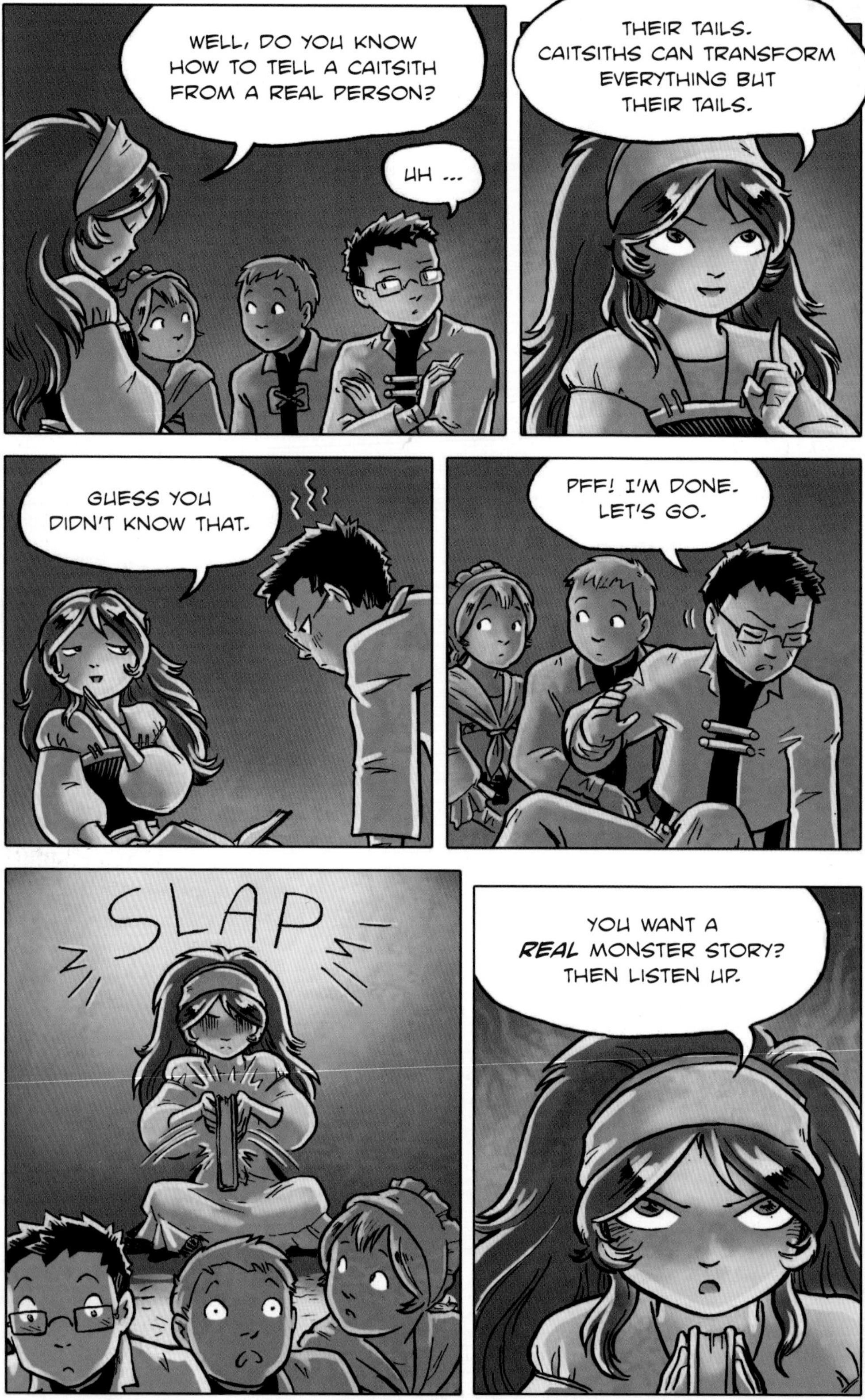
WELL, DO YOU KNOW HOW TO TELL A CAITSITH FROM A REAL PERSON?
UH ...
THEIR TAILS. CAITSITHS CAN TRANSFORM EVERYTHING BUT THEIR TAILS.
GUESS YOU DIDN'T KNOW THAT.
PFF! I'M DONE. LET'S GO.
SLAP
YOU WANT A *REAL* MONSTER STORY? THEN LISTEN UP.

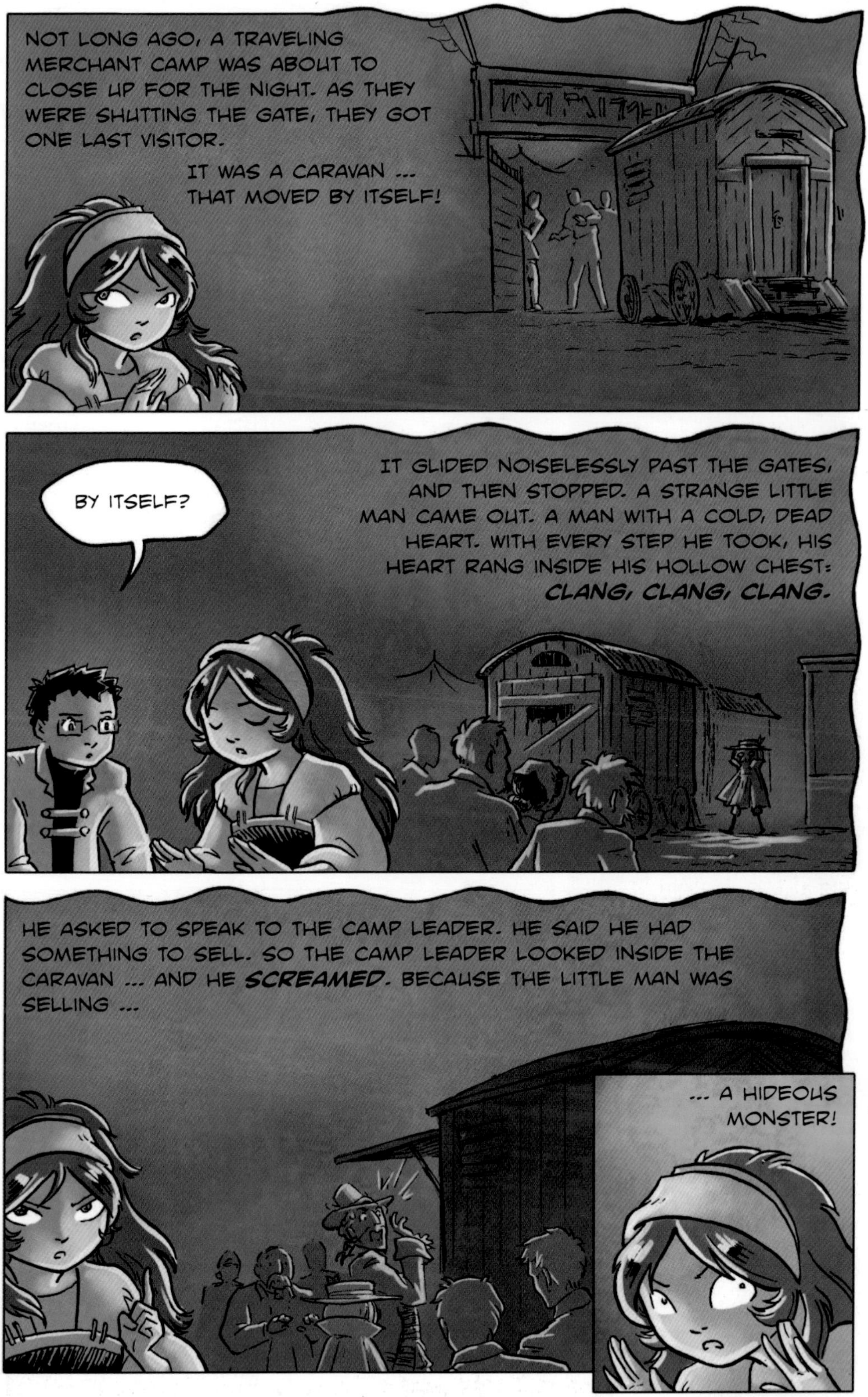
NOT LONG AGO, A TRAVELING MERCHANT CAMP WAS ABOUT TO CLOSE UP FOR THE NIGHT. AS THEY WERE SHUTTING THE GATE, THEY GOT ONE LAST VISITOR.
IT WAS A CARAVAN ... THAT MOVED BY ITSELF!
BY ITSELF?
IT GLIDED NOISELESSLY PAST THE GATES, AND THEN STOPPED. A STRANGE LITTLE MAN CAME OUT. A MAN WITH A COLD, DEAD HEART. WITH EVERY STEP HE TOOK, HIS HEART RANG INSIDE HIS HOLLOW CHEST: CLANG, CLANG, CLANG.
HE ASKED TO SPEAK TO THE CAMP LEADER. HE SAID HE HAD SOMETHING TO SELL. SO THE CAMP LEADER LOOKED INSIDE THE CARAVAN ... AND HE SCREAMED. BECAUSE THE LITTLE MAN WAS SELLING ...
... A HIDEOUS MONSTER!

HOW HIDEOUS?

TOO HIDEOUS TO COME OUT OF THE SHADOW OF THE CARAVAN. BUT HIS EYES BURNED LIKE EMBERS! AND HIS BLOOD-CURDLING WAILS COULD BE HEARD THROUGHOUT THE NIGHT.

AWOOO! AWOO!

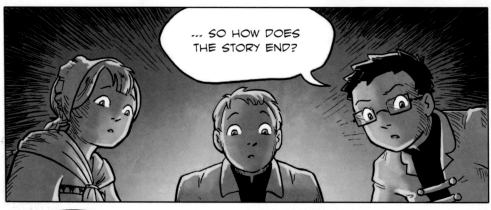

... SO HOW DOES THE STORY END?

IT DOESN'T. THE MONSTER'S STILL HERE, IN THIS CAMP!

WHAT?!

NO WAY!

FOLLOW ME!

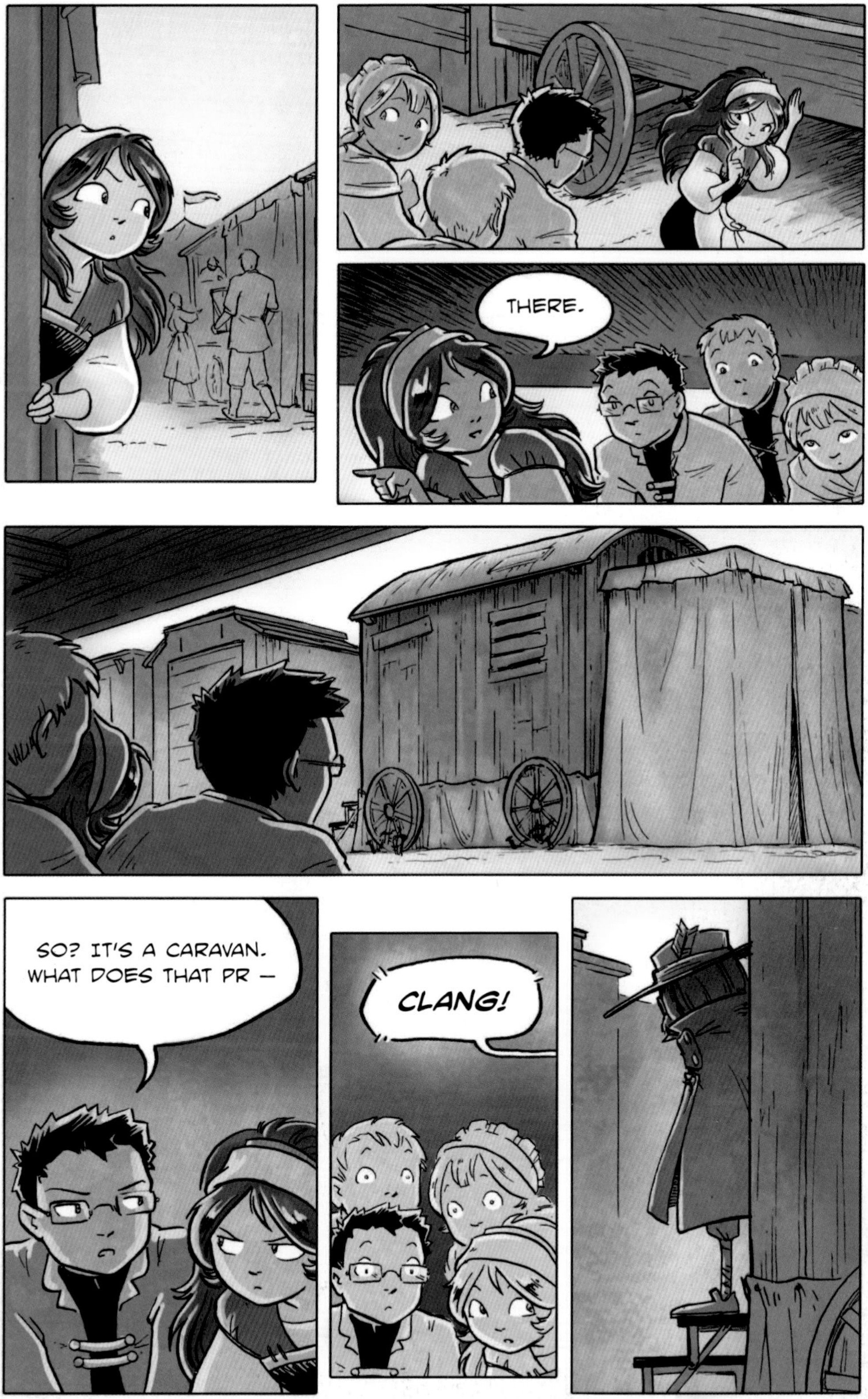
THERE.
SO? IT'S A CARAVAN. WHAT DOES THAT PR —
CLANG!

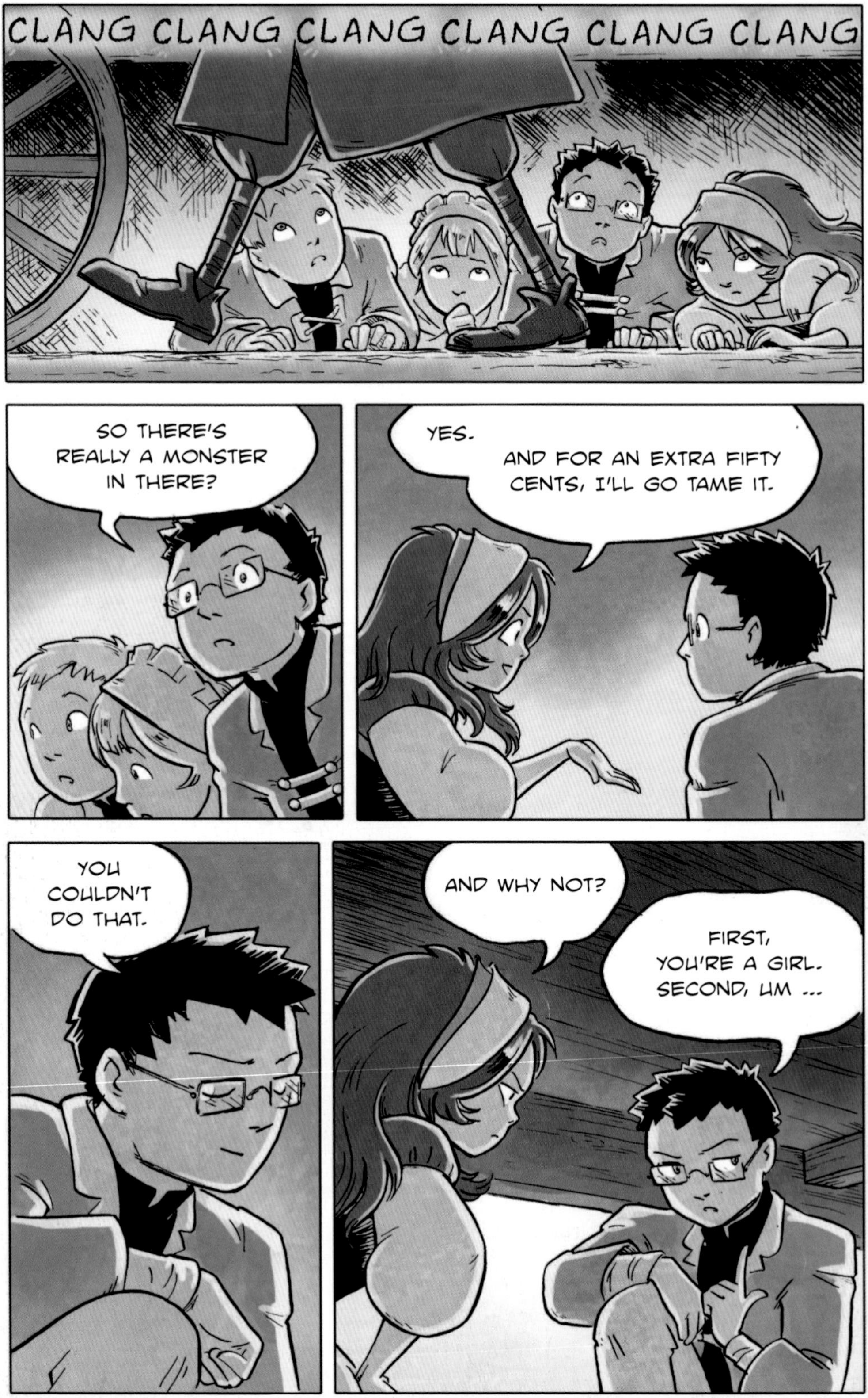
CLANG CLANG CLANG CLANG CLANG CLANG
SO THERE'S REALLY A MONSTER IN THERE?
YES.
AND FOR AN EXTRA FIFTY CENTS, I'LL GO TAME IT.
YOU COULDN'T DO THAT.
AND WHY NOT?
FIRST, YOU'RE A GIRL. SECOND, UM ...

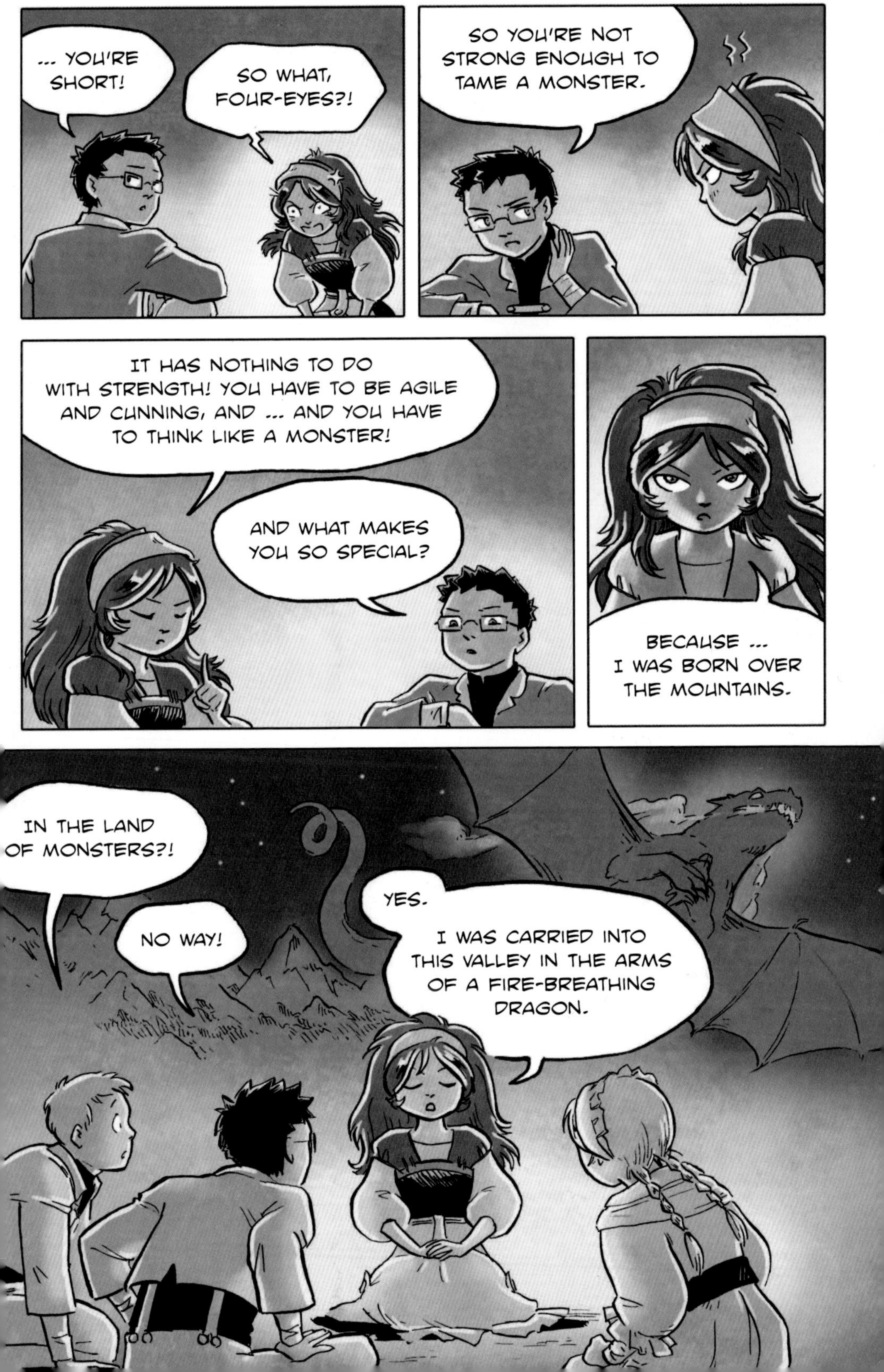
... YOU'RE SHORT!
SO WHAT, FOUR-EYES?!
SO YOU'RE NOT STRONG ENOUGH TO TAME A MONSTER.
IT HAS NOTHING TO DO WITH STRENGTH! YOU HAVE TO BE AGILE AND CUNNING, AND ... AND YOU HAVE TO THINK LIKE A MONSTER!
AND WHAT MAKES YOU SO SPECIAL?
BECAUSE ... I WAS BORN OVER THE MOUNTAINS.
IN THE LAND OF MONSTERS?!
NO WAY!
YES.
I WAS CARRIED INTO THIS VALLEY IN THE ARMS OF A FIRE-BREATHING DRAGON.

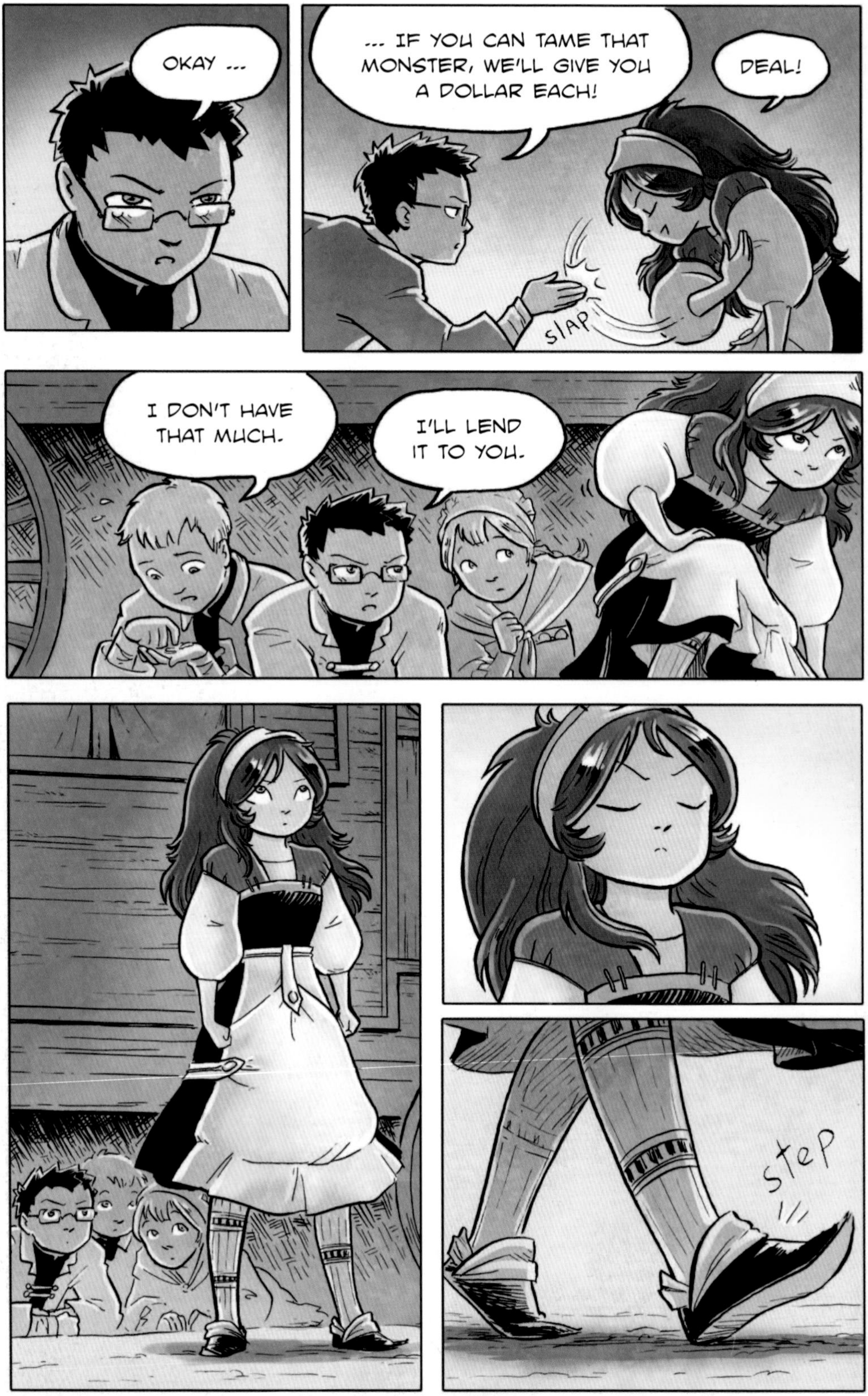
OKAY ...
... IF YOU CAN TAME THAT MONSTER, WE'LL GIVE YOU A DOLLAR EACH!
DEAL!
SLAP
I DON'T HAVE THAT MUCH.
I'LL LEND IT TO YOU.
STEP

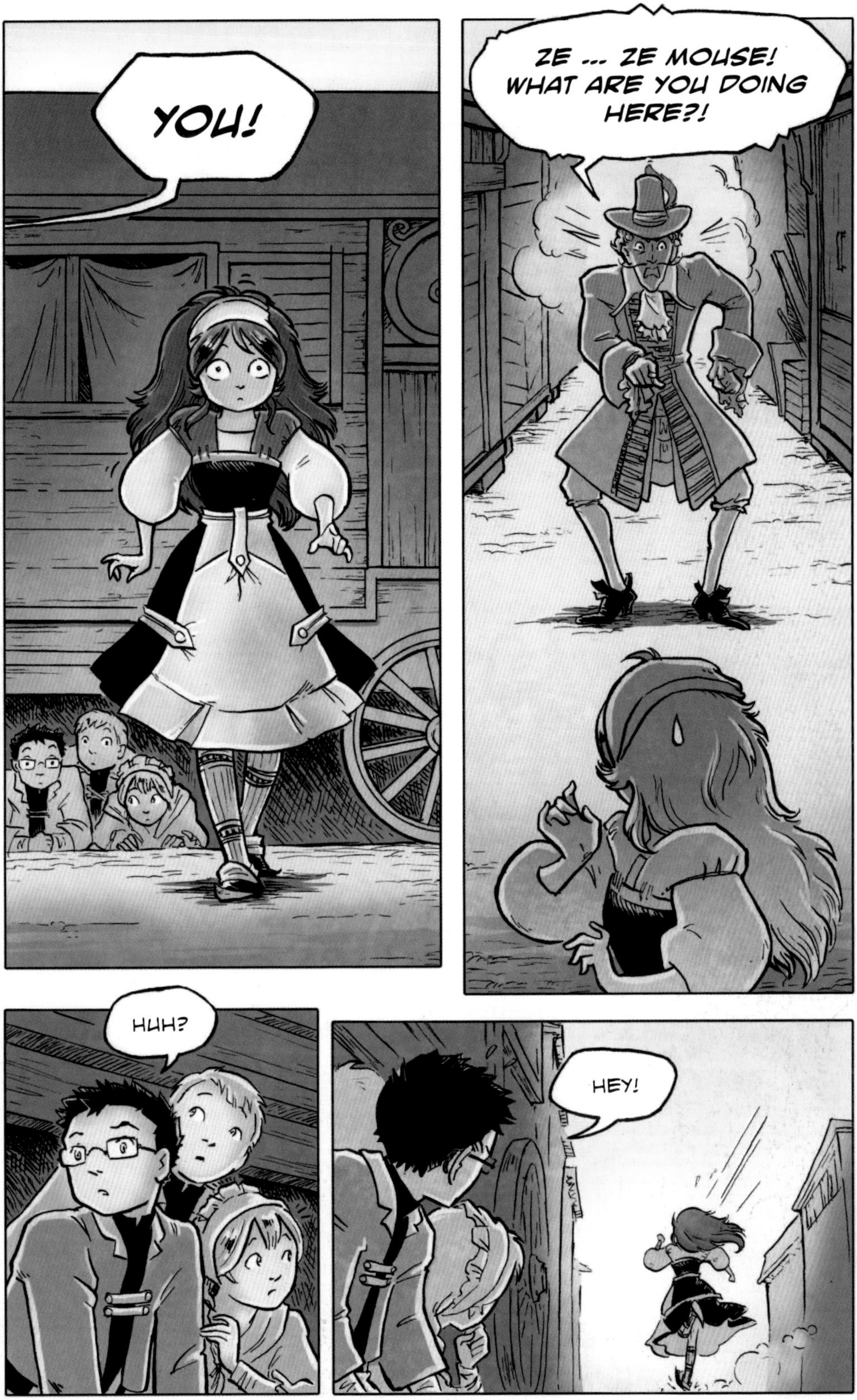
YOU!
ZE ... ZE MOUSE! WHAT ARE YOU DOING HERE?!
HUH?
HEY!

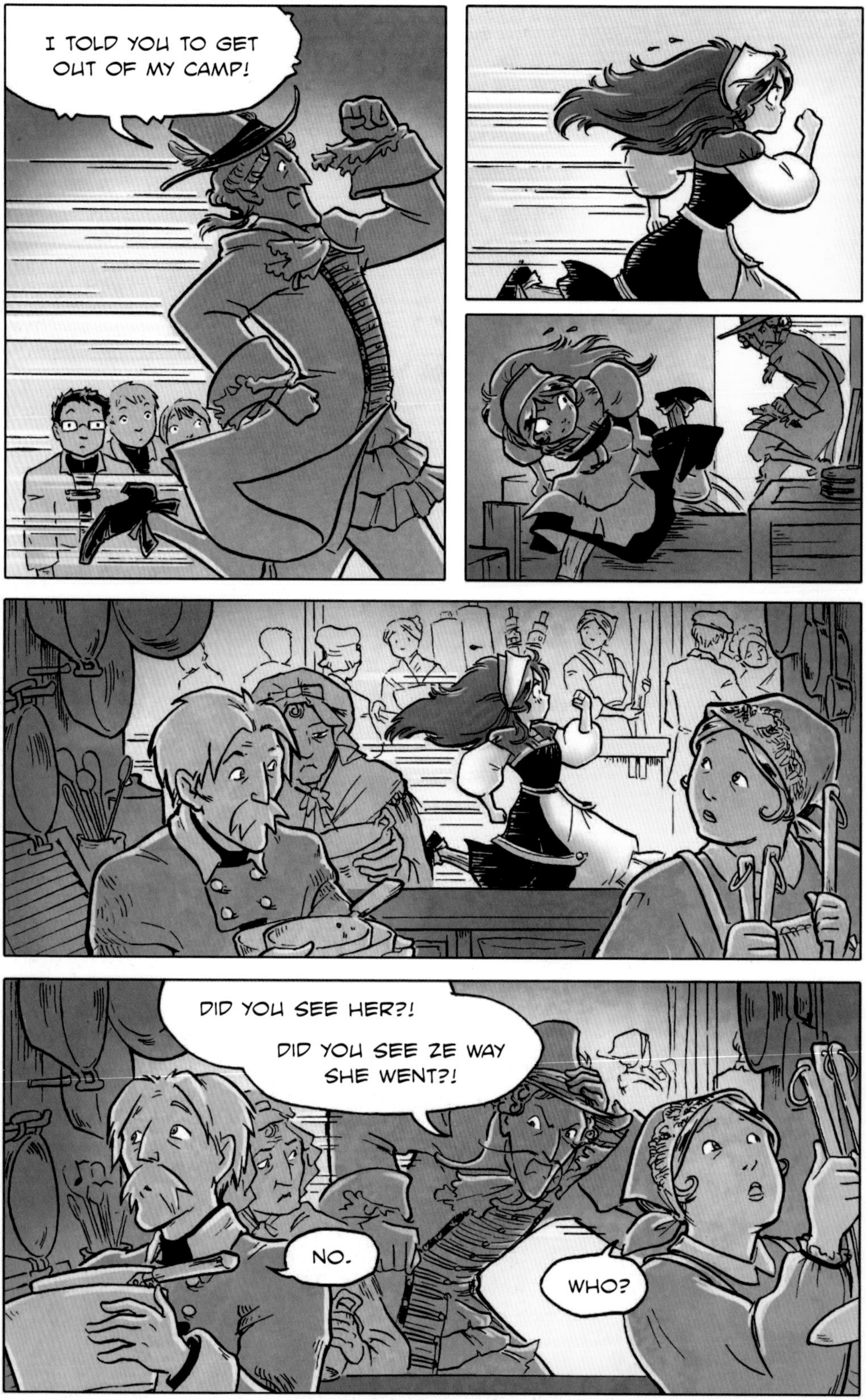
I TOLD YOU TO GET OUT OF MY CAMP!
DID YOU SEE HER?!
DID YOU SEE ZE WAY SHE WENT?!
NO.
WHO?

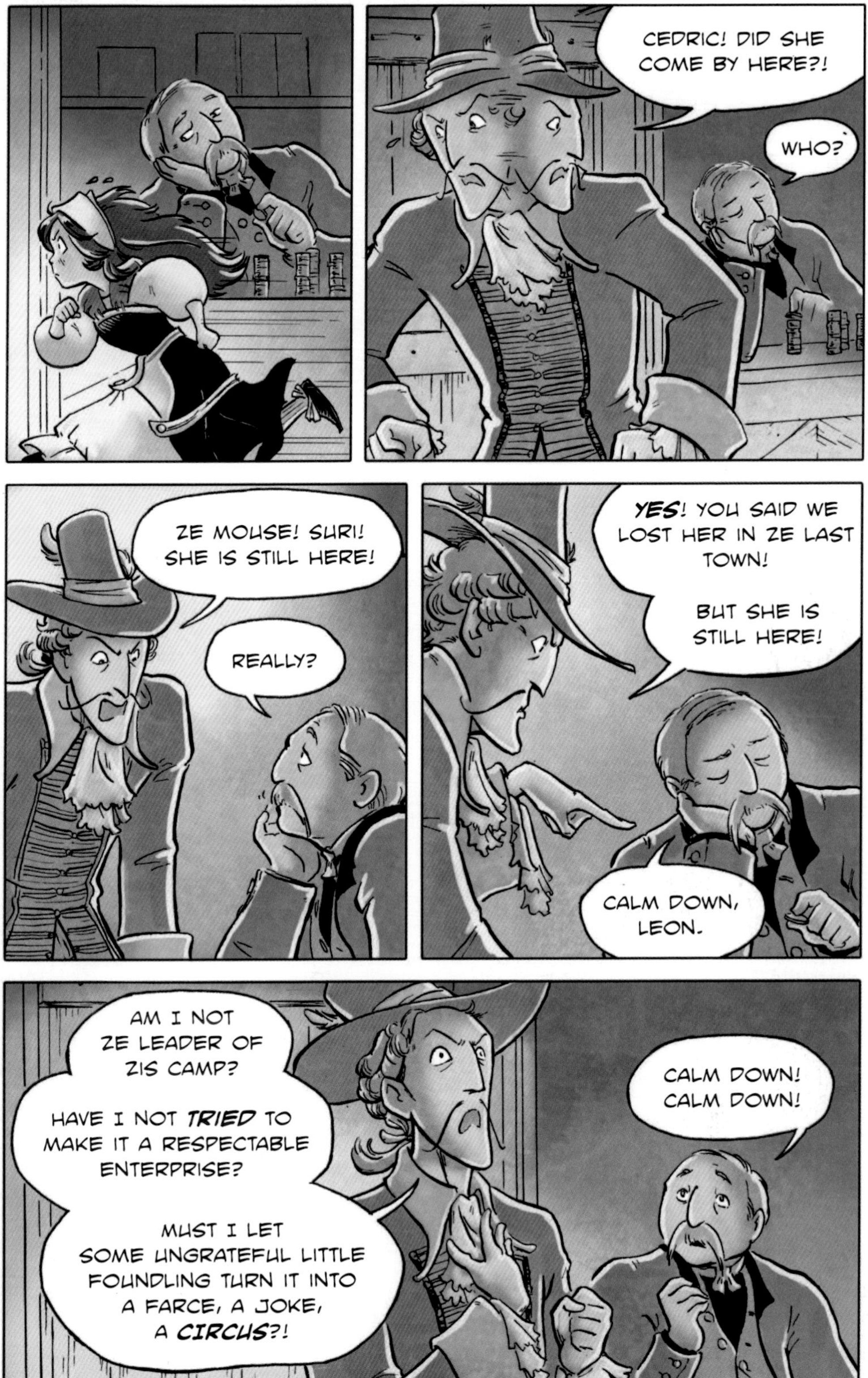
CEDRIC! DID SHE COME BY HERE?!
WHO?
ZE MOUSE! SURI! SHE IS STILL HERE!
REALLY?
YES! YOU SAID WE LOST HER IN ZE LAST TOWN!
BUT SHE IS STILL HERE!
CALM DOWN, LEON.
AM I NOT ZE LEADER OF ZIS CAMP?
HAVE I NOT TRIED TO MAKE IT A RESPECTABLE ENTERPRISE?
MUST I LET SOME UNGRATEFUL LITTLE FOUNDLING TURN IT INTO A FARCE, A JOKE, A CIRCUS?!
CALM DOWN! CALM DOWN!

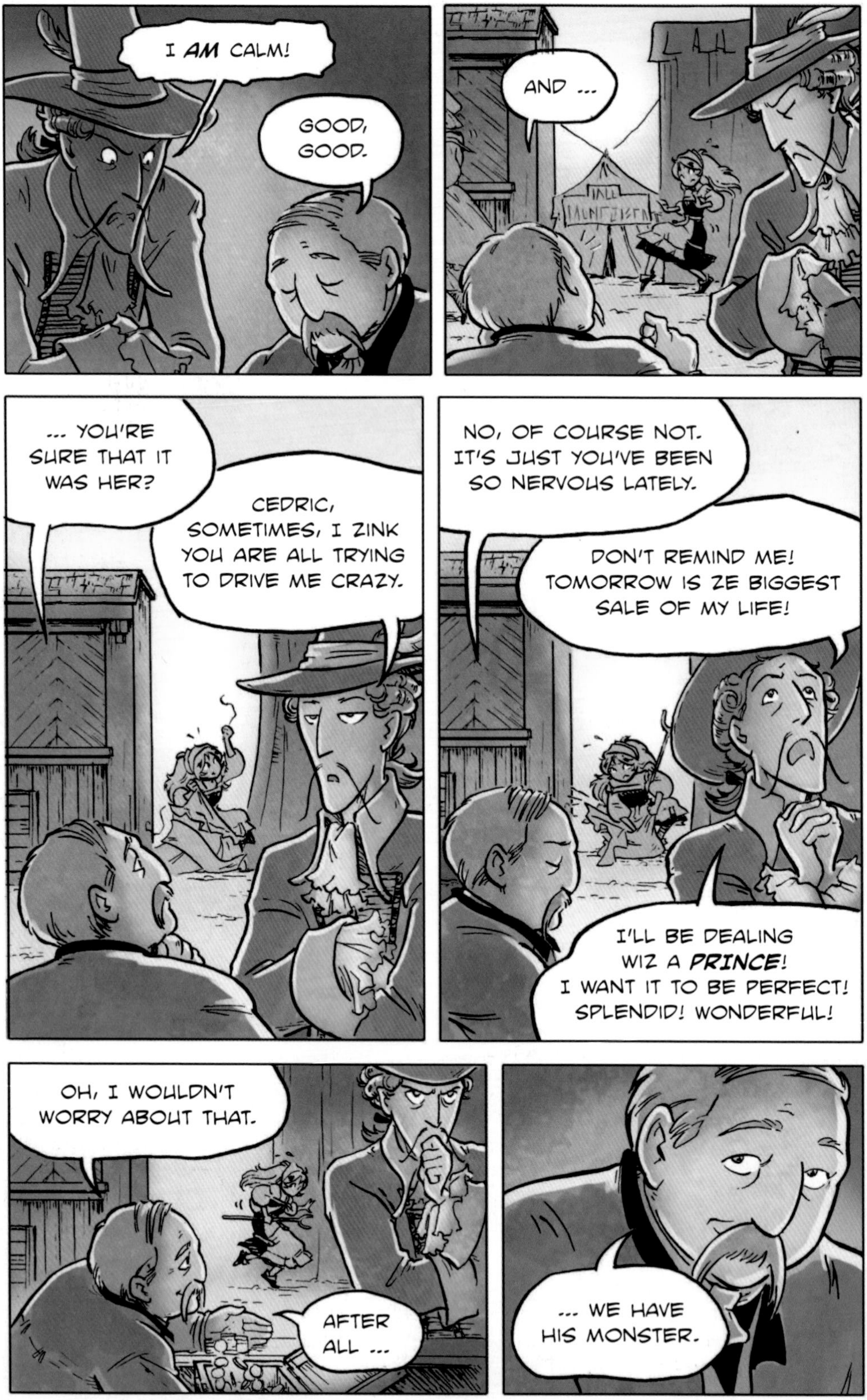
I AM CALM!
GOOD, GOOD.
AND ...
... YOU'RE SURE THAT IT WAS HER?
CEDRIC, SOMETIMES, I ZINK YOU ARE ALL TRYING TO DRIVE ME CRAZY.
NO, OF COURSE NOT. IT'S JUST YOU'VE BEEN SO NERVOUS LATELY.
DON'T REMIND ME! TOMORROW IS ZE BIGGEST SALE OF MY LIFE!
I'LL BE DEALING WIZ A PRINCE! I WANT IT TO BE PERFECT! SPLENDID! WONDERFUL!
OH, I WOULDN'T WORRY ABOUT THAT.
AFTER ALL ...
... WE HAVE HIS MONSTER.

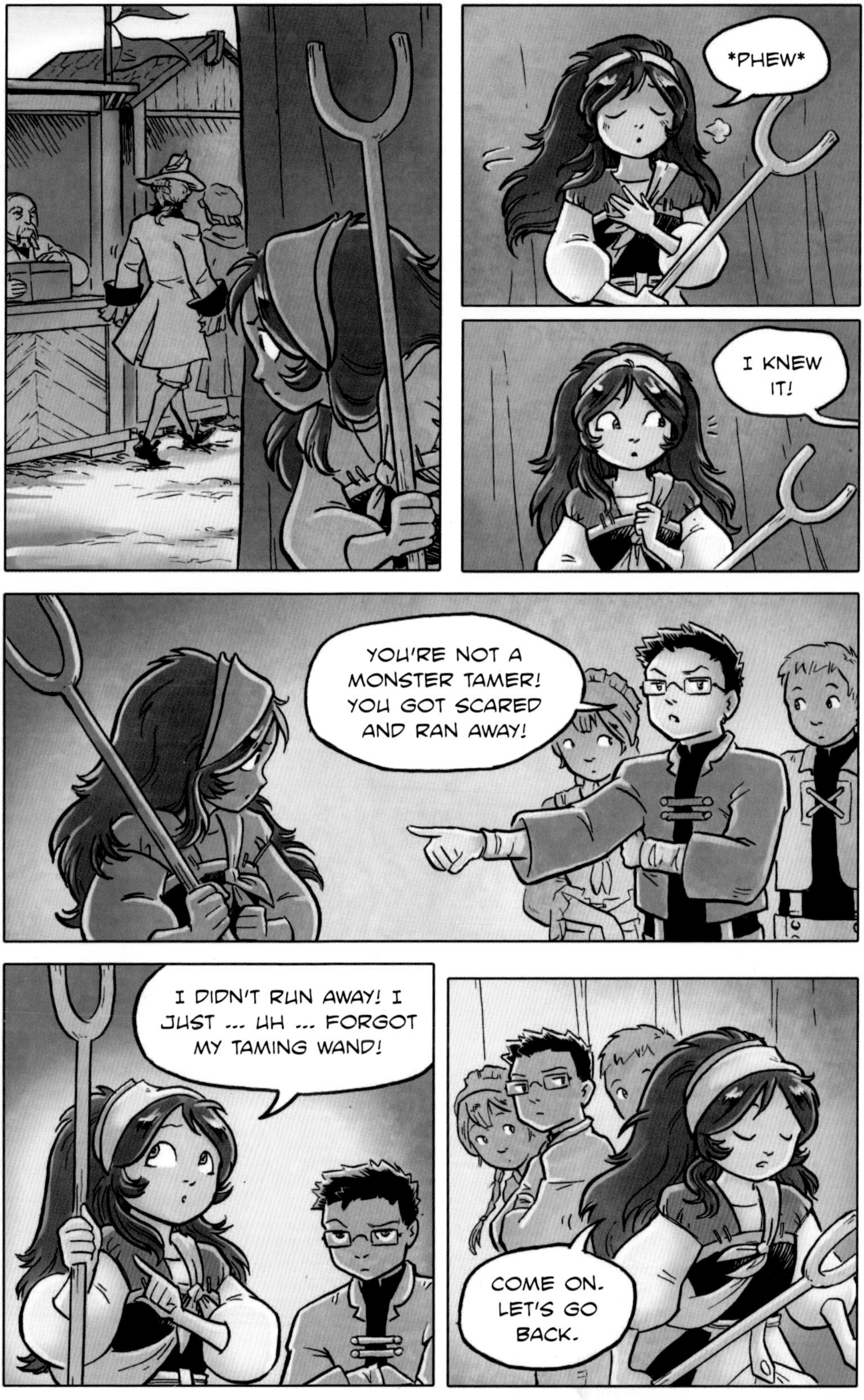
PHEW
I KNEW IT!
YOU'RE NOT A MONSTER TAMER! YOU GOT SCARED AND RAN AWAY!
I DIDN'T RUN AWAY! I JUST ... UH ... FORGOT MY TAMING WAND!
COME ON. LET'S GO BACK.

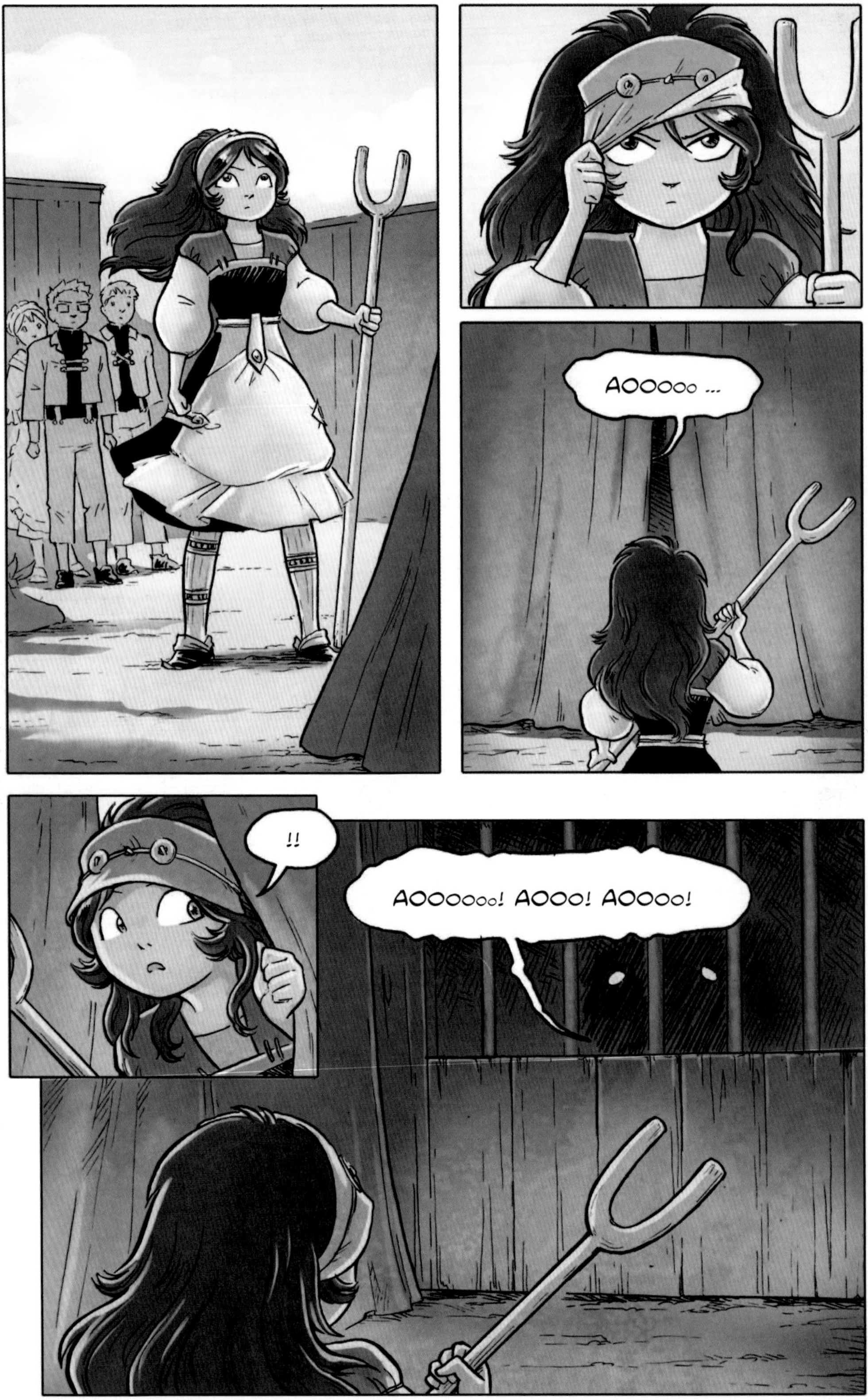
AOOOoo ...
!!
AOOOoooo! AOOO! AOOOo!

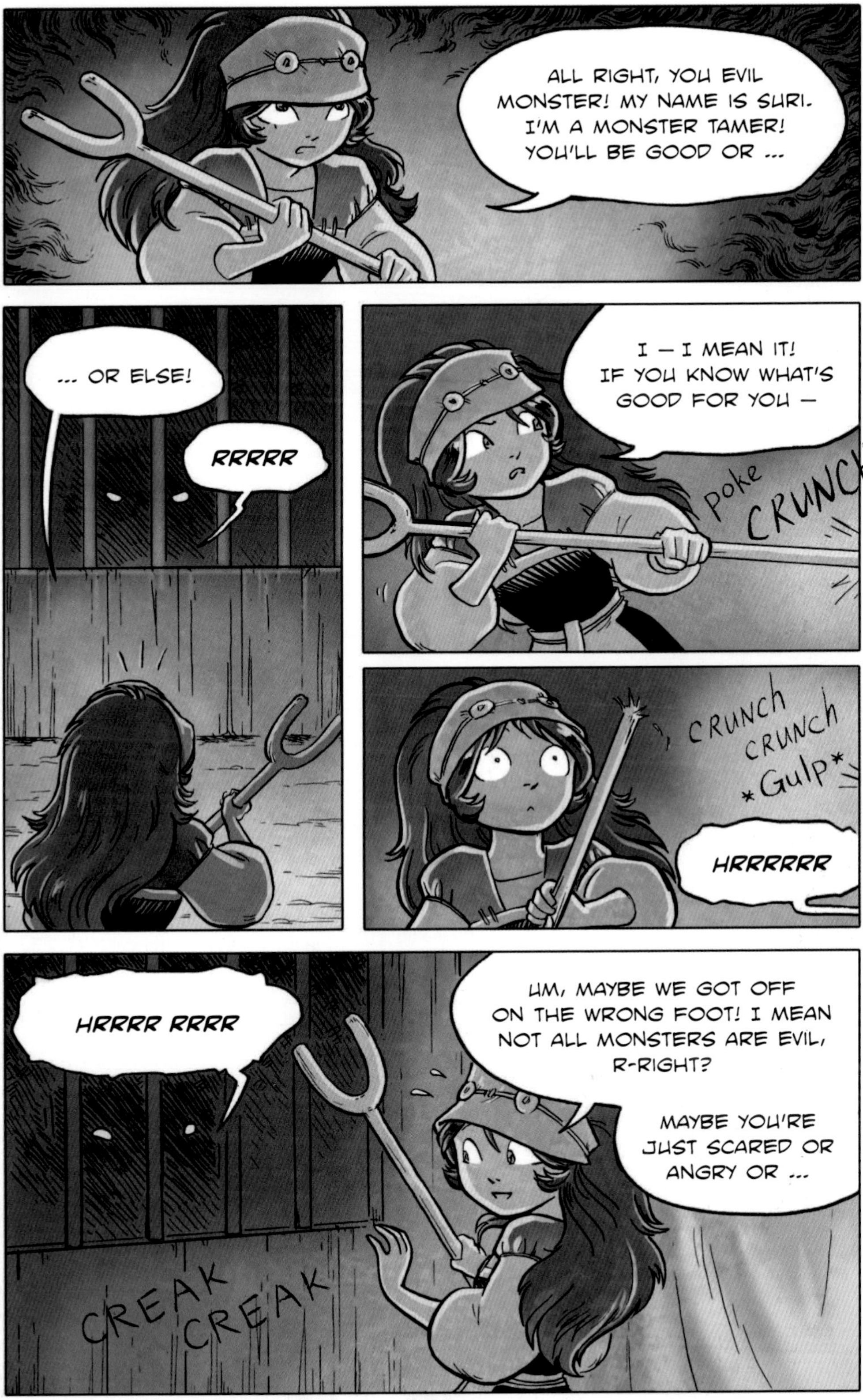
ALL RIGHT, YOU EVIL MONSTER! MY NAME IS SURI. I'M A MONSTER TAMER! YOU'LL BE GOOD OR ...
... OR ELSE!
RRRRR
I — I MEAN IT! IF YOU KNOW WHAT'S GOOD FOR YOU —
poke
CRUNCH
CRUNCH
CRUNCH
Gulp
HRRRRRR
HRRRR RRRR
UM, MAYBE WE GOT OFF ON THE WRONG FOOT! I MEAN NOT ALL MONSTERS ARE EVIL, R-RIGHT?
MAYBE YOU'RE JUST SCARED OR ANGRY OR ...
CREAK
CREAK

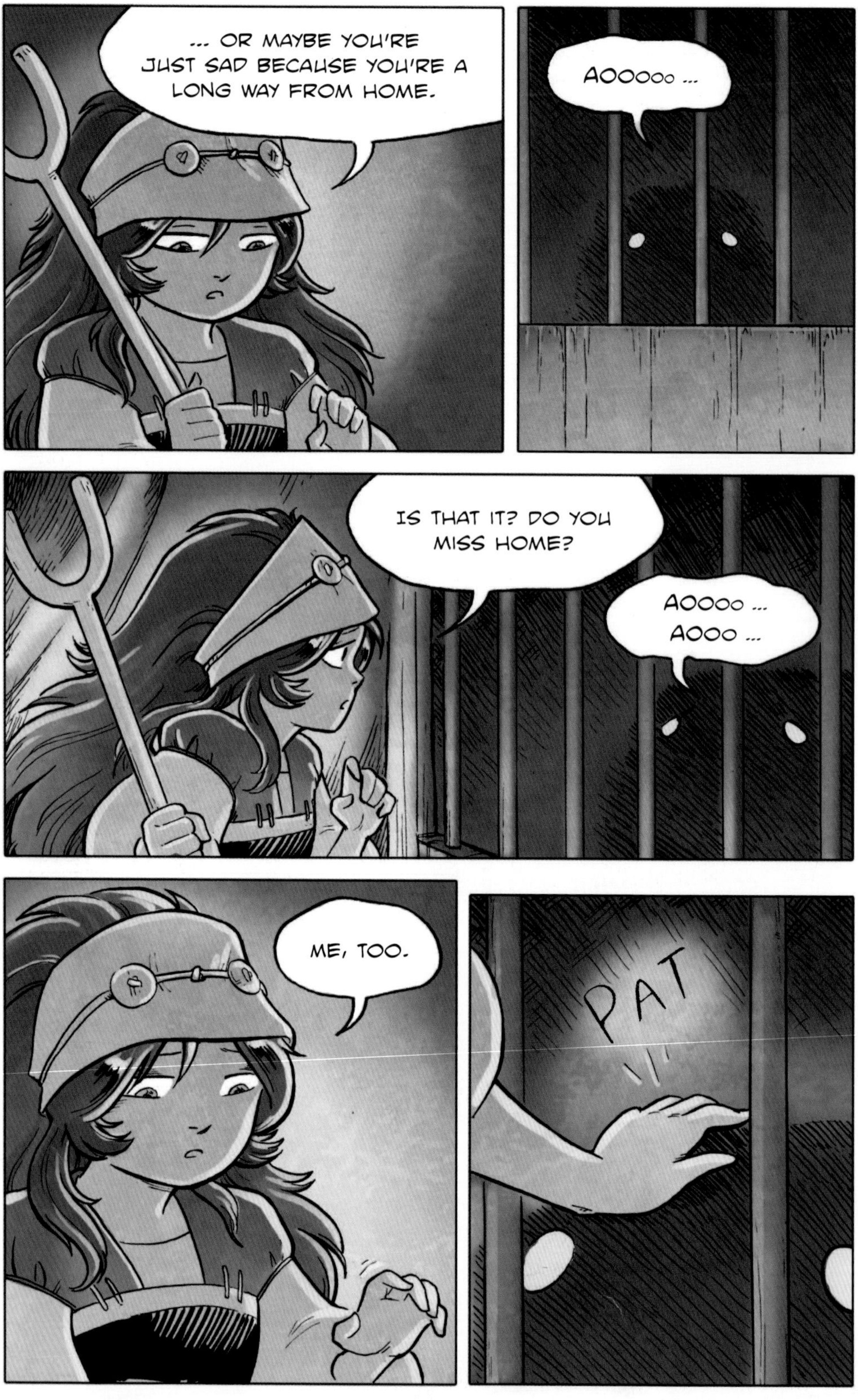
... OR MAYBE YOU'RE JUST SAD BECAUSE YOU'RE A LONG WAY FROM HOME.
AOOOoo ...
IS THAT IT? DO YOU MISS HOME?
AOOOo ... AOOO ...
ME, TOO.
PAT

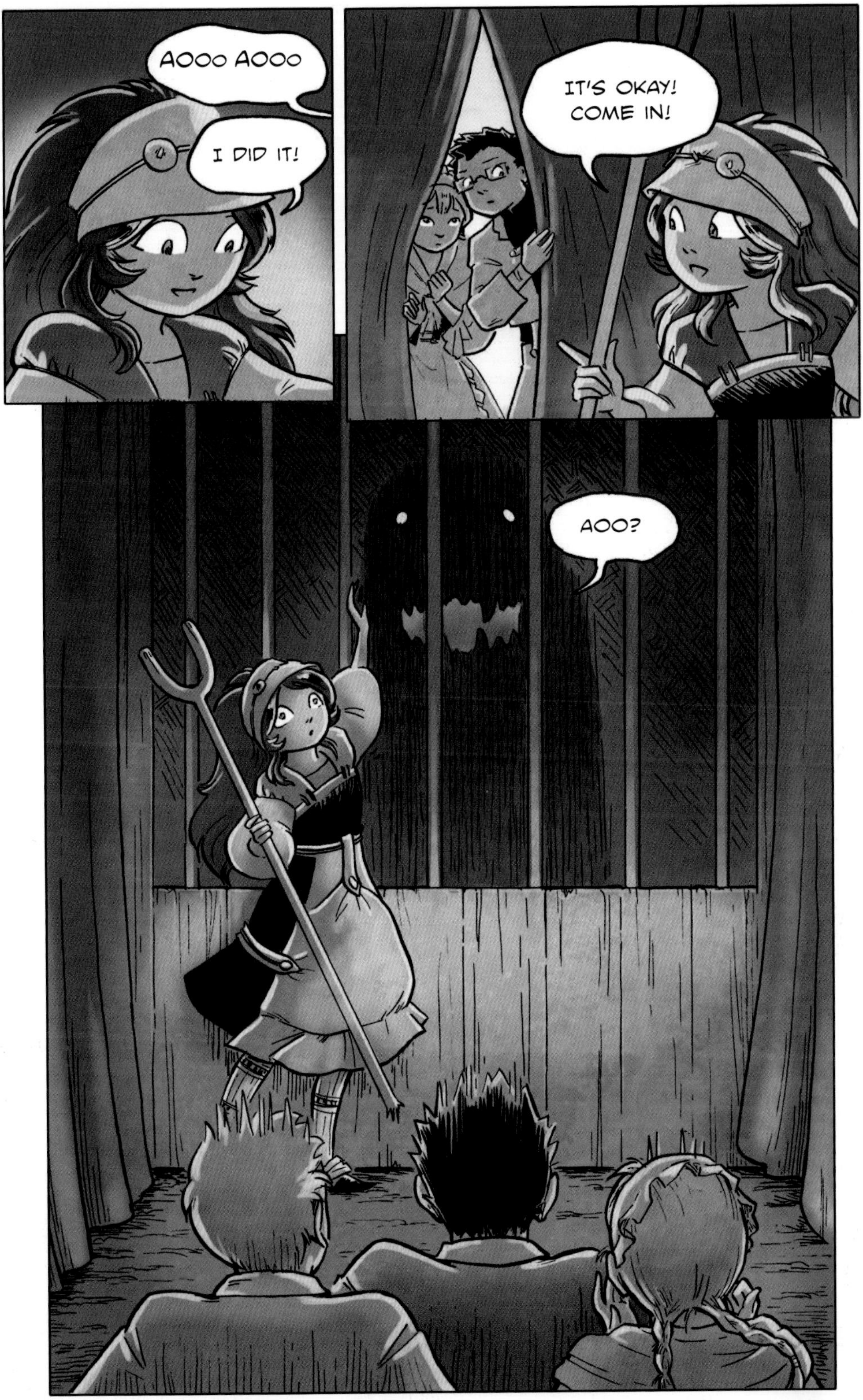
AOOo AOOo
I DID IT!
IT'S OKAY! COME IN!
AOO?

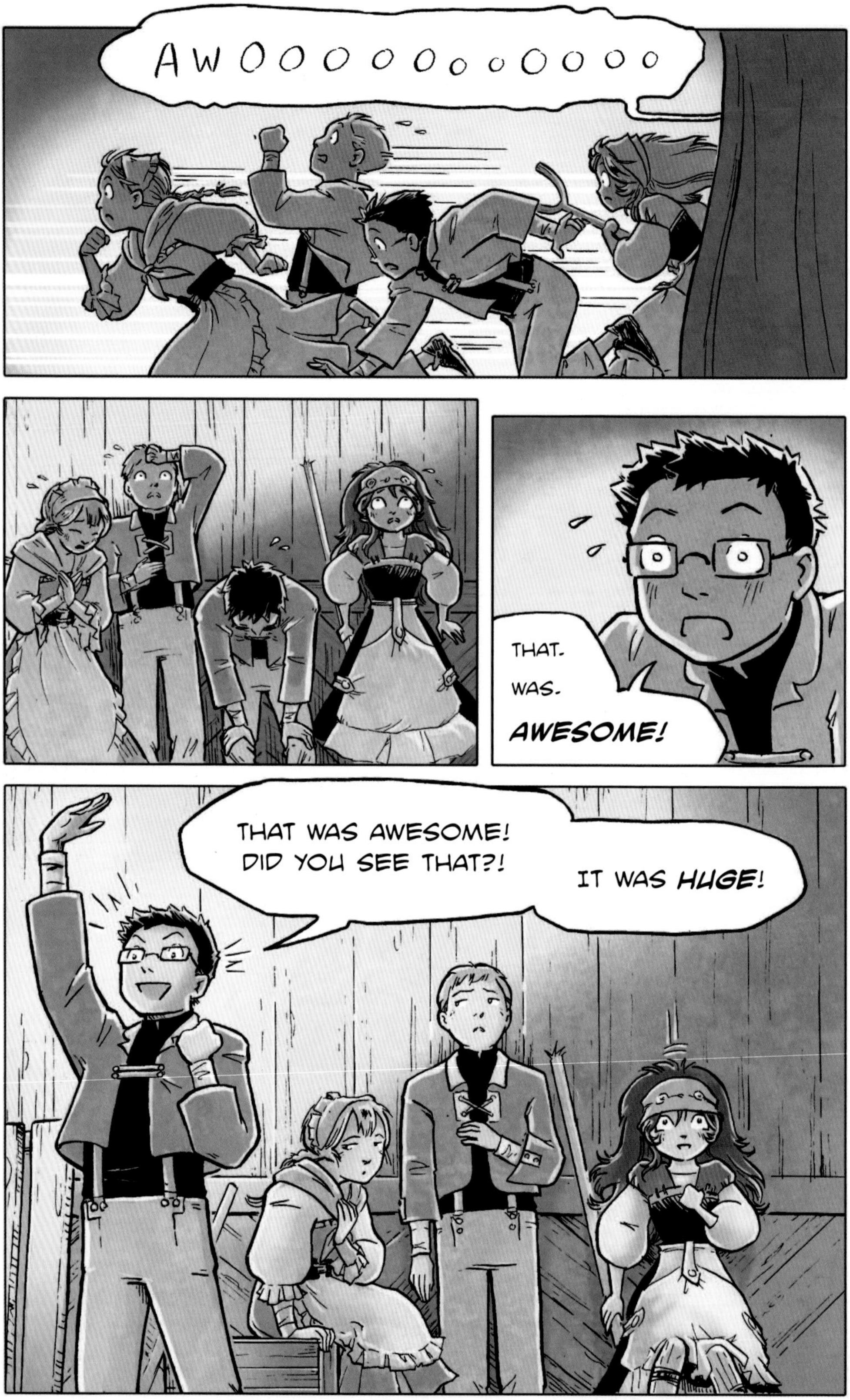
AWOOOOOOoOOOOO
THAT.
WAS.
AWESOME!
THAT WAS AWESOME!
DID YOU SEE THAT?!
IT WAS *HUGE*!

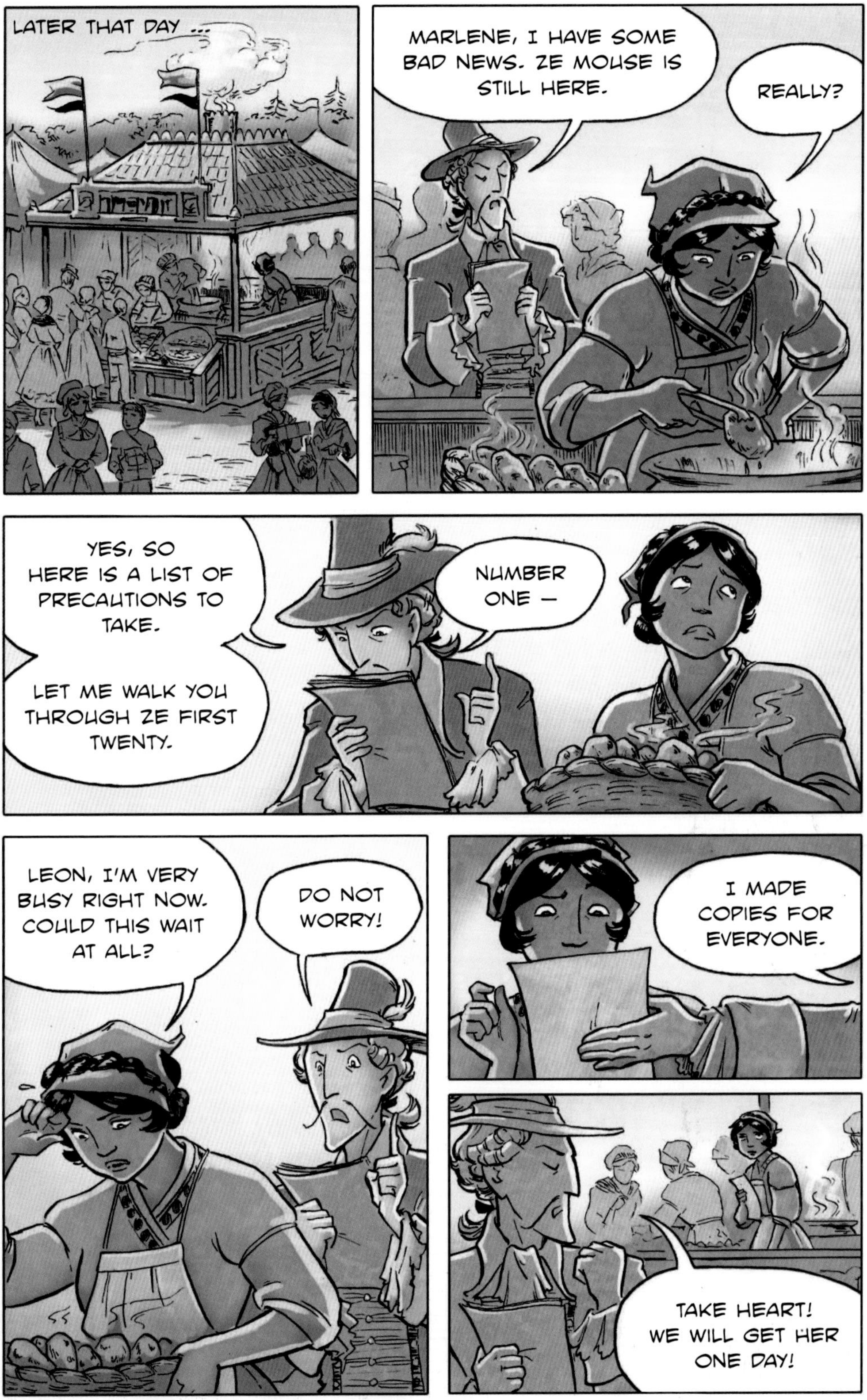

LATER THAT DAY ...
MARLENE, I HAVE SOME BAD NEWS. ZE MOUSE IS STILL HERE.
REALLY?
YES, SO HERE IS A LIST OF PRECAUTIONS TO TAKE.
LET ME WALK YOU THROUGH ZE FIRST TWENTY.
NUMBER ONE —
LEON, I'M VERY BUSY RIGHT NOW. COULD THIS WAIT AT ALL?
DO NOT WORRY!
I MADE COPIES FOR EVERYONE.
TAKE HEART! WE WILL GET HER ONE DAY!

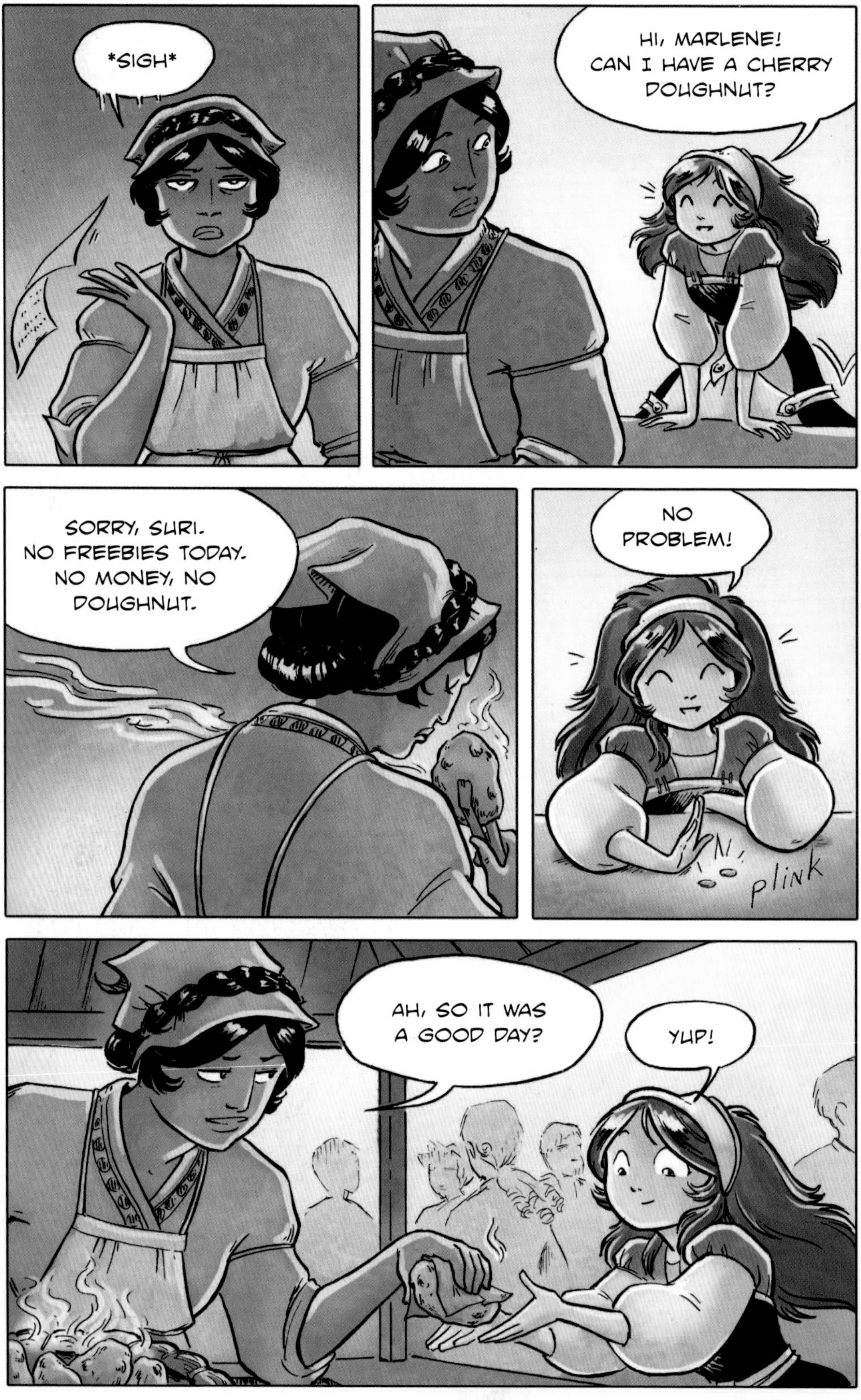
SIGH
HI, MARLENE! CAN I HAVE A CHERRY DOUGHNUT?
SORRY, SURI. NO FREEBIES TODAY. NO MONEY, NO DOUGHNUT.
NO PROBLEM!
plink
AH, SO IT WAS A GOOD DAY?
YUP!

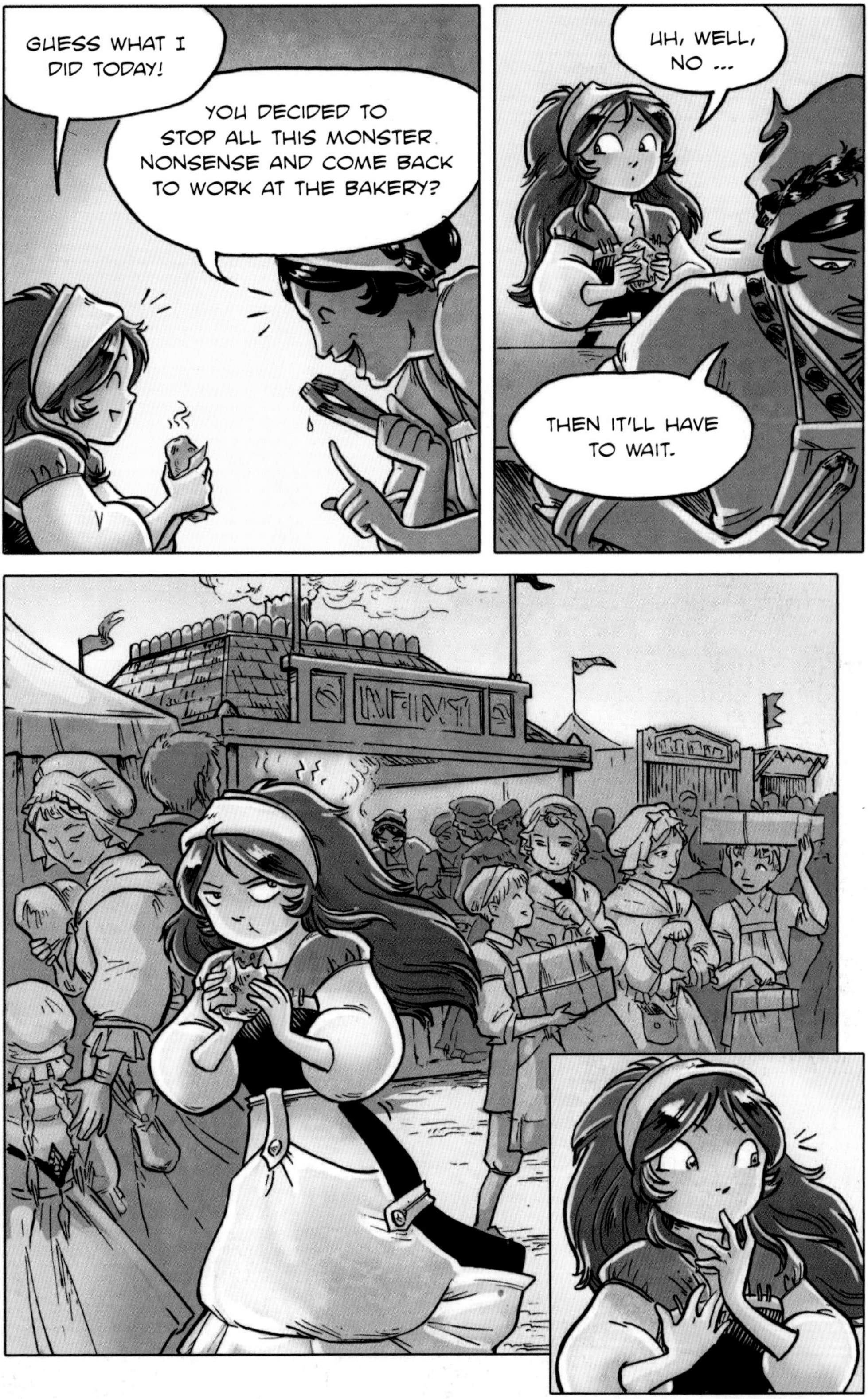
GUESS WHAT I DID TODAY!
YOU DECIDED TO STOP ALL THIS MONSTER NONSENSE AND COME BACK TO WORK AT THE BAKERY?
UH, WELL, NO ...
THEN IT'LL HAVE TO WAIT.

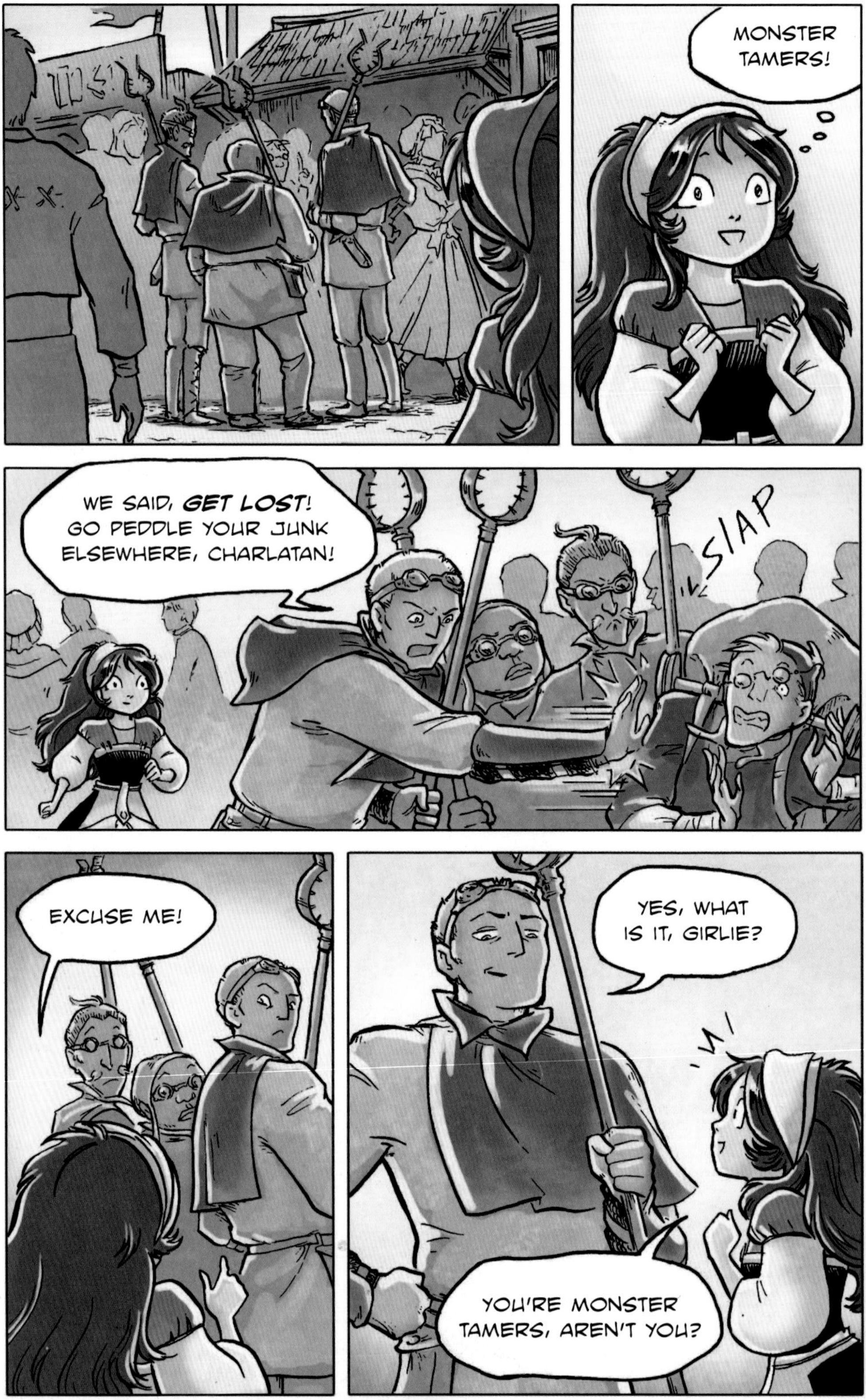
MONSTER TAMERS!
WE SAID, **GET LOST**! GO PEDDLE YOUR JUNK ELSEWHERE, CHARLATAN!
SLAP
EXCUSE ME!
YES, WHAT IS IT, GIRLIE?
YOU'RE MONSTER TAMERS, AREN'T YOU?

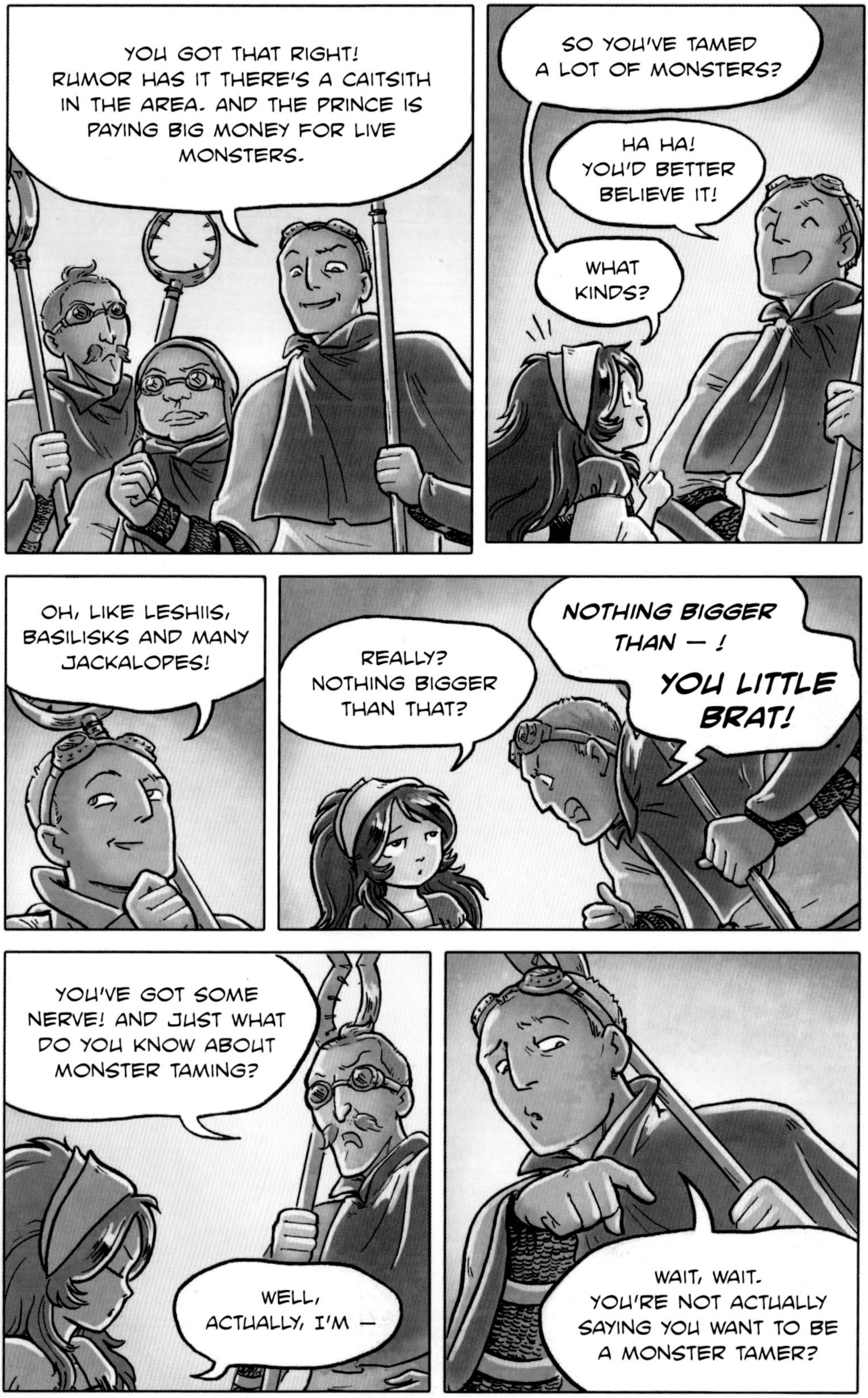
YOU GOT THAT RIGHT! RUMOR HAS IT THERE'S A CAITSITH IN THE AREA. AND THE PRINCE IS PAYING BIG MONEY FOR LIVE MONSTERS.
SO YOU'VE TAMED A LOT OF MONSTERS?
HA HA! YOU'D BETTER BELIEVE IT!
WHAT KINDS?
OH, LIKE LESHIIS, BASILISKS AND MANY JACKALOPES!
REALLY? NOTHING BIGGER THAN THAT?
NOTHING BIGGER THAN — !
YOU LITTLE BRAT!
YOU'VE GOT SOME NERVE! AND JUST WHAT DO YOU KNOW ABOUT MONSTER TAMING?
WELL, ACTUALLY, I'M —
WAIT, WAIT. YOU'RE NOT ACTUALLY SAYING YOU WANT TO BE A MONSTER TAMER?

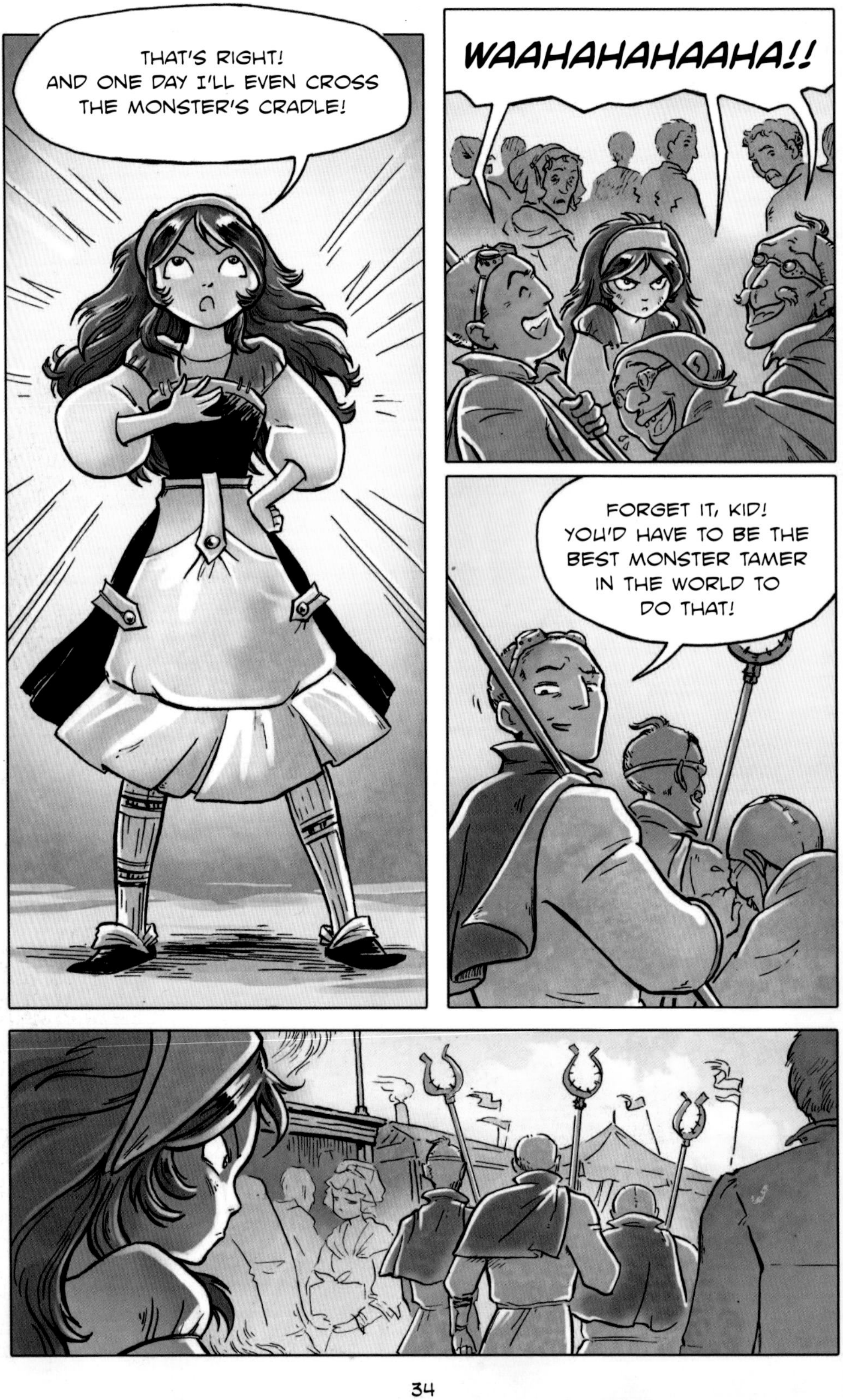
THAT'S RIGHT! AND ONE DAY I'LL EVEN CROSS THE MONSTER'S CRADLE!
WAAHAHAHAAHA!!
FORGET IT, KID! YOU'D HAVE TO BE THE BEST MONSTER TAMER IN THE WORLD TO DO THAT!

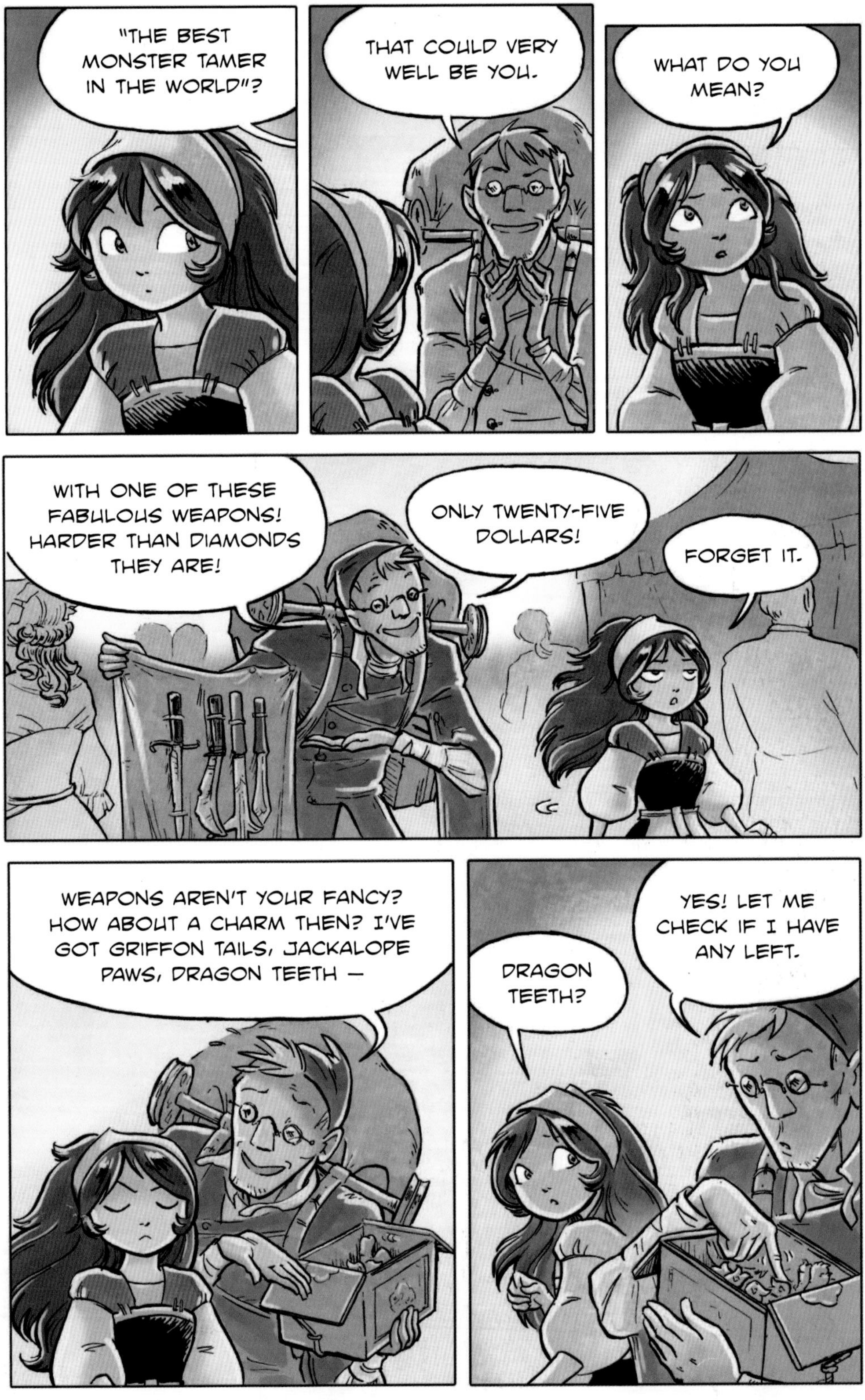
"THE BEST MONSTER TAMER IN THE WORLD"?
THAT COULD VERY WELL BE YOU.
WHAT DO YOU MEAN?
WITH ONE OF THESE FABULOUS WEAPONS! HARDER THAN DIAMONDS THEY ARE!
ONLY TWENTY-FIVE DOLLARS!
FORGET IT.
WEAPONS AREN'T YOUR FANCY? HOW ABOUT A CHARM THEN? I'VE GOT GRIFFON TAILS, JACKALOPE PAWS, DRAGON TEETH –
DRAGON TEETH?
YES! LET ME CHECK IF I HAVE ANY LEFT.

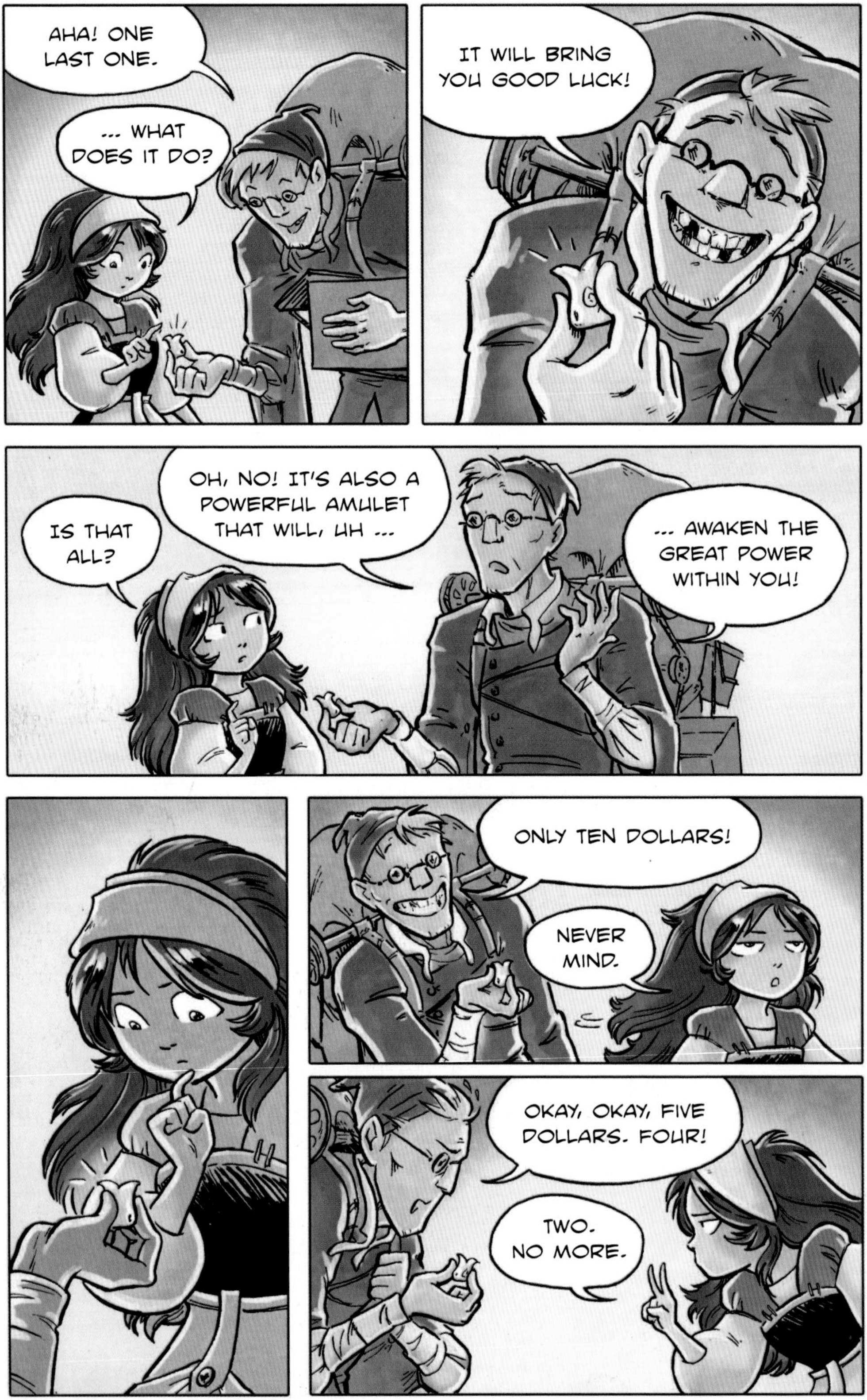
AHA! ONE LAST ONE.
... WHAT DOES IT DO?
IT WILL BRING YOU GOOD LUCK!
IS THAT ALL?
OH, NO! IT'S ALSO A POWERFUL AMULET THAT WILL, UH ...
... AWAKEN THE GREAT POWER WITHIN YOU!
ONLY TEN DOLLARS!
NEVER MIND.
OKAY, OKAY, FIVE DOLLARS. FOUR!
TWO. NO MORE.

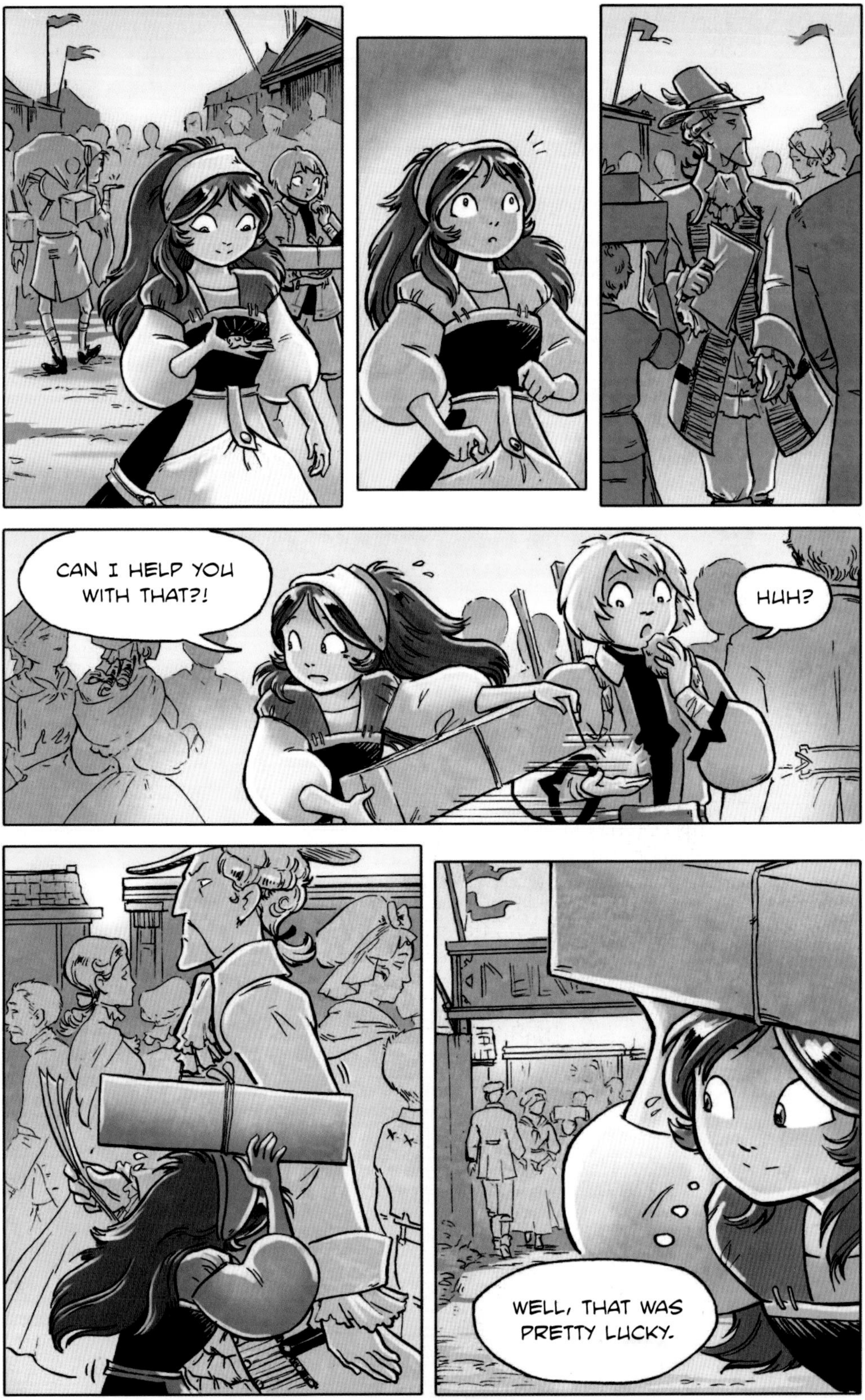
CAN I HELP YOU WITH THAT?!
HUH?
WELL, THAT WAS PRETTY LUCKY.

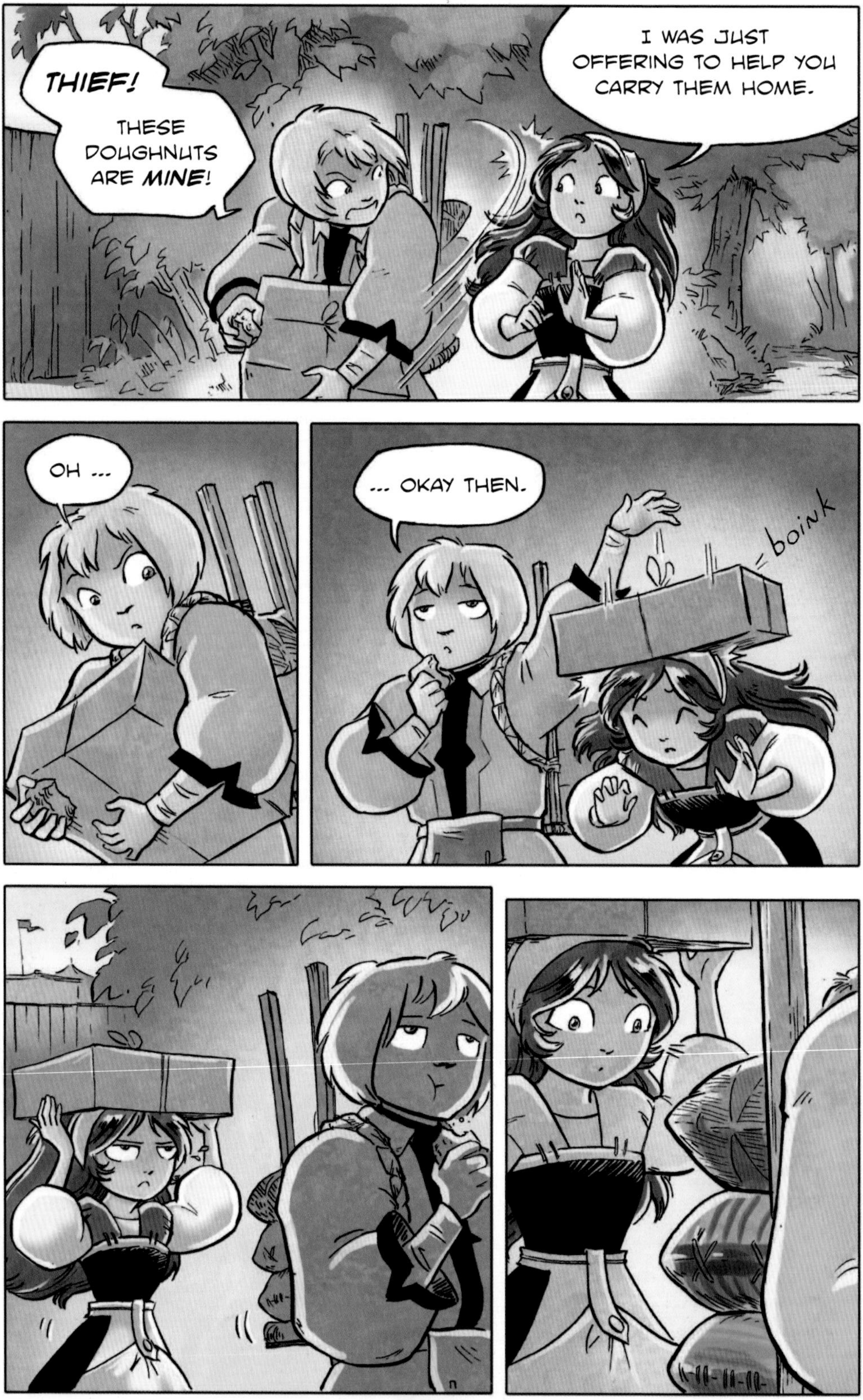
THIEF!
THESE DOUGHNUTS ARE MINE!
I WAS JUST OFFERING TO HELP YOU CARRY THEM HOME.
OH ...
... OKAY THEN.
boink

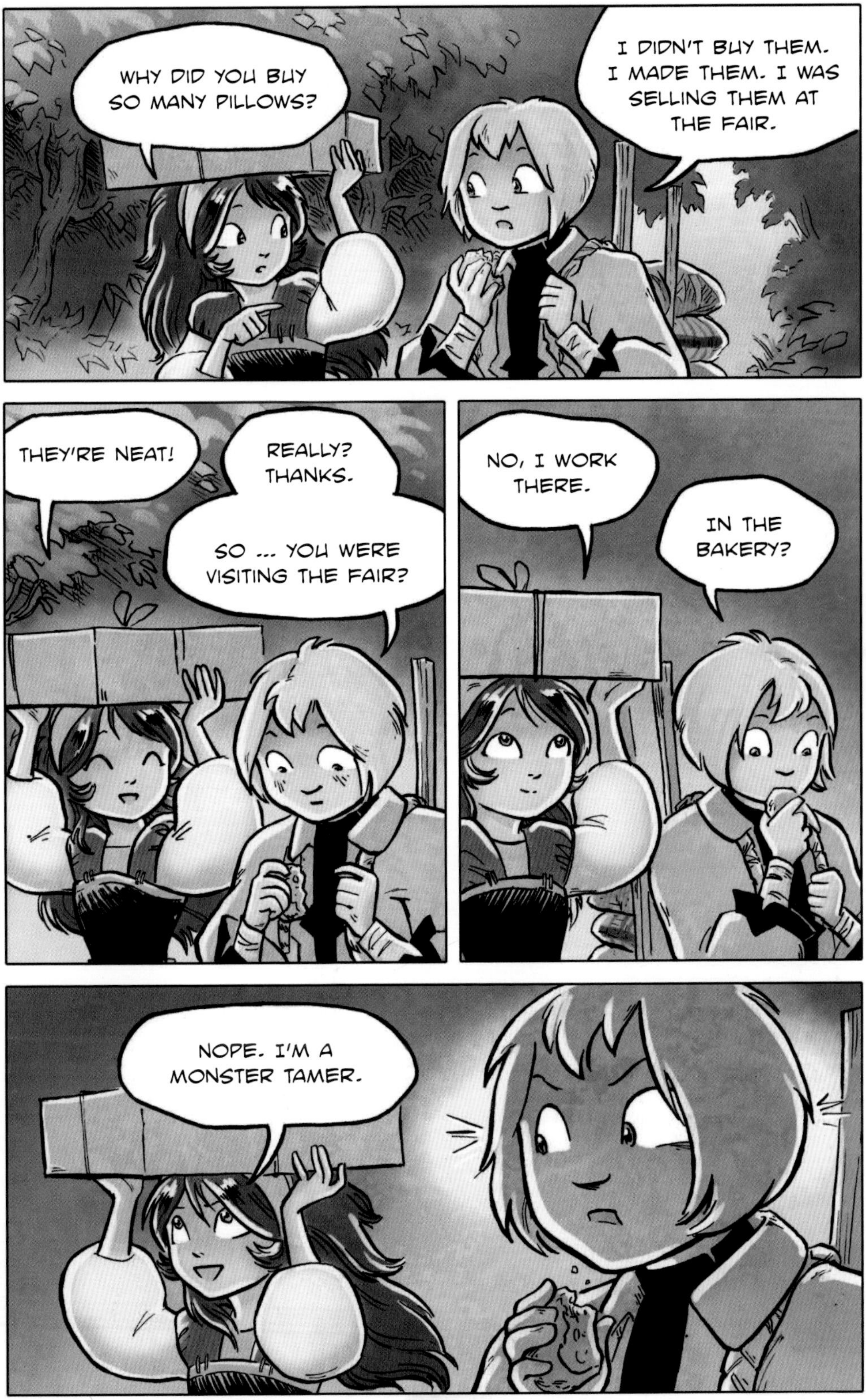
WHY DID YOU BUY SO MANY PILLOWS?
I DIDN'T BUY THEM. I MADE THEM. I WAS SELLING THEM AT THE FAIR.
THEY'RE NEAT!
REALLY? THANKS.
SO ... YOU WERE VISITING THE FAIR?
NO, I WORK THERE.
IN THE BAKERY?
NOPE. I'M A MONSTER TAMER.

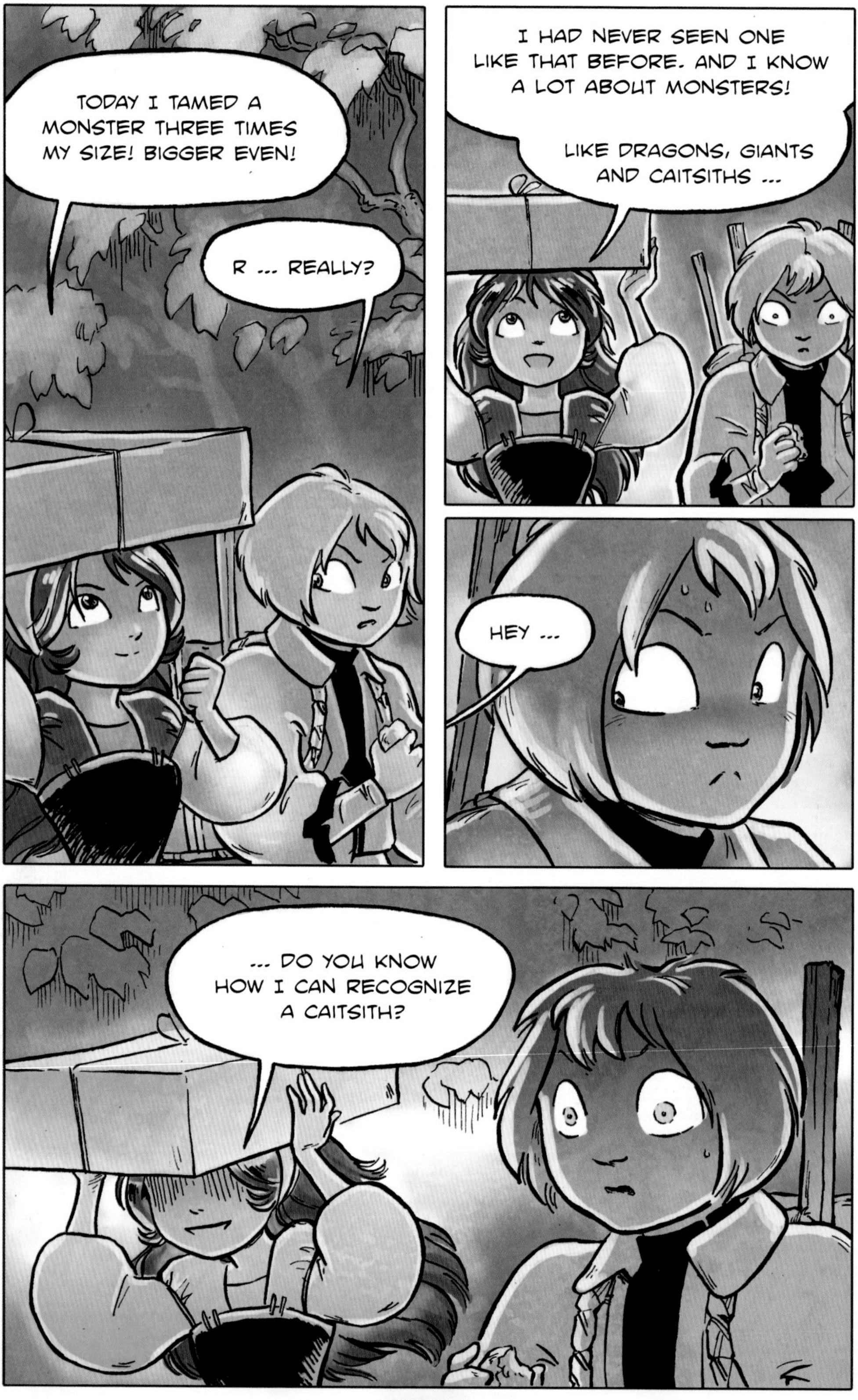
TODAY I TAMED A MONSTER THREE TIMES MY SIZE! BIGGER EVEN!
R ... REALLY?
I HAD NEVER SEEN ONE LIKE THAT BEFORE. AND I KNOW A LOT ABOUT MONSTERS!
LIKE DRAGONS, GIANTS AND CAITSITHS ...
HEY ...
... DO YOU KNOW HOW I CAN RECOGNIZE A CAITSITH?

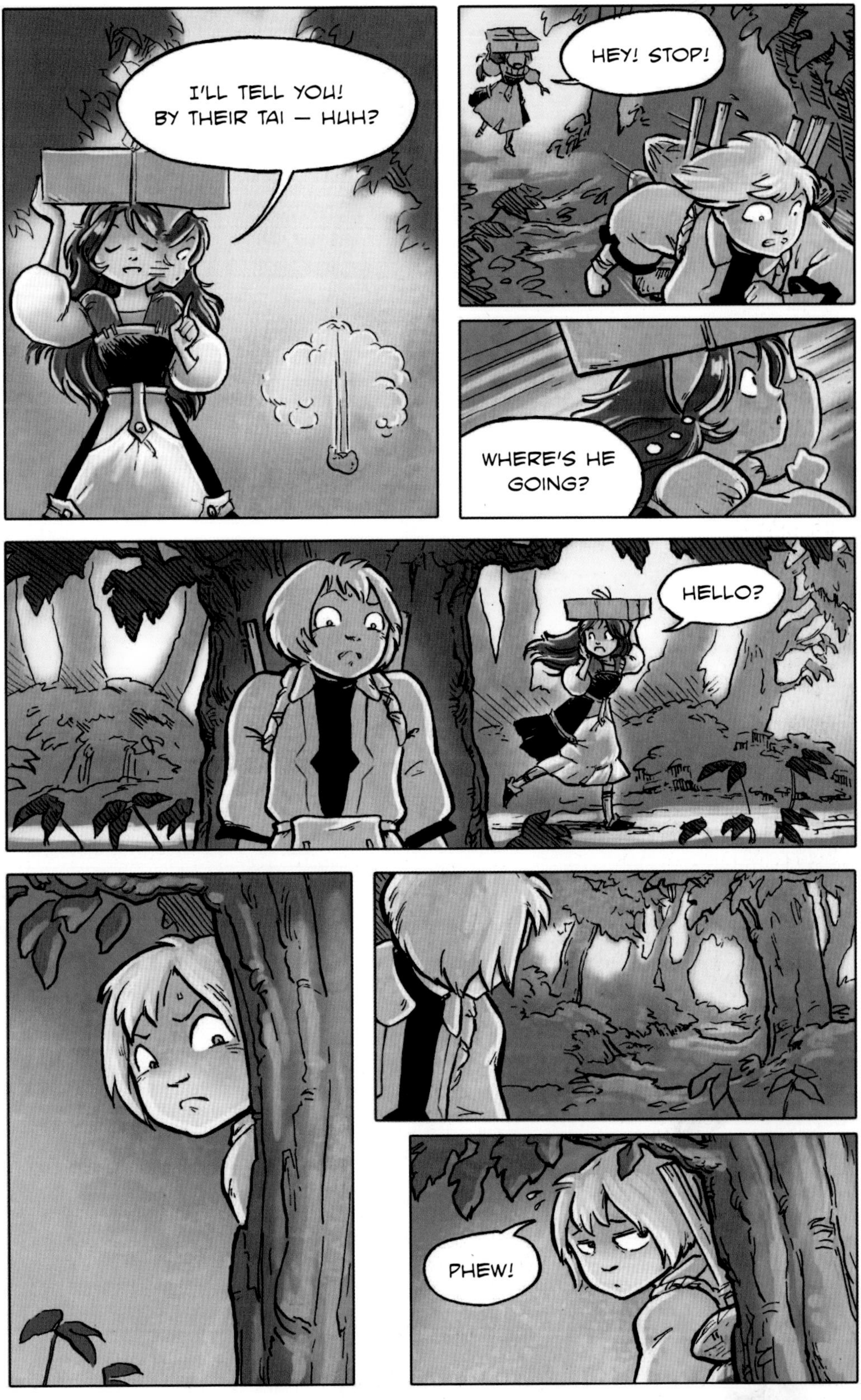
I'LL TELL YOU!
BY THEIR TAI — HUH?
HEY! STOP!
WHERE'S HE GOING?
HELLO?
PHEW!

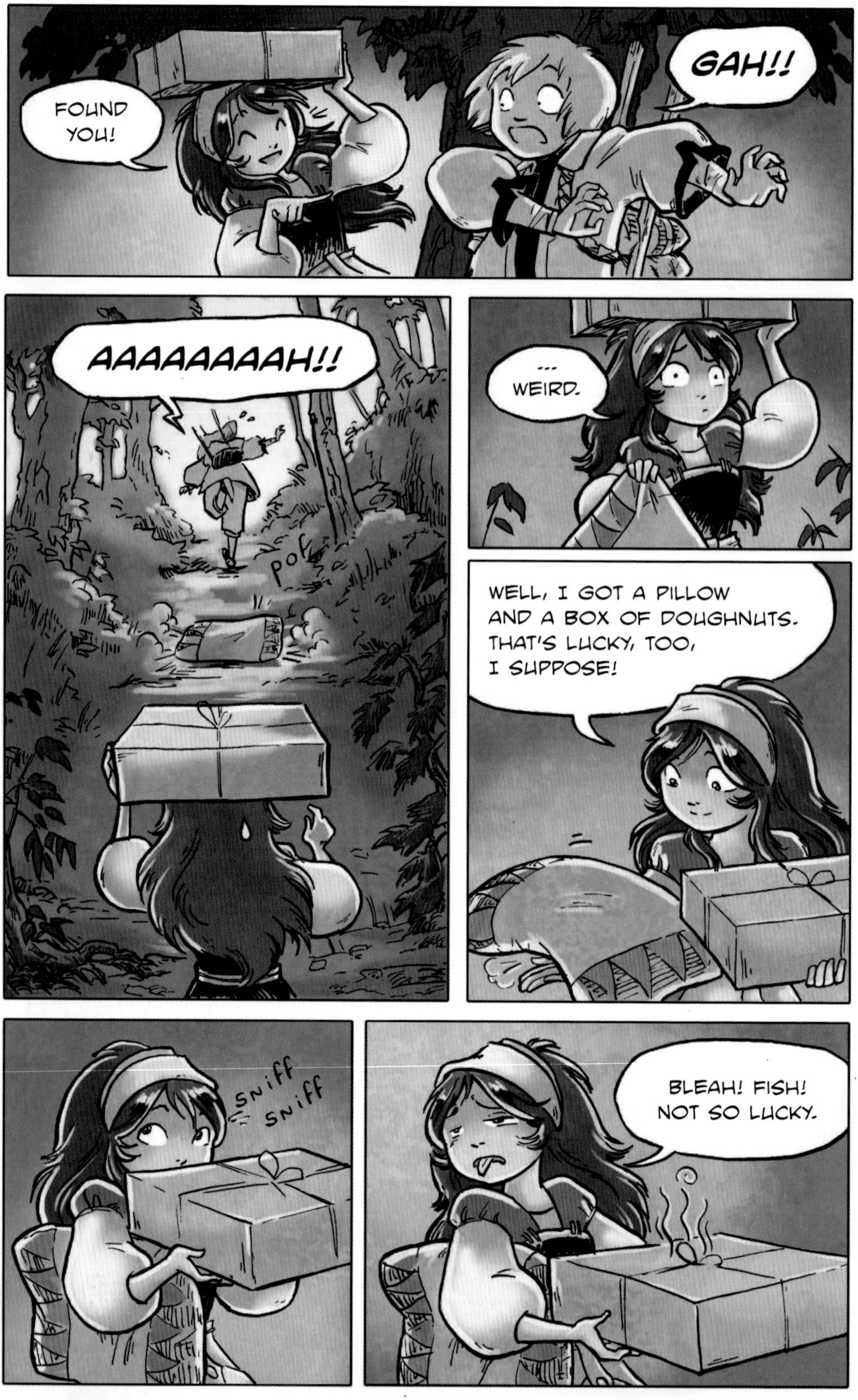
FOUND YOU!
GAH!!
AAAAAAAAH!!
pof
... WEIRD.
WELL, I GOT A PILLOW AND A BOX OF DOUGHNUTS. THAT'S LUCKY, TOO, I SUPPOSE!
SNIFF SNIFF
BLEAH! FISH! NOT SO LUCKY.

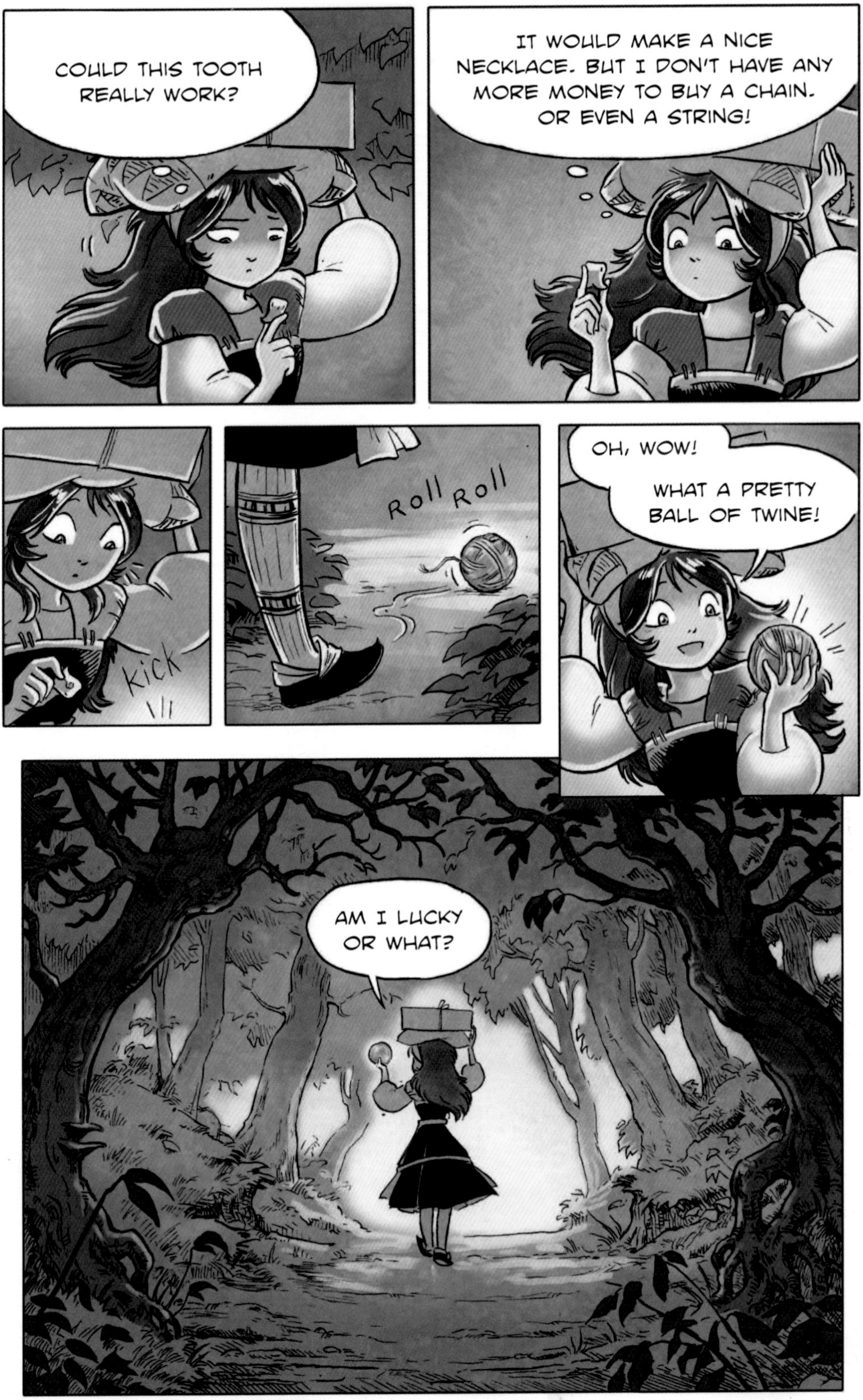
COULD THIS TOOTH REALLY WORK?
IT WOULD MAKE A NICE NECKLACE. BUT I DON'T HAVE ANY MORE MONEY TO BUY A CHAIN. OR EVEN A STRING!
KICK
ROLL ROLL
OH, WOW!
WHAT A PRETTY BALL OF TWINE!
AM I LUCKY OR WHAT?

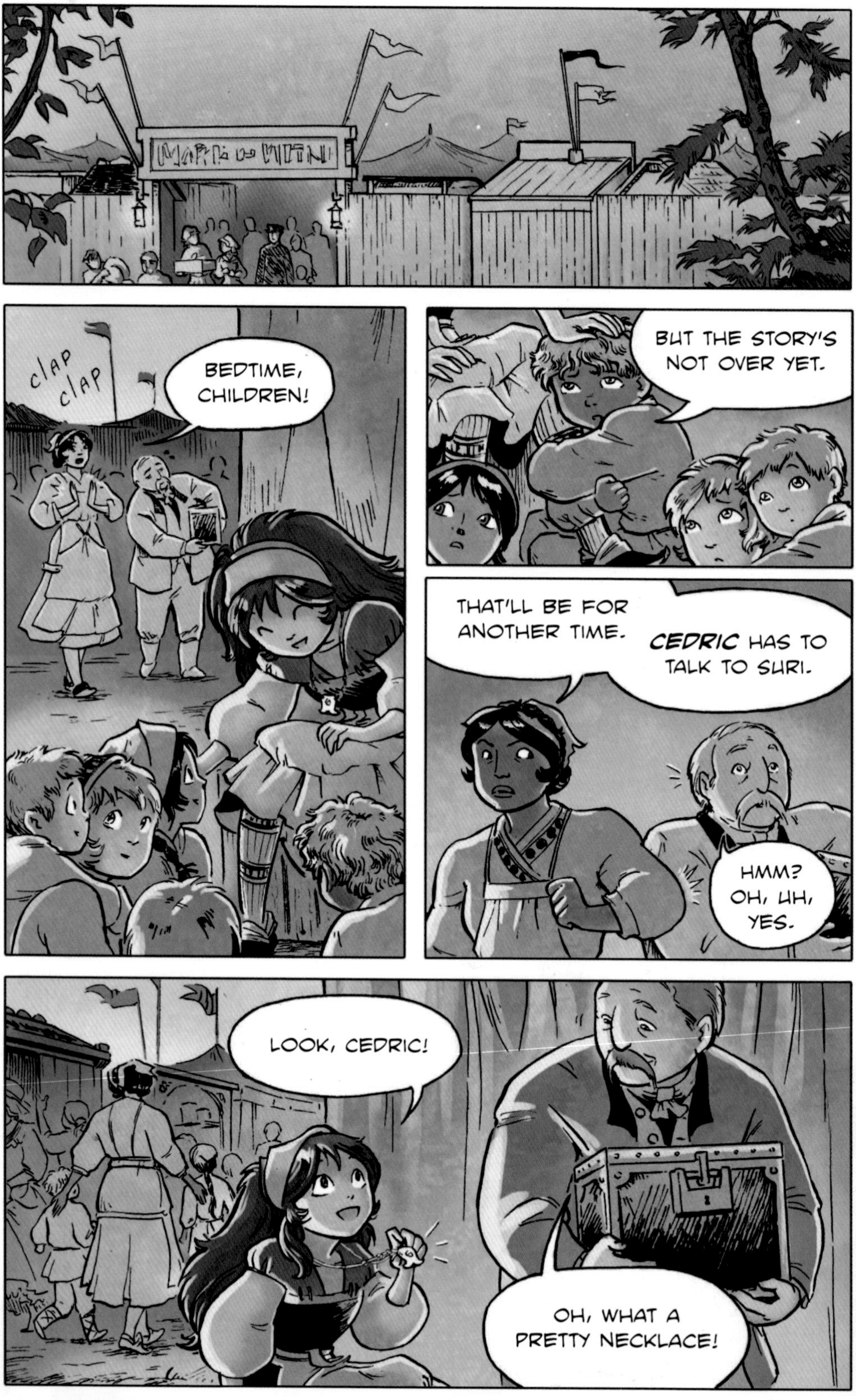
CLAP CLAP
BEDTIME, CHILDREN!
BUT THE STORY'S NOT OVER YET.
THAT'LL BE FOR ANOTHER TIME.
CEDRIC HAS TO TALK TO SURI.
HMM? OH, UH, YES.
LOOK, CEDRIC!
OH, WHAT A PRETTY NECKLACE!

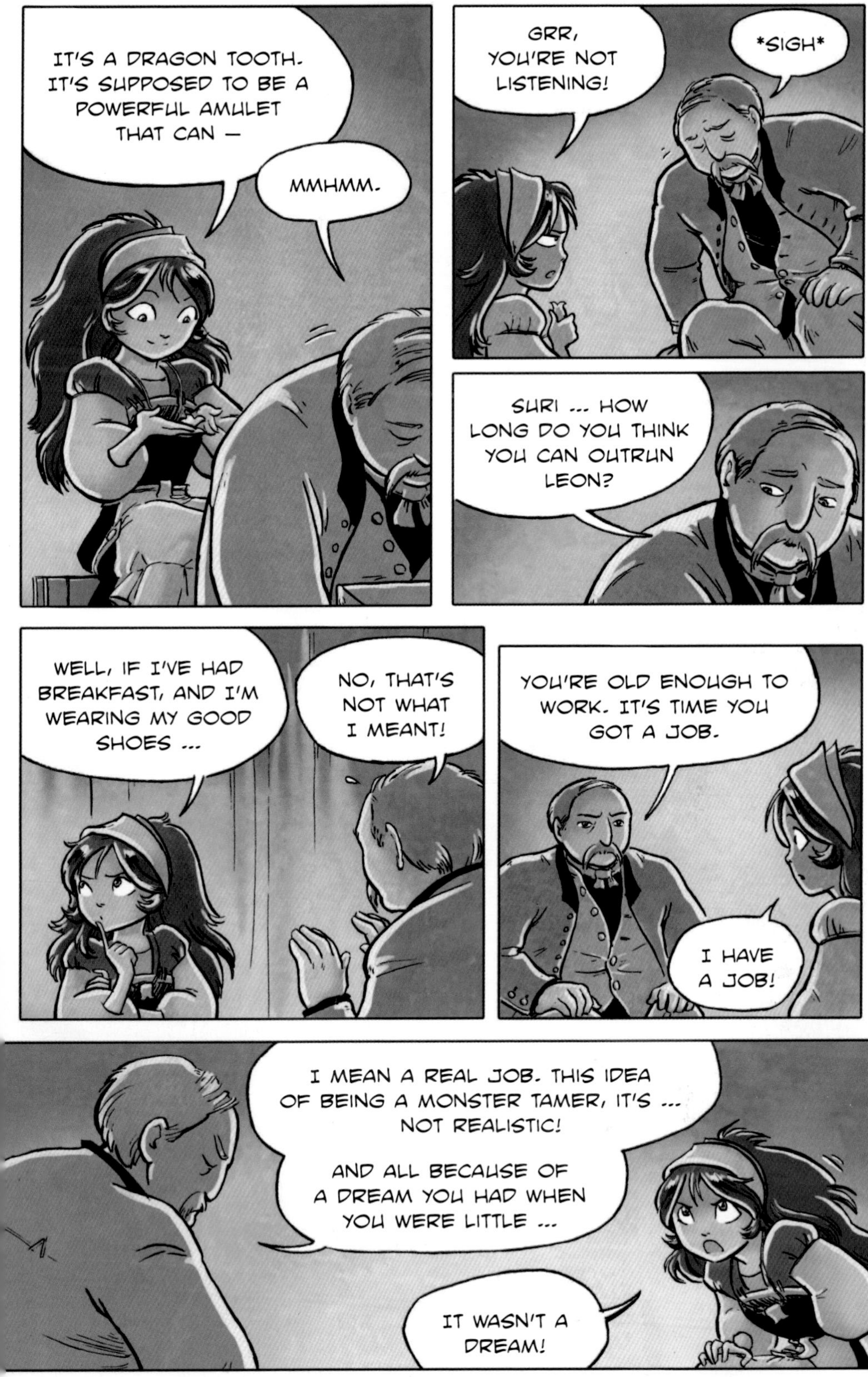
IT'S A DRAGON TOOTH. IT'S SUPPOSED TO BE A POWERFUL AMULET THAT CAN —
MMHMM.
GRR, YOU'RE NOT LISTENING!
SIGH
SURI ... HOW LONG DO YOU THINK YOU CAN OUTRUN LEON?
WELL, IF I'VE HAD BREAKFAST, AND I'M WEARING MY GOOD SHOES ...
NO, THAT'S NOT WHAT I MEANT!
YOU'RE OLD ENOUGH TO WORK. IT'S TIME YOU GOT A JOB.
I HAVE A JOB!
I MEAN A REAL JOB. THIS IDEA OF BEING A MONSTER TAMER, IT'S ... NOT REALISTIC!
AND ALL BECAUSE OF A DREAM YOU HAD WHEN YOU WERE LITTLE ...
IT WASN'T A DREAM!

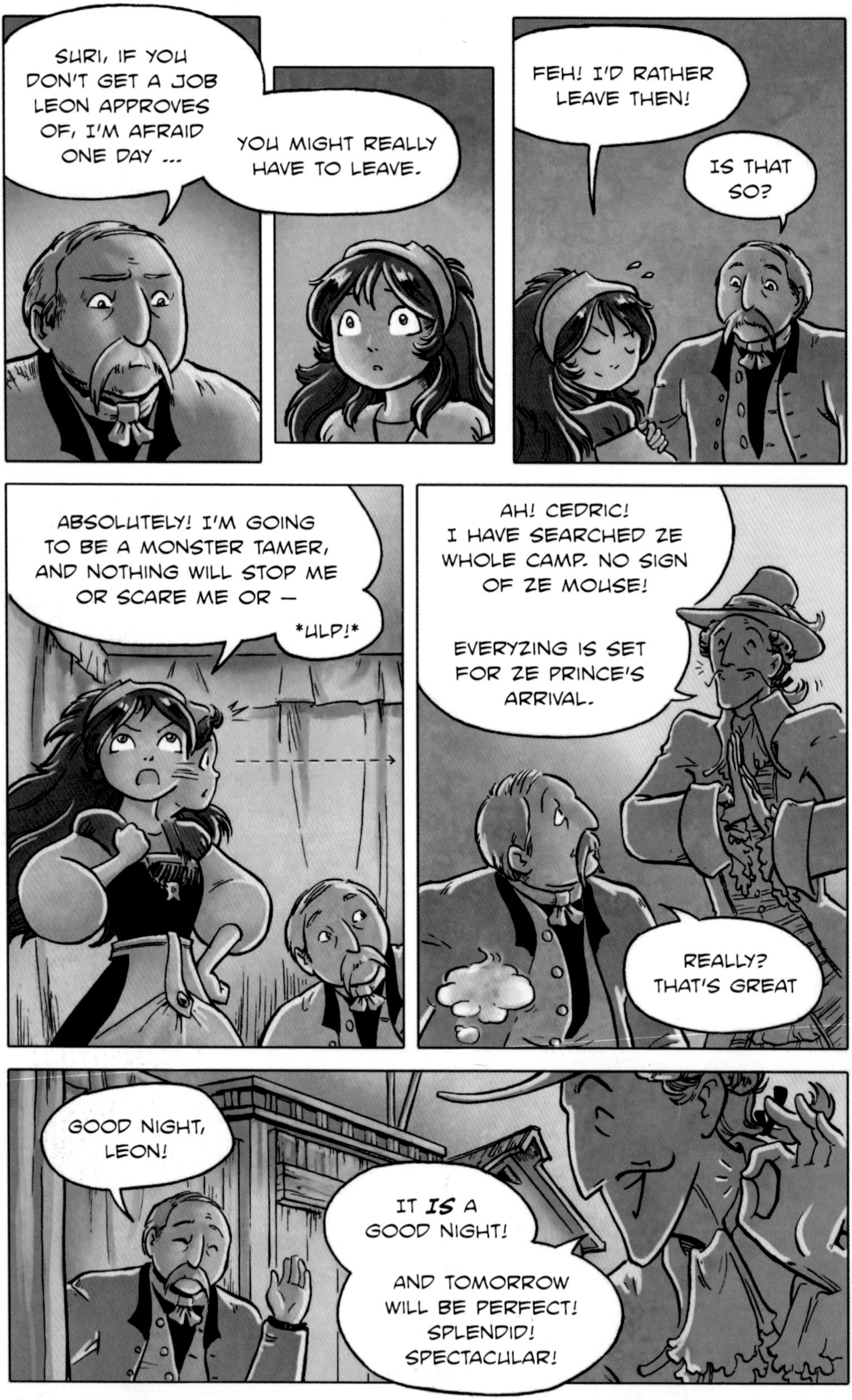
SURI, IF YOU DON'T GET A JOB LEON APPROVES OF, I'M AFRAID ONE DAY ...
YOU MIGHT REALLY HAVE TO LEAVE.
FEH! I'D RATHER LEAVE THEN!
IS THAT SO?
ABSOLUTELY! I'M GOING TO BE A MONSTER TAMER, AND NOTHING WILL STOP ME OR SCARE ME OR —
ULP!
AH! CEDRIC! I HAVE SEARCHED ZE WHOLE CAMP. NO SIGN OF ZE MOUSE!
EVERYZING IS SET FOR ZE PRINCE'S ARRIVAL.
REALLY? THAT'S GREAT
GOOD NIGHT, LEON!
IT IS A GOOD NIGHT!
AND TOMORROW WILL BE PERFECT! SPLENDID! SPECTACULAR!

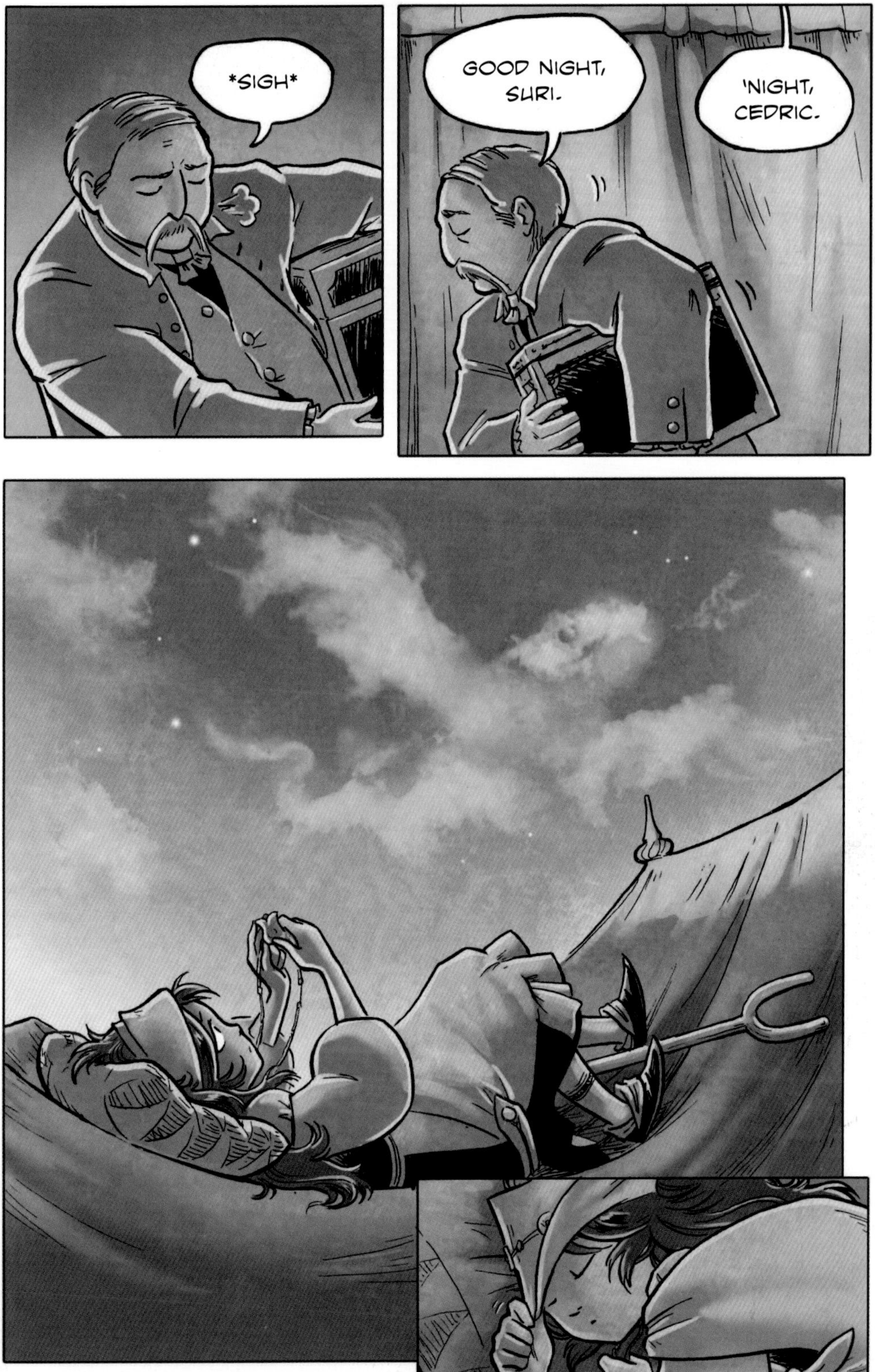
SIGH
GOOD NIGHT, SURI.
'NIGHT, CEDRIC.

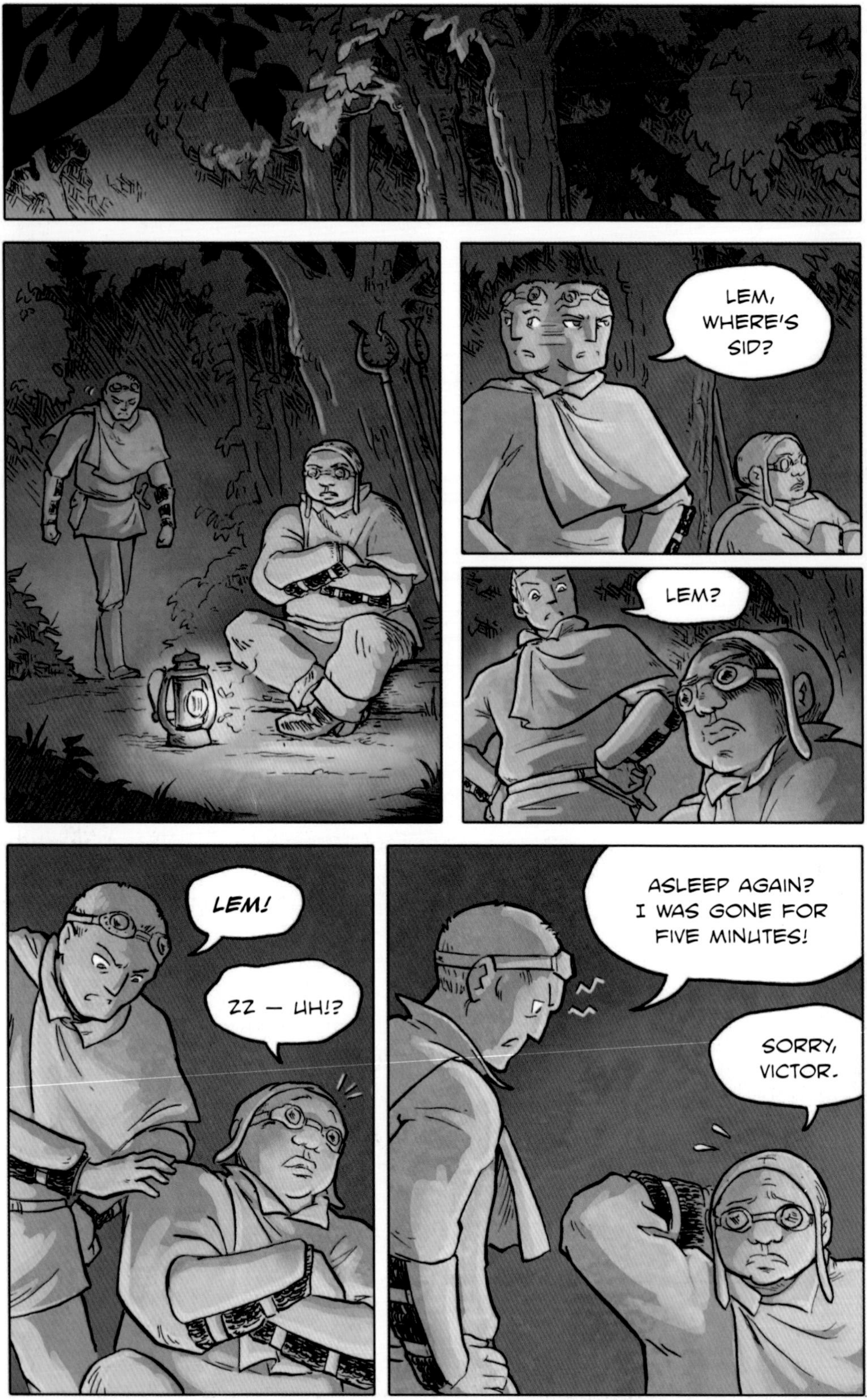
LEM, WHERE'S SID?
LEM?
LEM!
ZZ — UH!?
ASLEEP AGAIN? I WAS GONE FOR FIVE MINUTES!
SORRY, VICTOR.

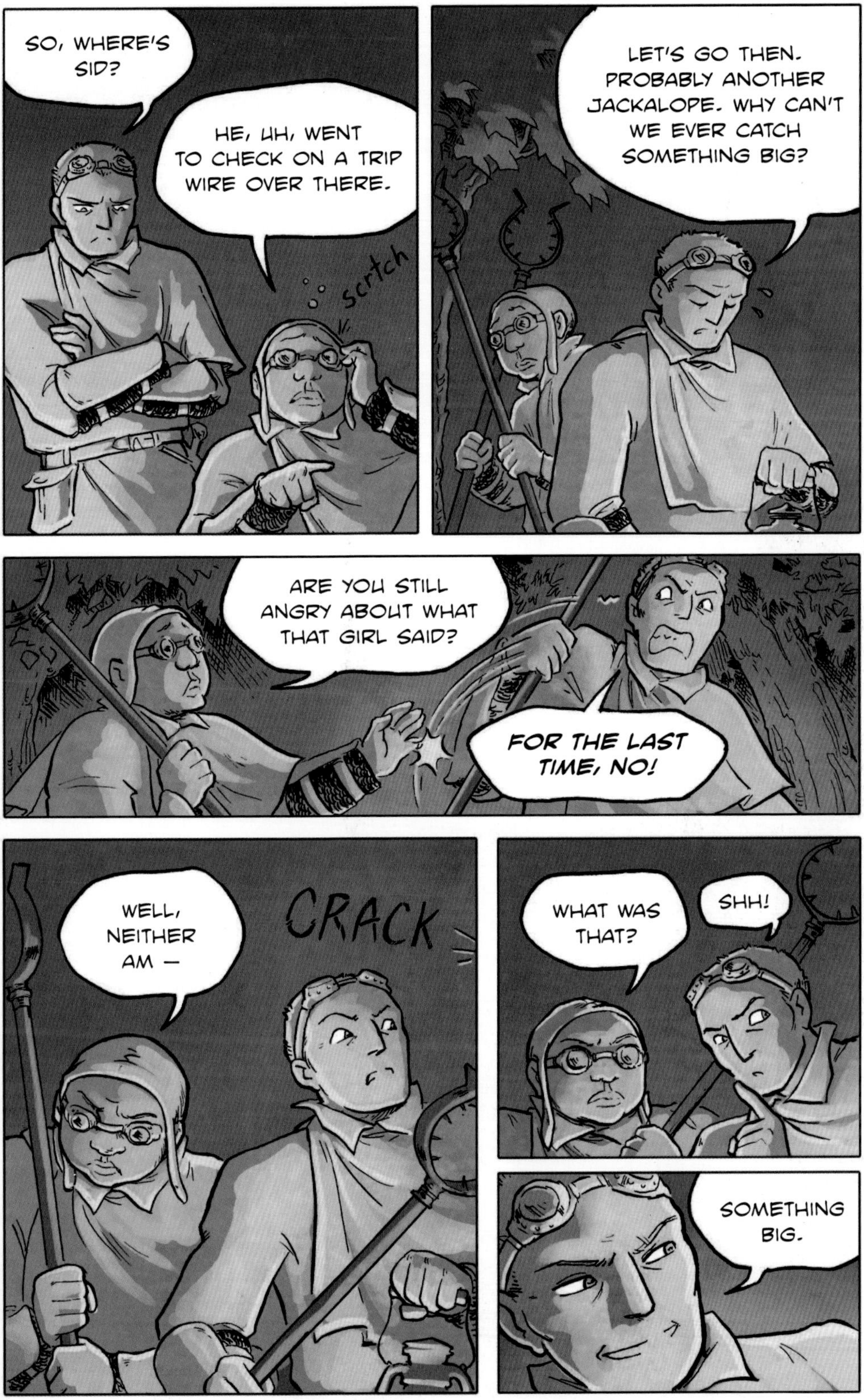
SO, WHERE'S SID?
HE, UH, WENT TO CHECK ON A TRIP WIRE OVER THERE.
scrtch
LET'S GO THEN. PROBABLY ANOTHER JACKALOPE. WHY CAN'T WE EVER CATCH SOMETHING BIG?
ARE YOU STILL ANGRY ABOUT WHAT THAT GIRL SAID?
FOR THE LAST TIME, NO!
WELL, NEITHER AM —
CRACK
WHAT WAS THAT?
SHH!
SOMETHING BIG.

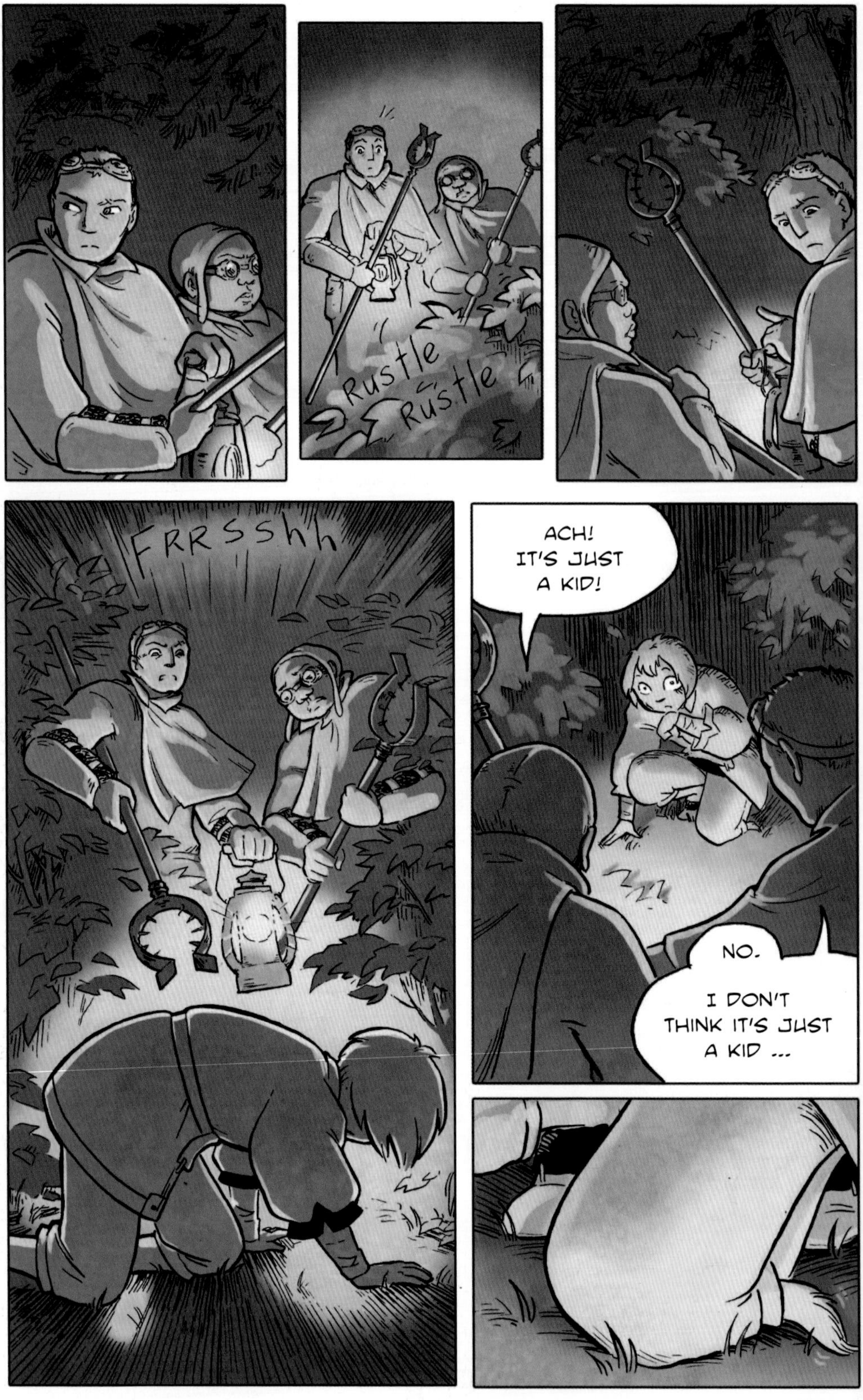
Rustle
Rustle
FRRSShh
ACH! IT'S JUST A KID!
NO.
I DON'T THINK IT'S JUST A KID ...

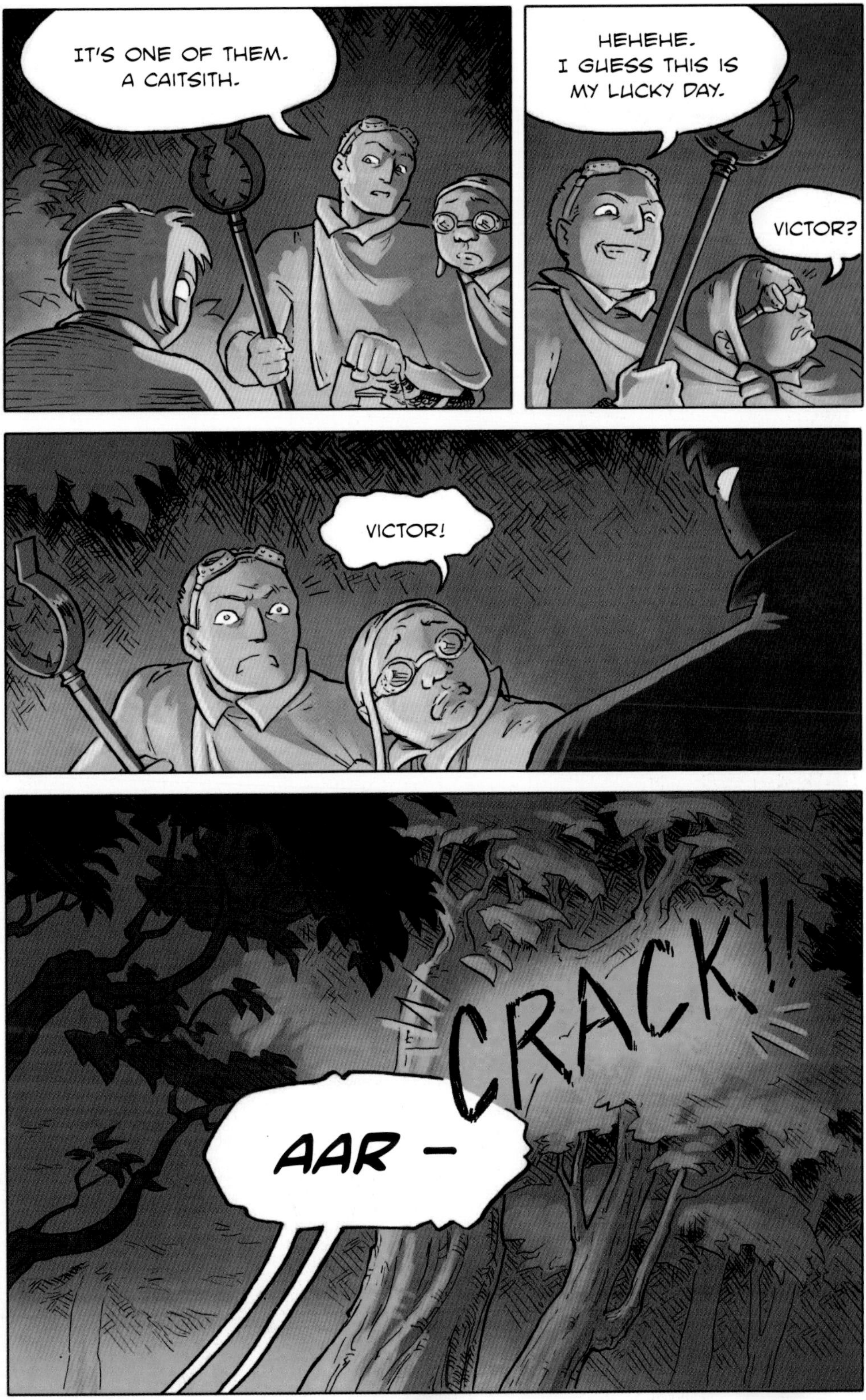
IT'S ONE OF THEM. A CAITSITH.
HEHEHE. I GUESS THIS IS MY LUCKY DAY.
VICTOR?
VICTOR!
CRACK!!
AAR –

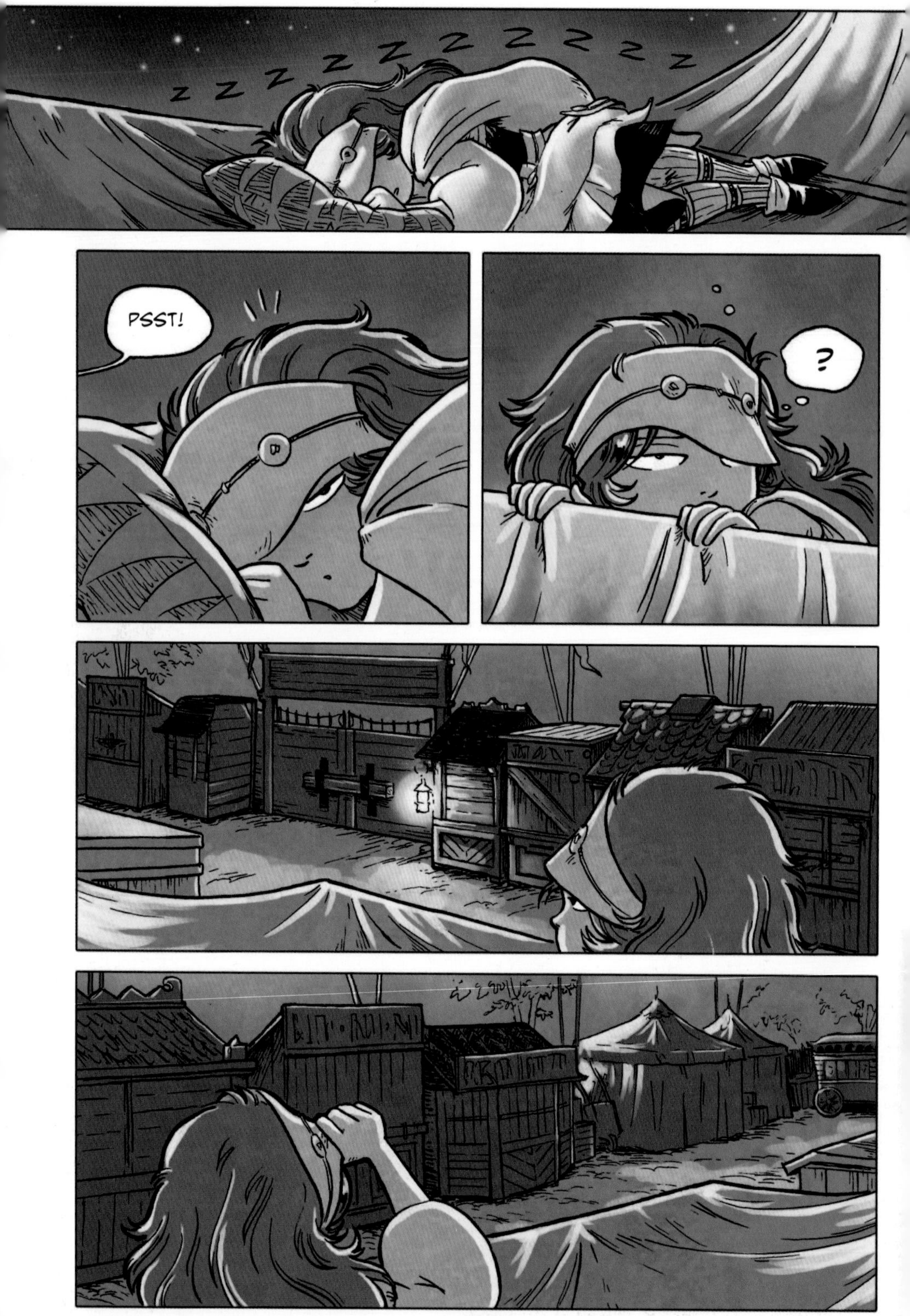
Z Z Z Z Z Z Z Z Z Z
PSST!
?

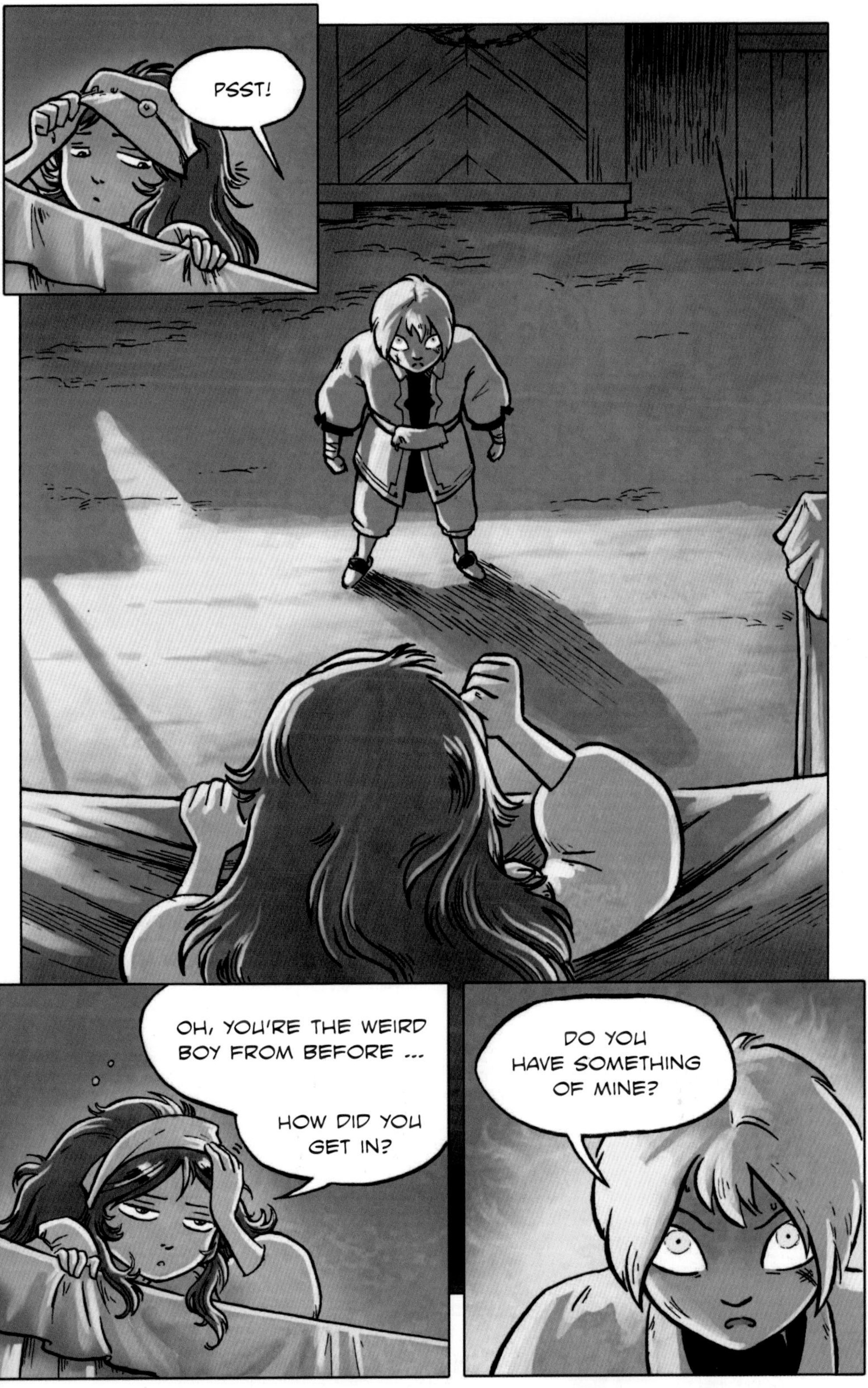
PSST!
OH, YOU'RE THE WEIRD BOY FROM BEFORE ...
HOW DID YOU GET IN?
DO YOU HAVE SOMETHING OF MINE?

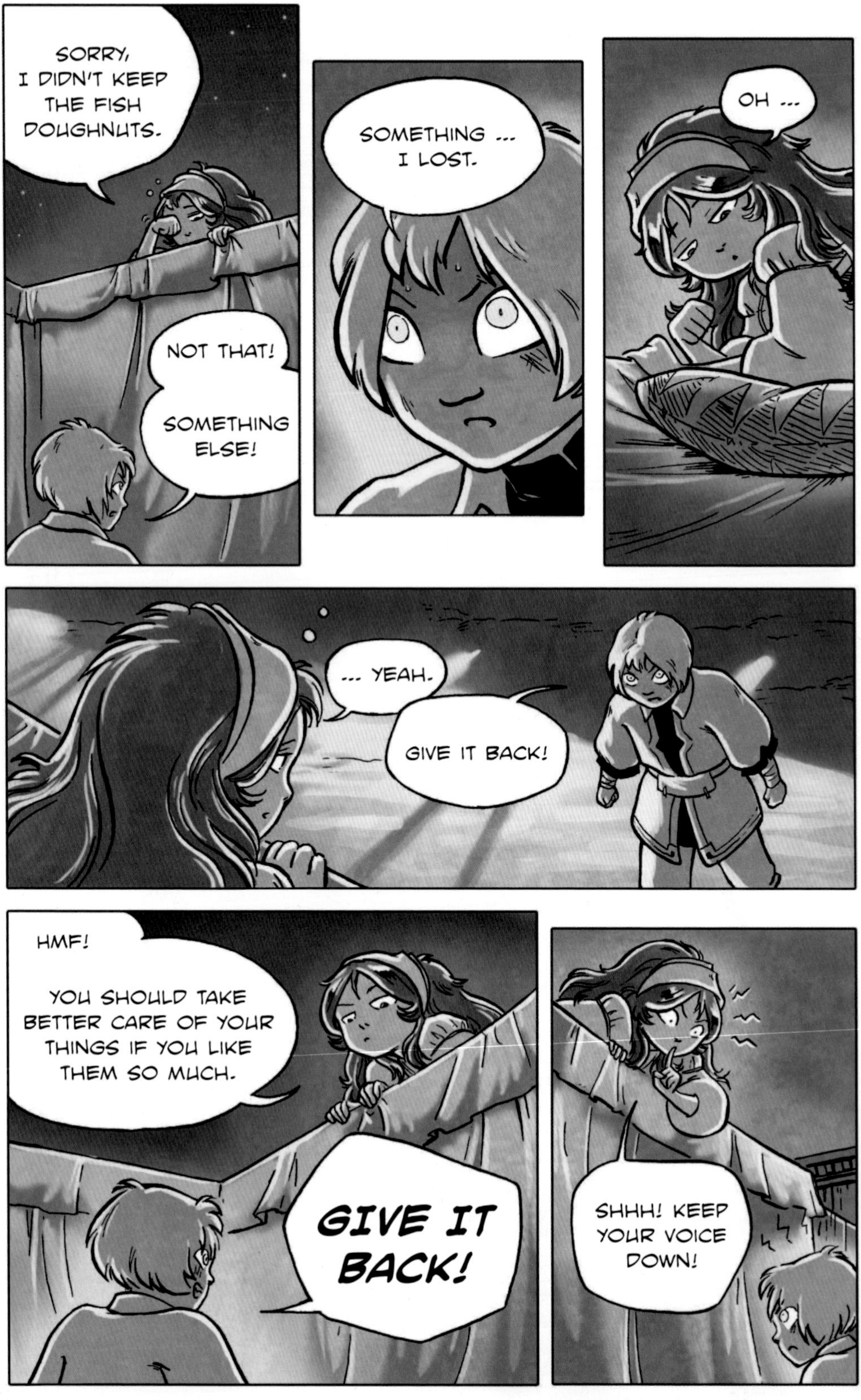
SORRY, I DIDN'T KEEP THE FISH DOUGHNUTS.
NOT THAT!
SOMETHING ELSE!
SOMETHING ... I LOST.
OH ...
... YEAH.
GIVE IT BACK!
HMF!
YOU SHOULD TAKE BETTER CARE OF YOUR THINGS IF YOU LIKE THEM SO MUCH.
GIVE IT BACK!
SHHH! KEEP YOUR VOICE DOWN!

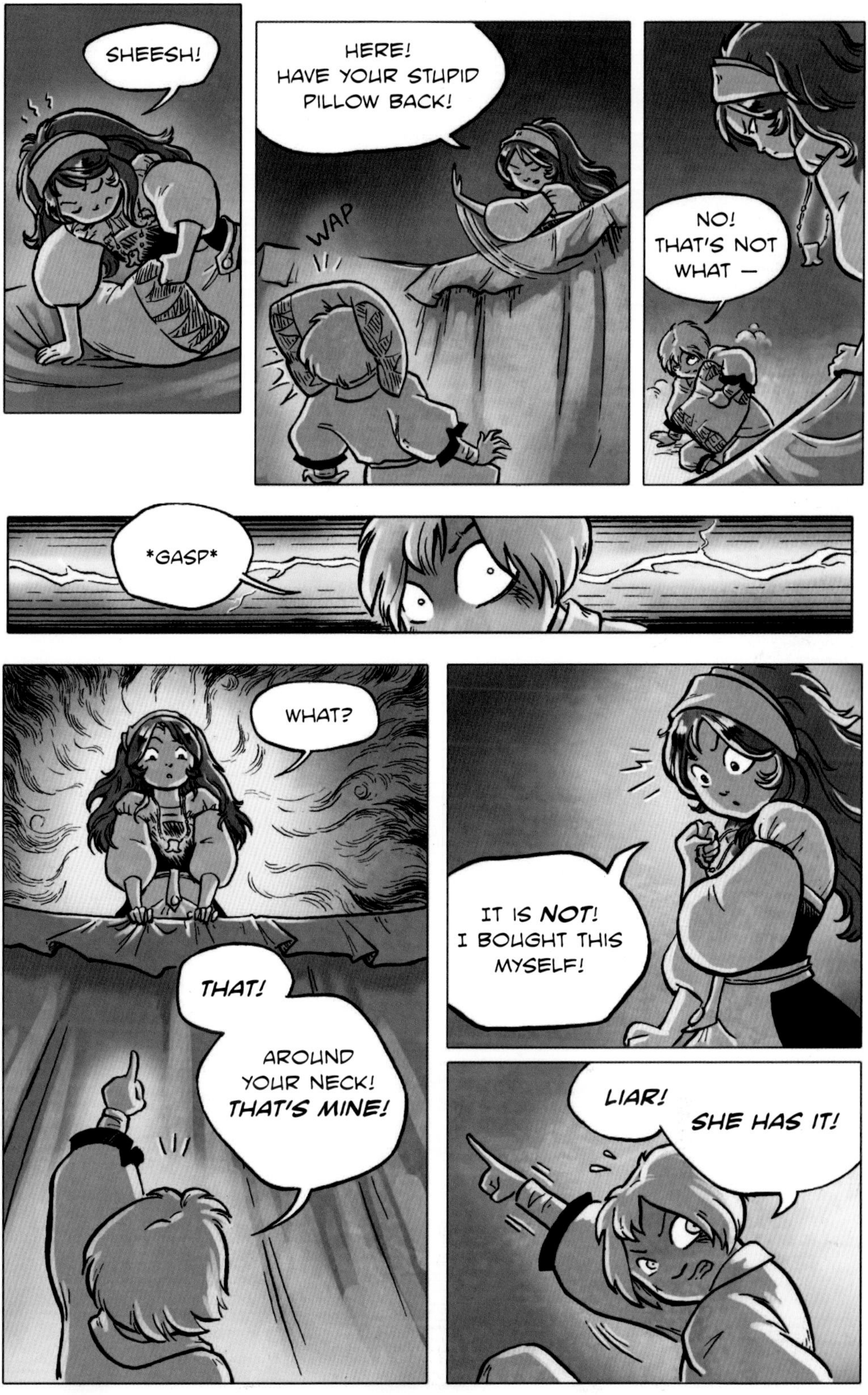
SHEESH!
HERE! HAVE YOUR STUPID PILLOW BACK!
WAP
NO! THAT'S NOT WHAT —
GASP
WHAT?
THAT!
AROUND YOUR NECK! THAT'S MINE!
IT IS NOT! I BOUGHT THIS MYSELF!
LIAR!
SHE HAS IT!

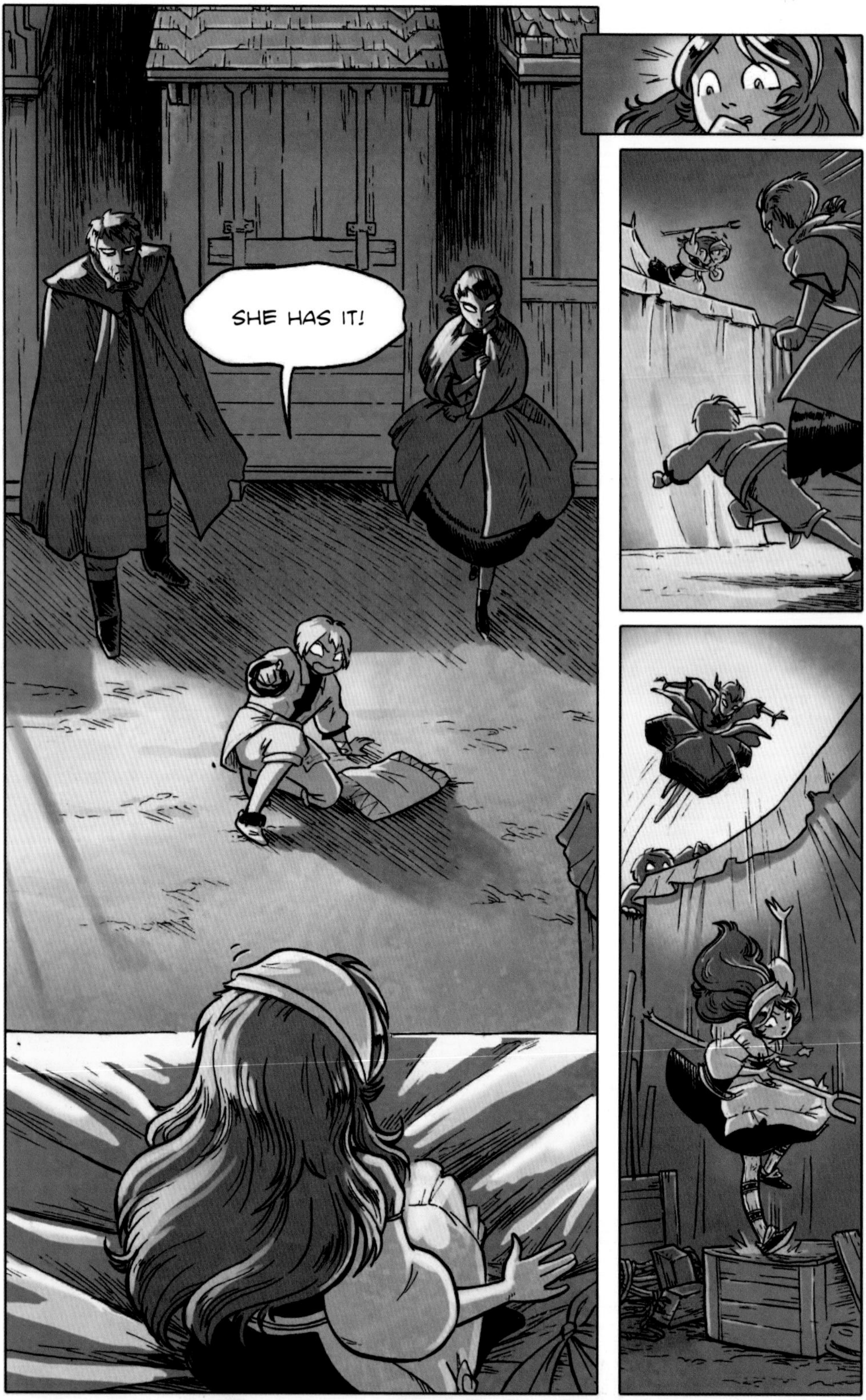
SHE HAS IT!

THAT WEIRDO BROUGHT HIS WHOLE FAM —
GAH! THEY'RE FAST!

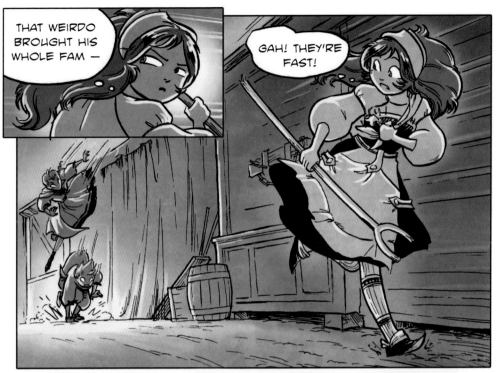

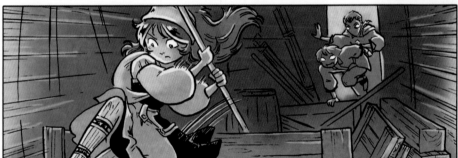

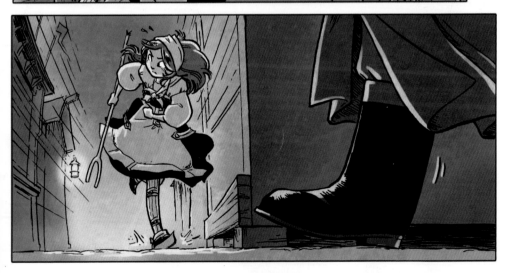

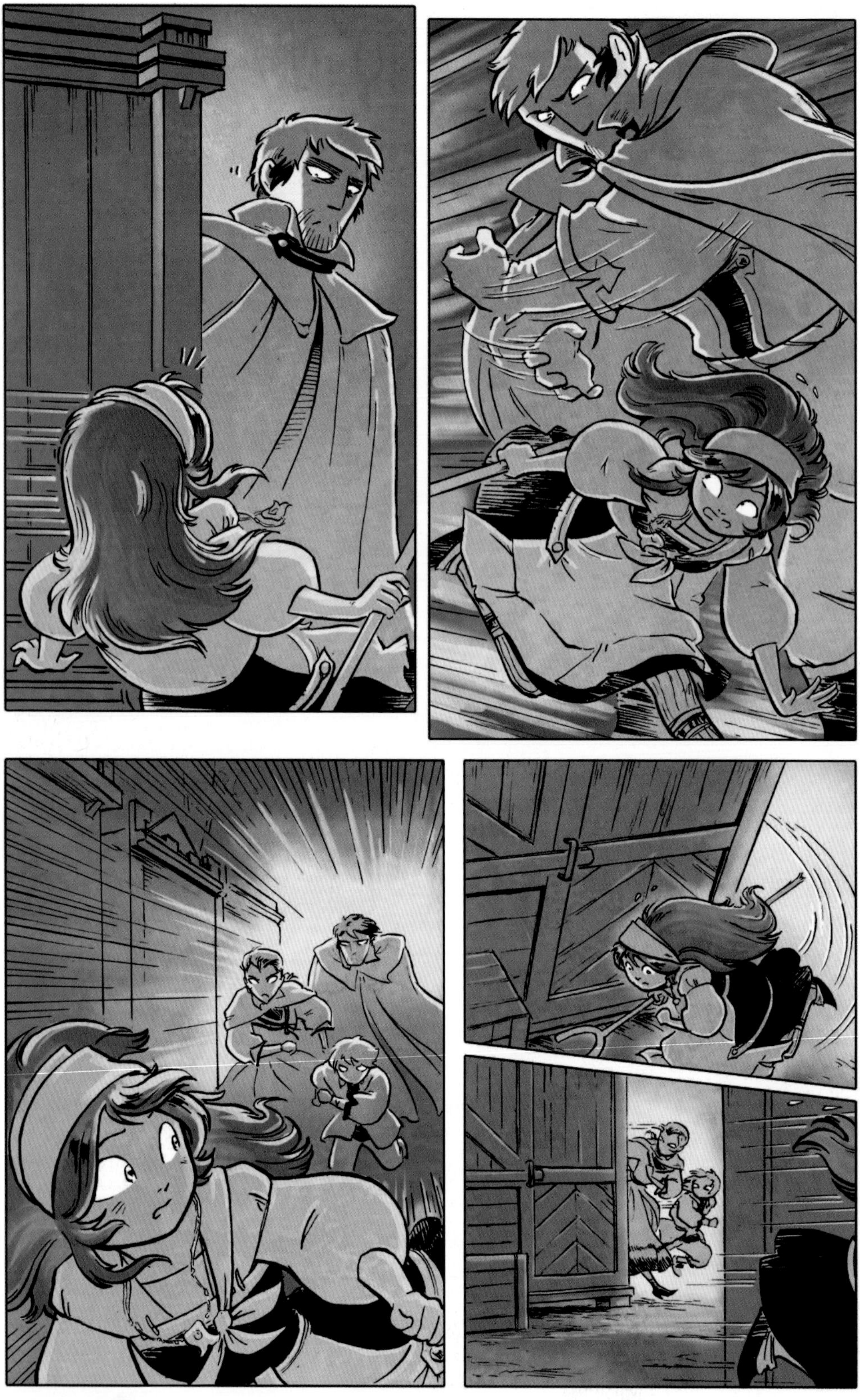

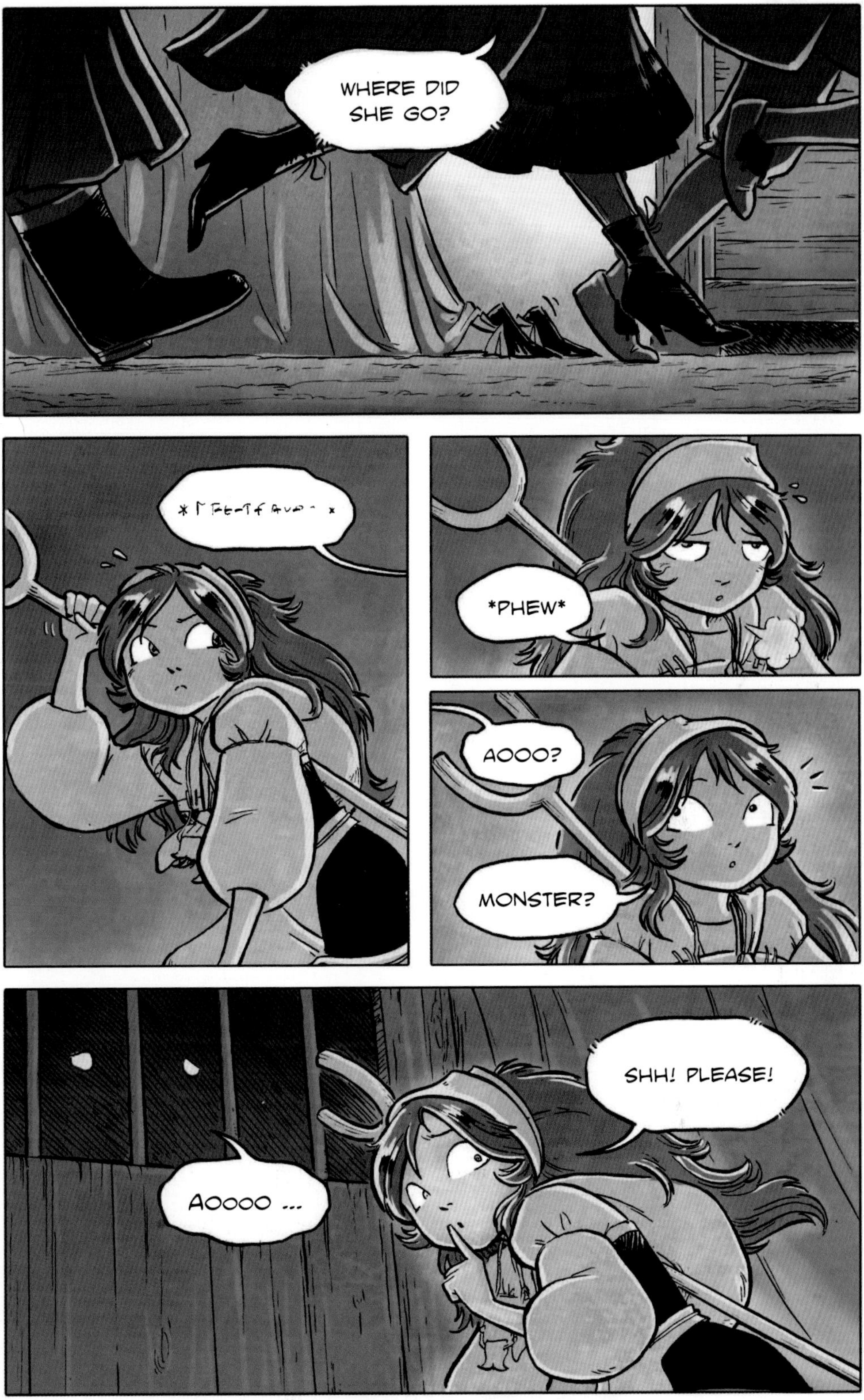
WHERE DID SHE GO?
PHEW
AOOO?
MONSTER?
SHH! PLEASE!
AOOOO ...

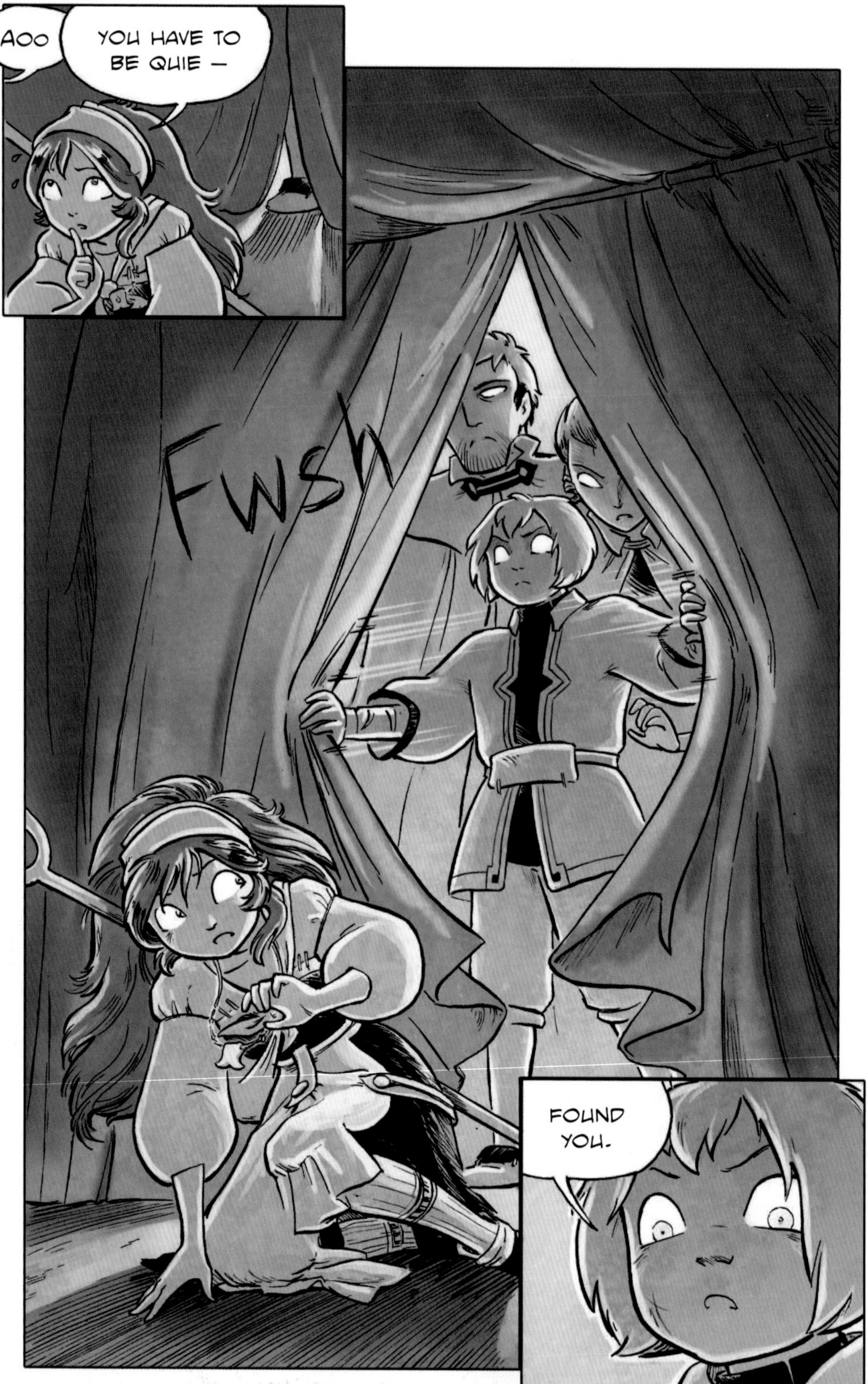
AOO
YOU HAVE TO BE QUIE –
Fwsh
FOUND YOU.

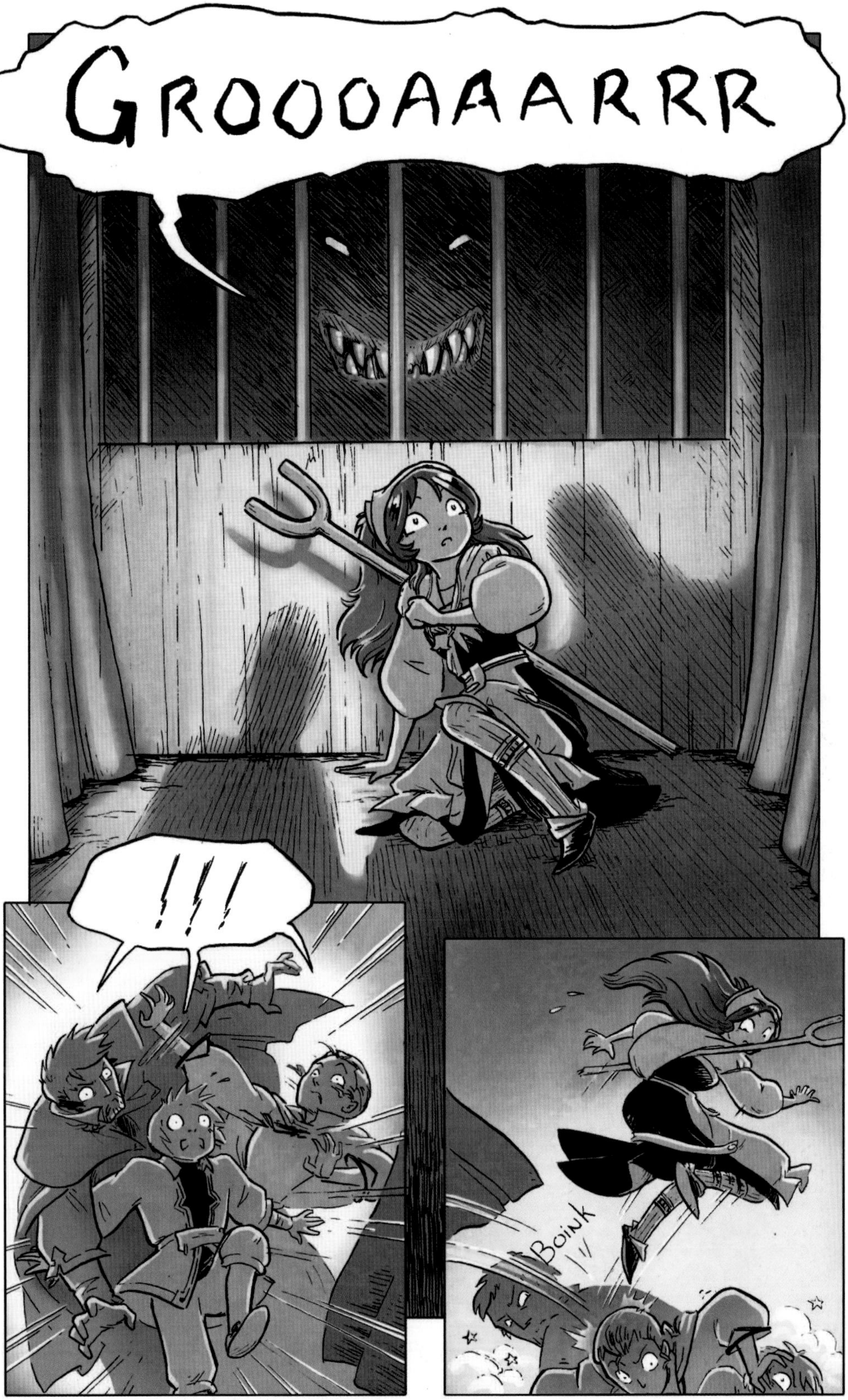
GROOOAAARRR
!!!
BOINK

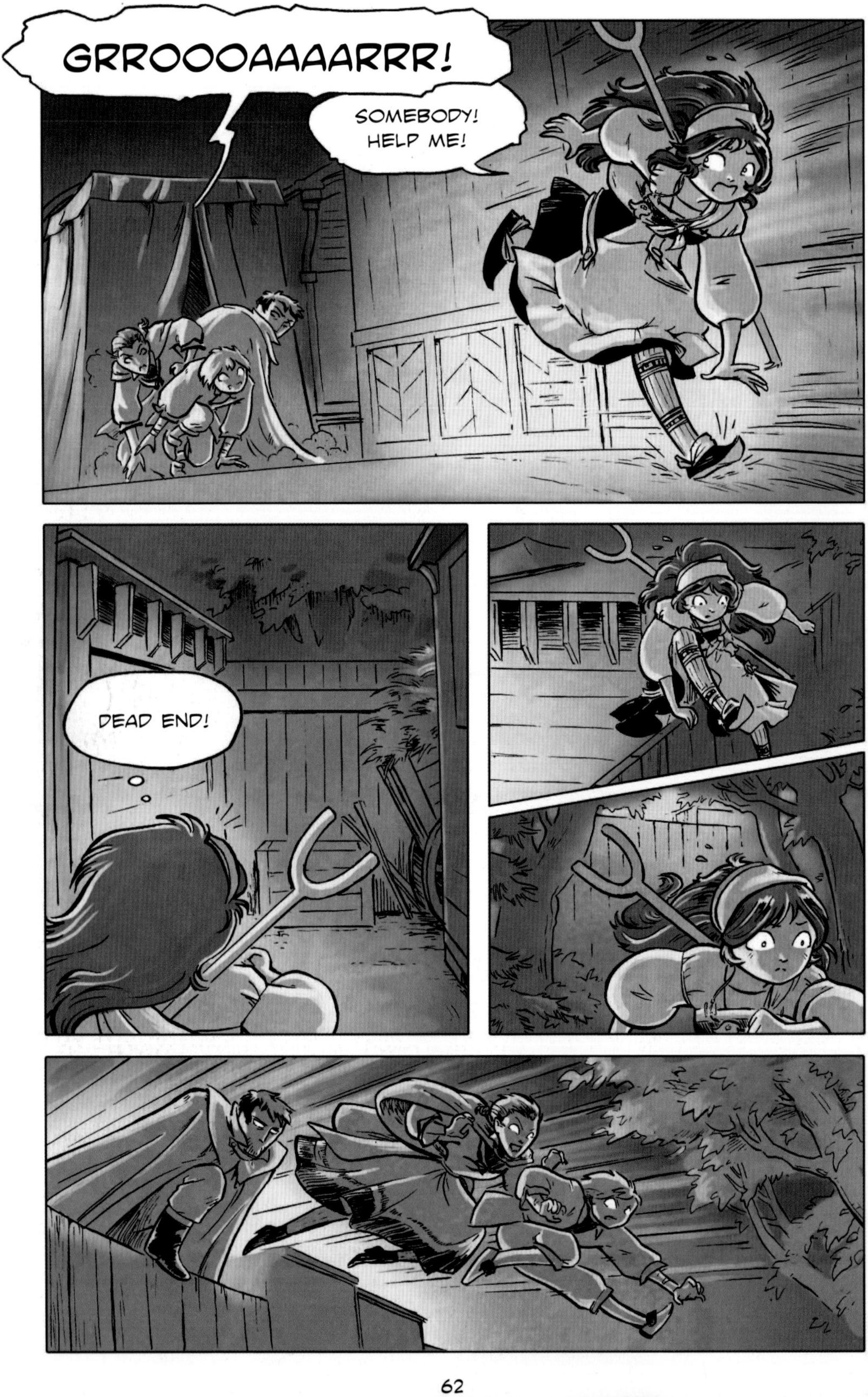
GRROOOAAAARRR!
SOMEBODY! HELP ME!
DEAD END!

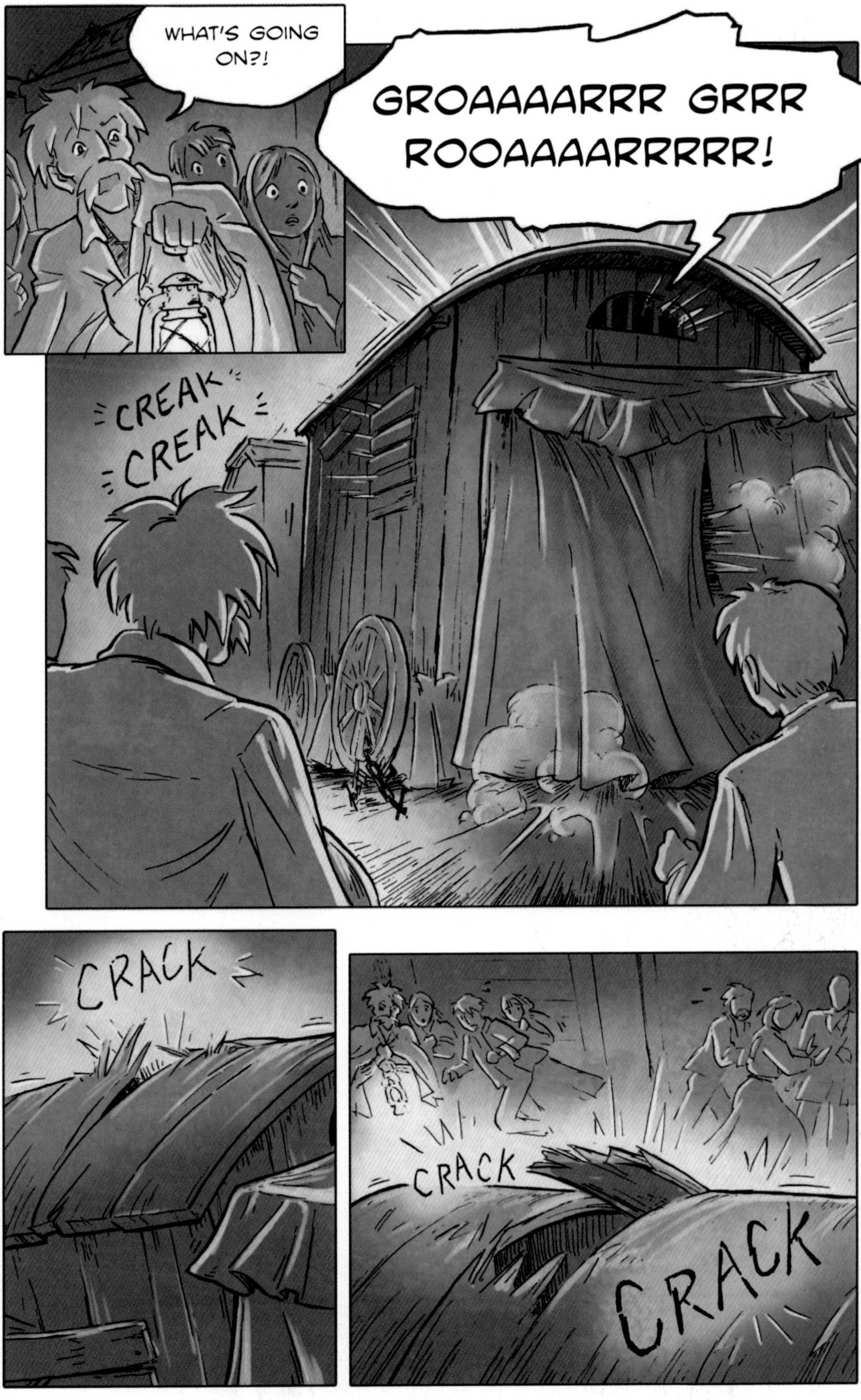
WHAT'S GOING ON?!
GROAAAARRR GRRR ROOAAAARRRRR!
CREAK CREAK
CRACK
CRACK
CRACK

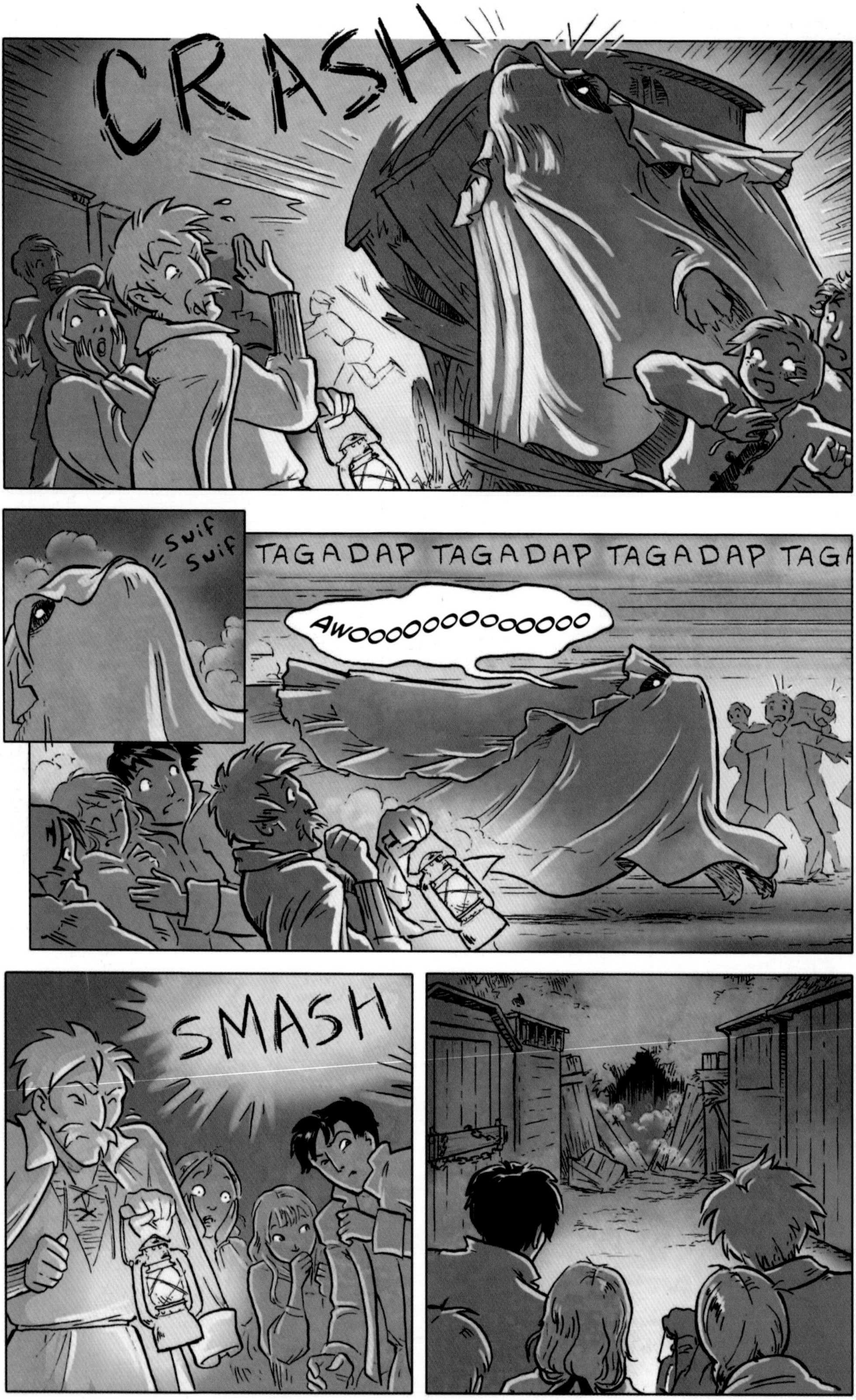
CRASH
Swif Swif
TAGADAP TAGADAP TAGADAP TAGA
AWOOOOOOOOOOOOOO
SMASH

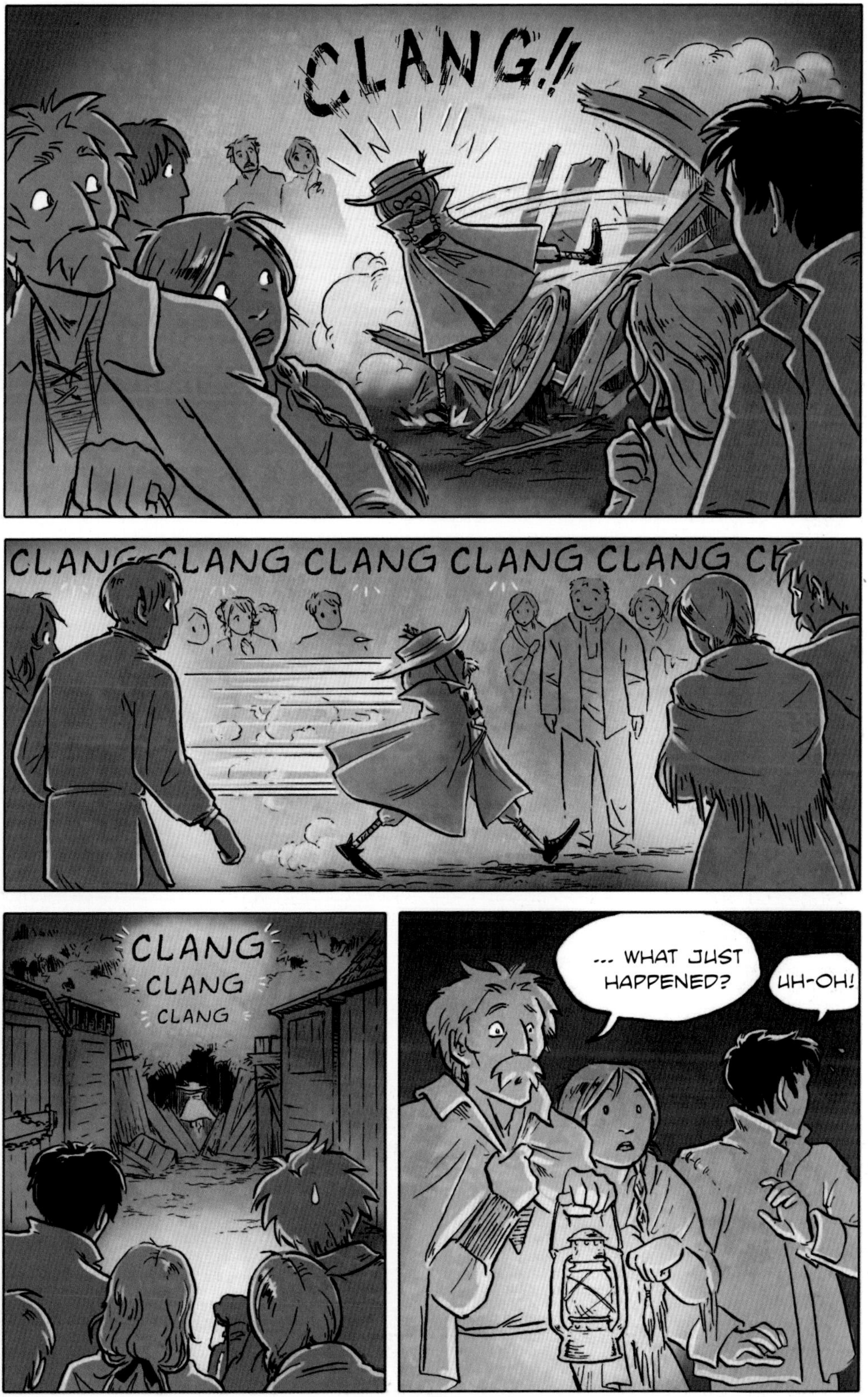
CLANG!!
CLANG CLANG CLANG CLANG CLANG CL
CLANG
CLANG
CLANG
... WHAT JUST HAPPENED?
UH-OH!

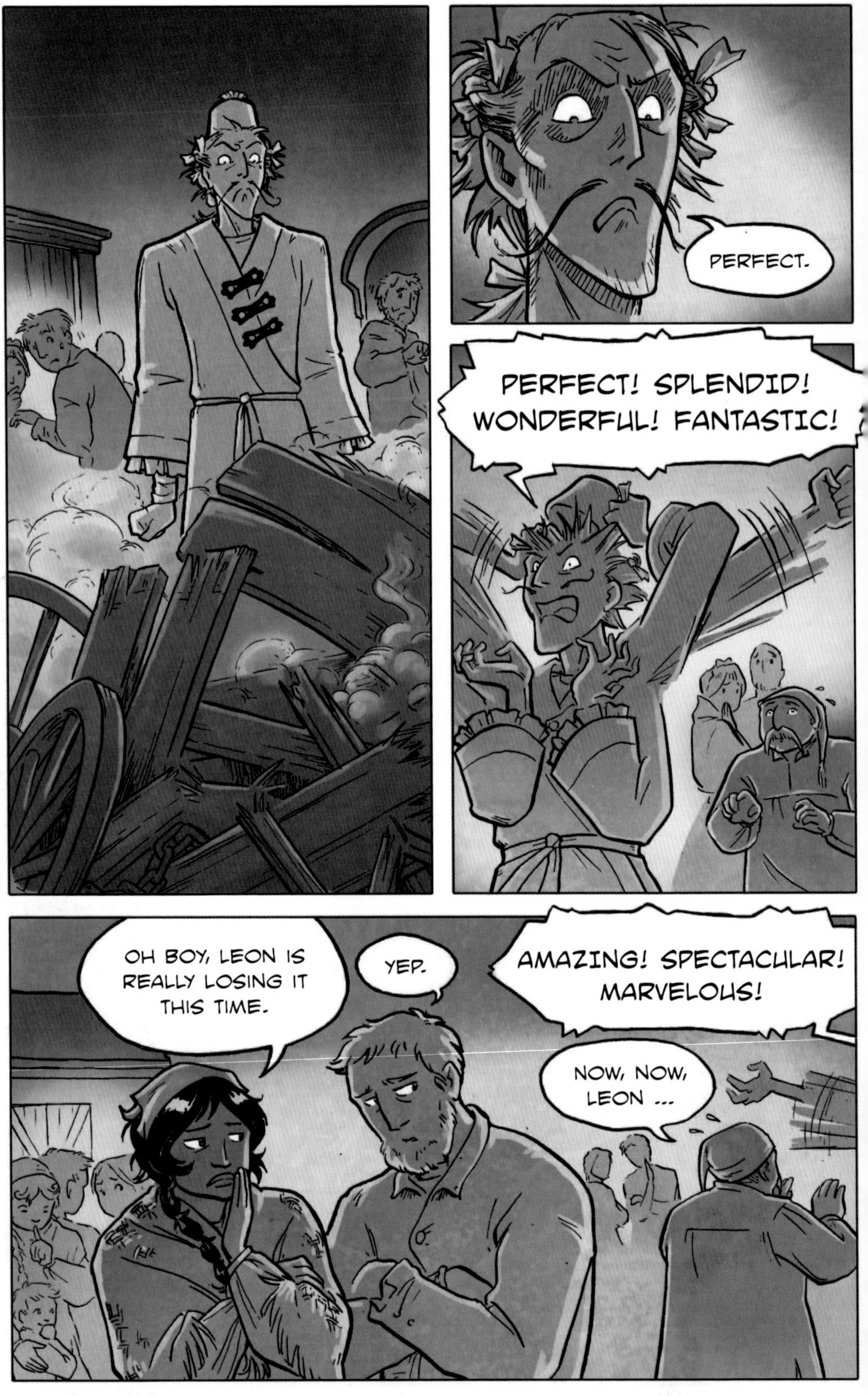
PERFECT.
PERFECT! SPLENDID! WONDERFUL! FANTASTIC!
OH BOY, LEON IS REALLY LOSING IT THIS TIME.
YEP.
AMAZING! SPECTACULAR! MARVELOUS!
NOW, NOW, LEON ...

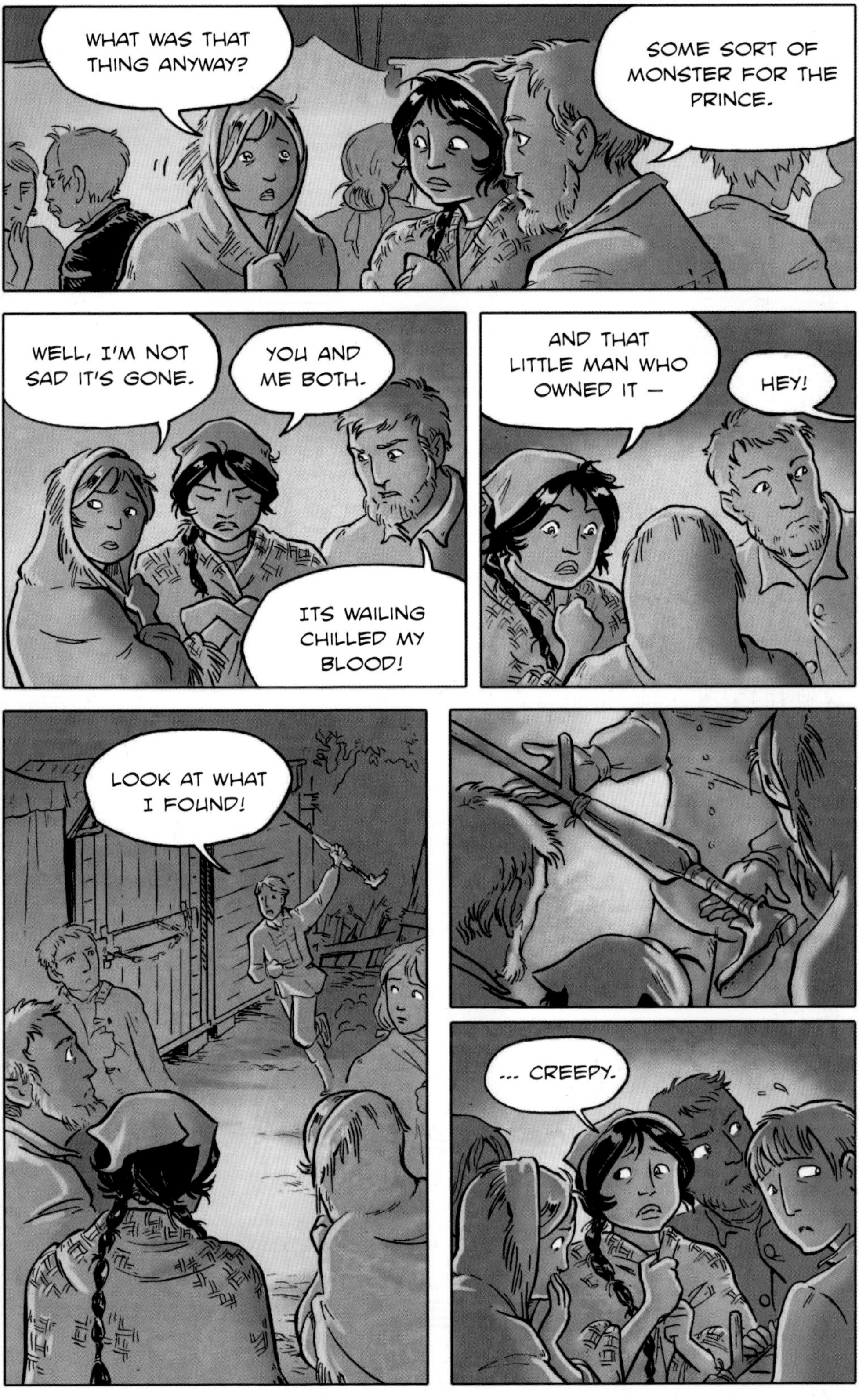
WHAT WAS THAT THING ANYWAY?
SOME SORT OF MONSTER FOR THE PRINCE.
WELL, I'M NOT SAD IT'S GONE.
YOU AND ME BOTH.
ITS WAILING CHILLED MY BLOOD!
AND THAT LITTLE MAN WHO OWNED IT —
HEY!
LOOK AT WHAT I FOUND!
... CREEPY.

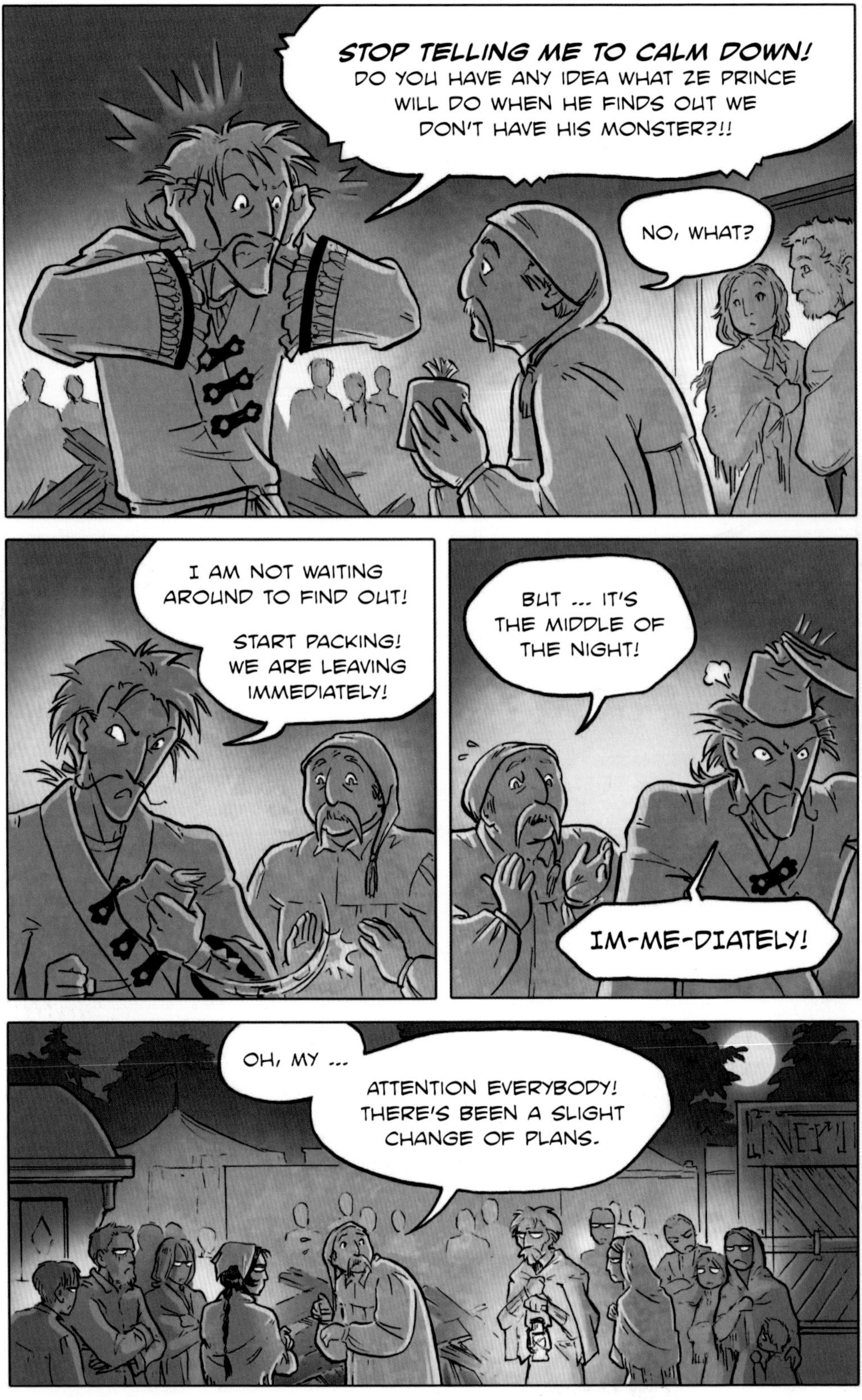
STOP TELLING ME TO CALM DOWN! DO YOU HAVE ANY IDEA WHAT ZE PRINCE WILL DO WHEN HE FINDS OUT WE DON'T HAVE HIS MONSTER?!!
NO, WHAT?
I AM NOT WAITING AROUND TO FIND OUT!
START PACKING! WE ARE LEAVING IMMEDIATELY!
BUT ... IT'S THE MIDDLE OF THE NIGHT!
IM-ME-DIATELY!
OH, MY ...
ATTENTION EVERYBODY! THERE'S BEEN A SLIGHT CHANGE OF PLANS.

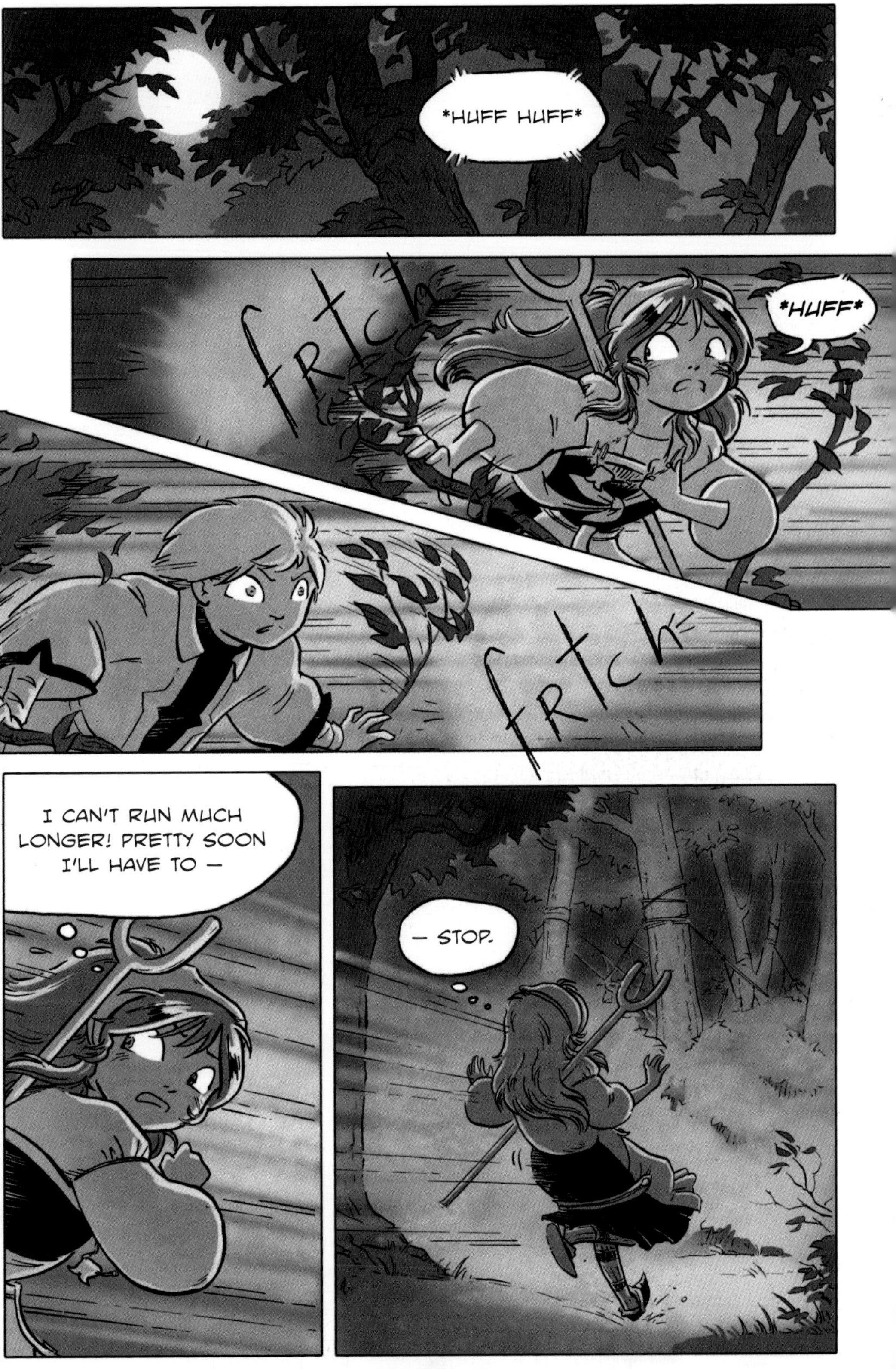
HUFF HUFF
FRTCH
HUFF
FRTCH
I CAN'T RUN MUCH LONGER! PRETTY SOON I'LL HAVE TO —
— STOP.

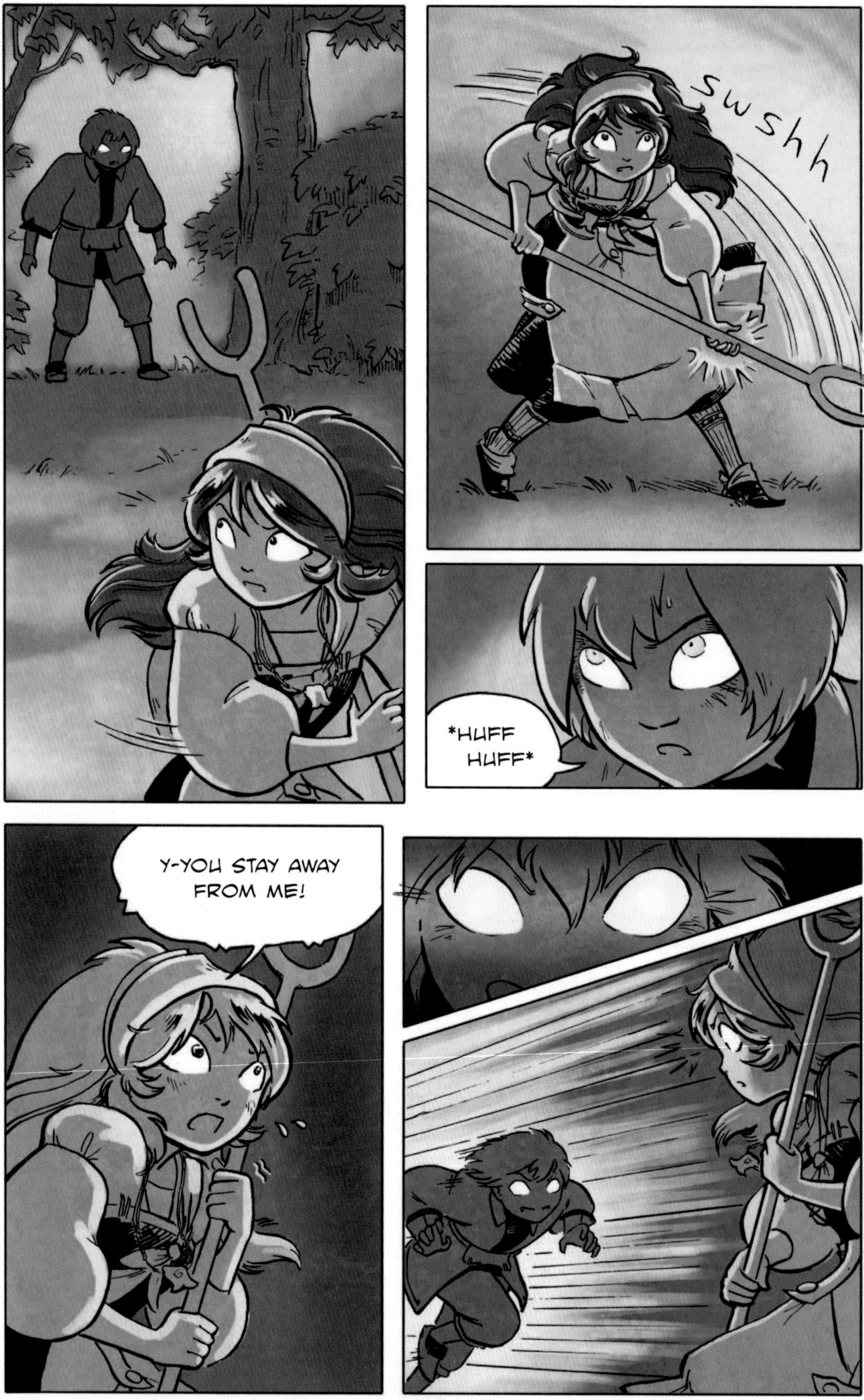
SWSHH
*HUFF
HUFF*
Y-YOU STAY AWAY FROM ME!

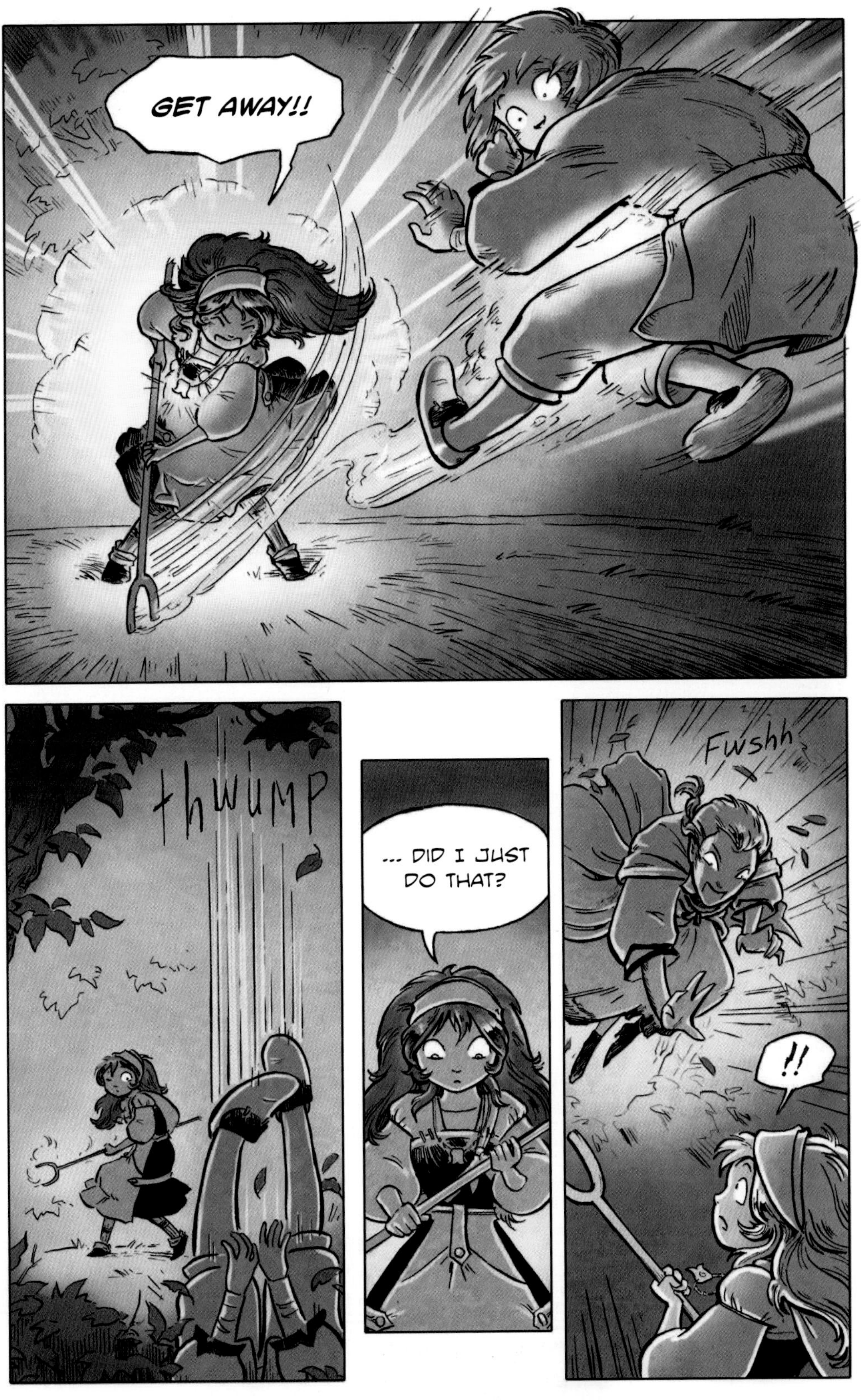
GET AWAY!!
thwump
... DID I JUST DO THAT?
Fwshh
!!

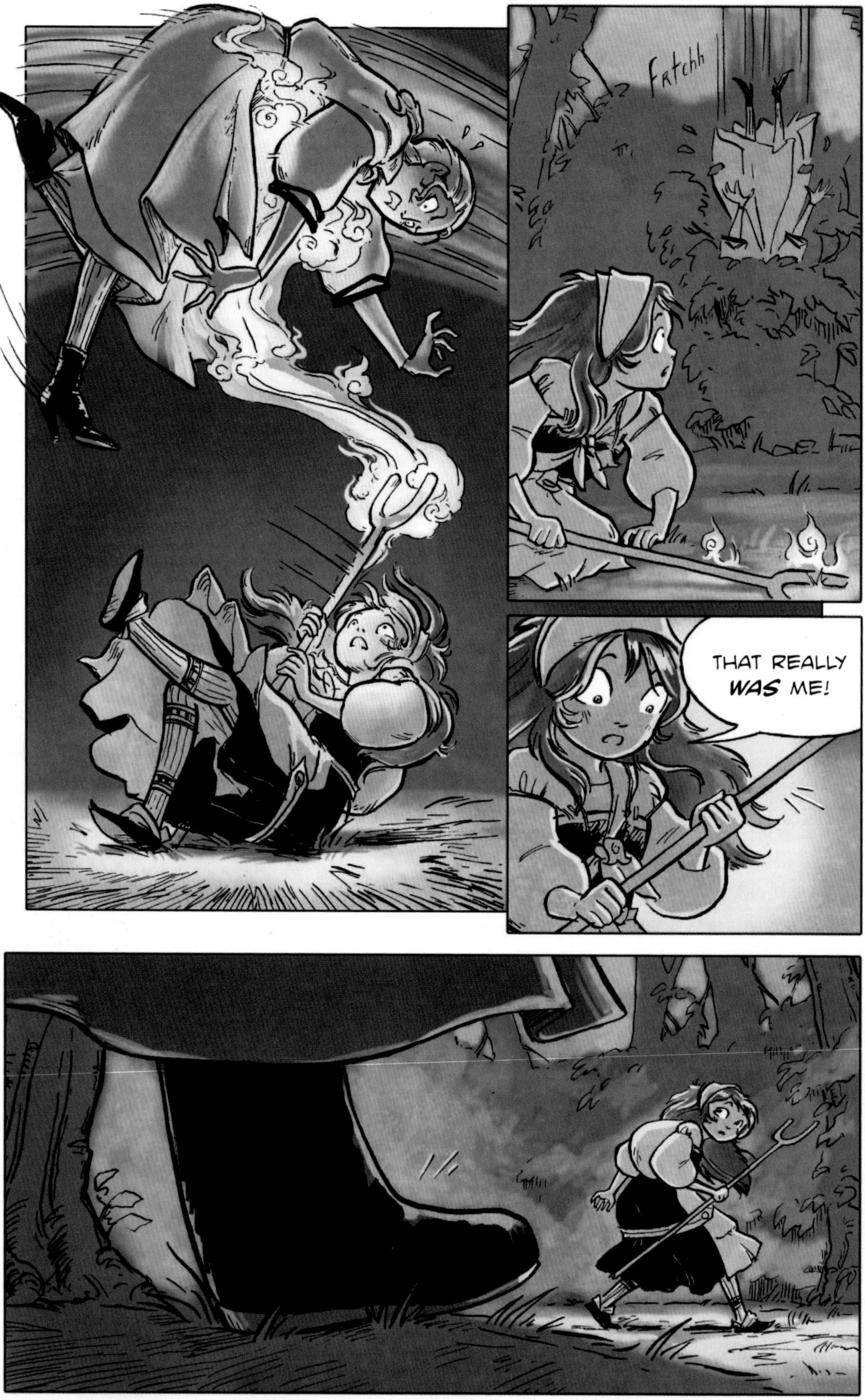
Frtchh
THAT REALLY WAS ME!

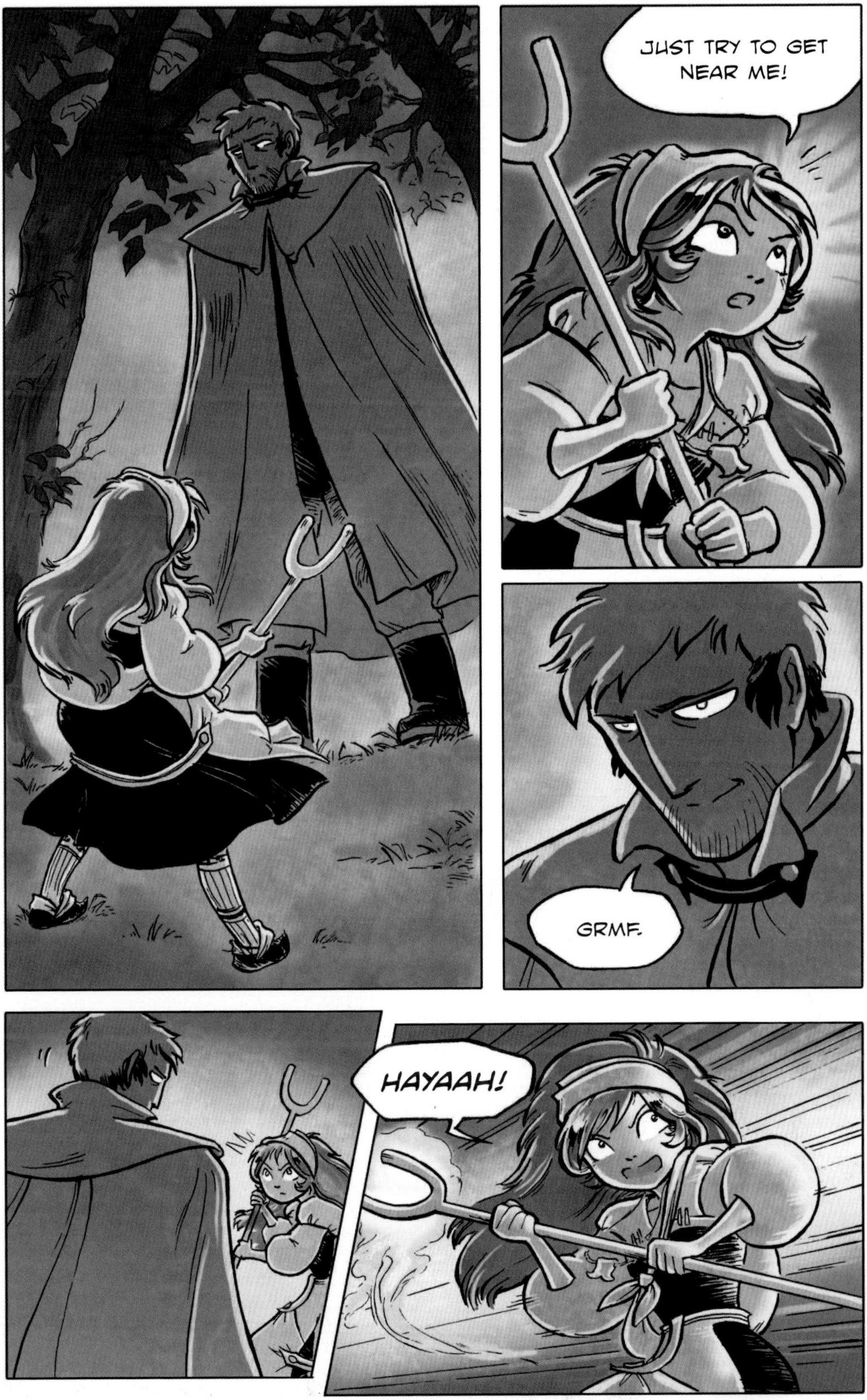
JUST TRY TO GET NEAR ME!
GRMF.
HAYAAH!

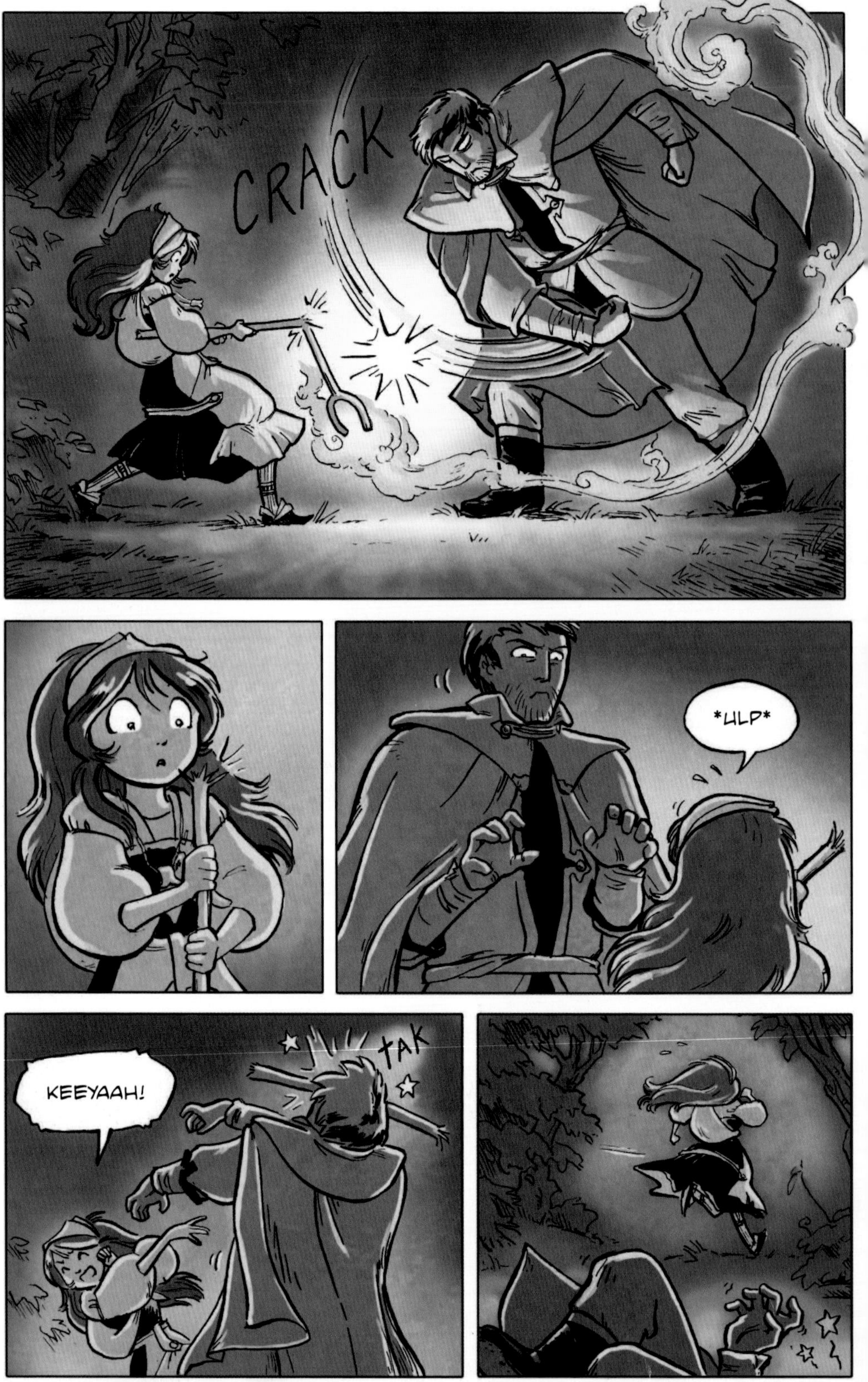
CRACK
ULP
KEEYAAH!
TAK

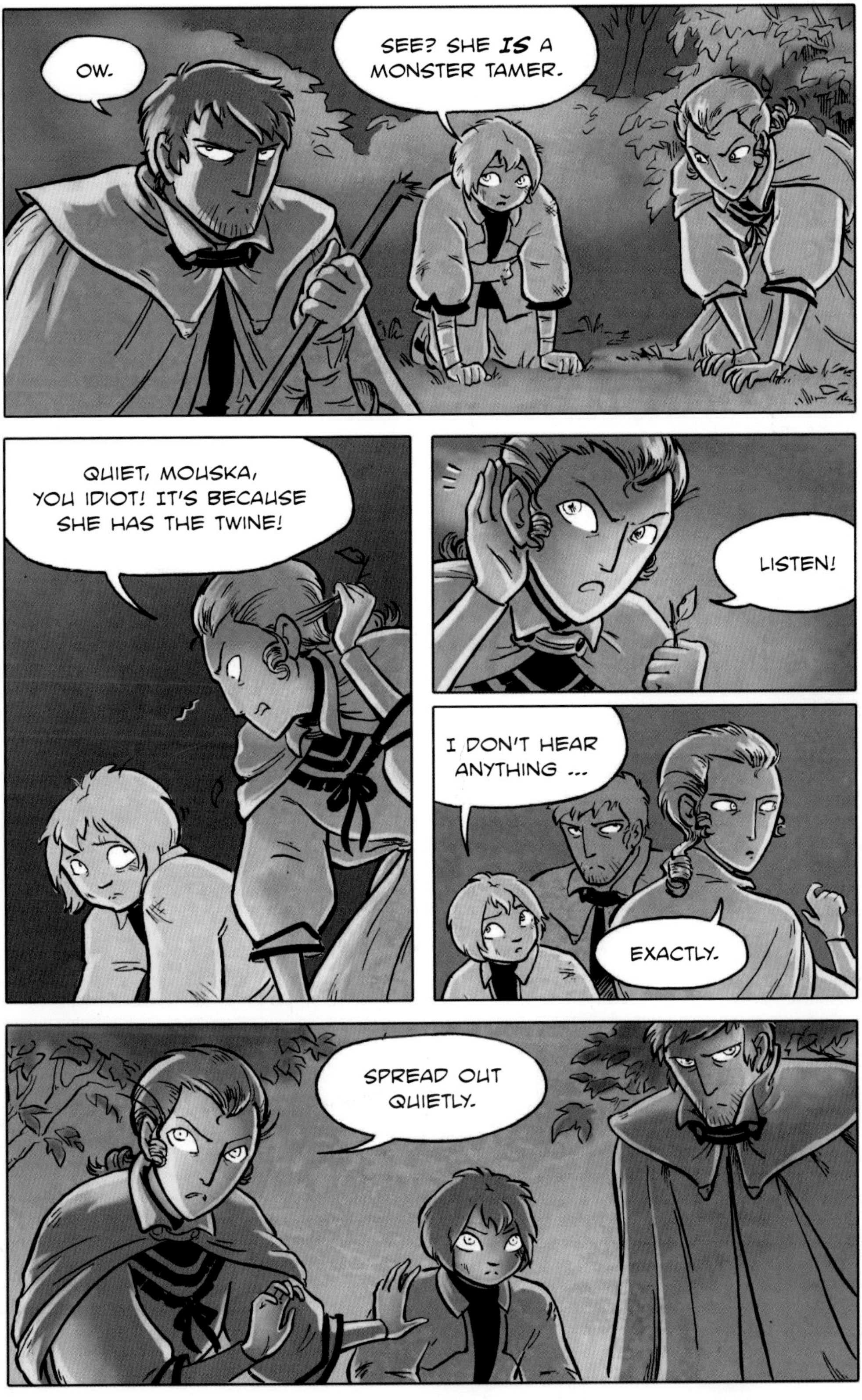
OW.
SEE? SHE IS A MONSTER TAMER.
QUIET, MOUSKA, YOU IDIOT! IT'S BECAUSE SHE HAS THE TWINE!
LISTEN!
I DON'T HEAR ANYTHING ...
EXACTLY.
SPREAD OUT QUIETLY.

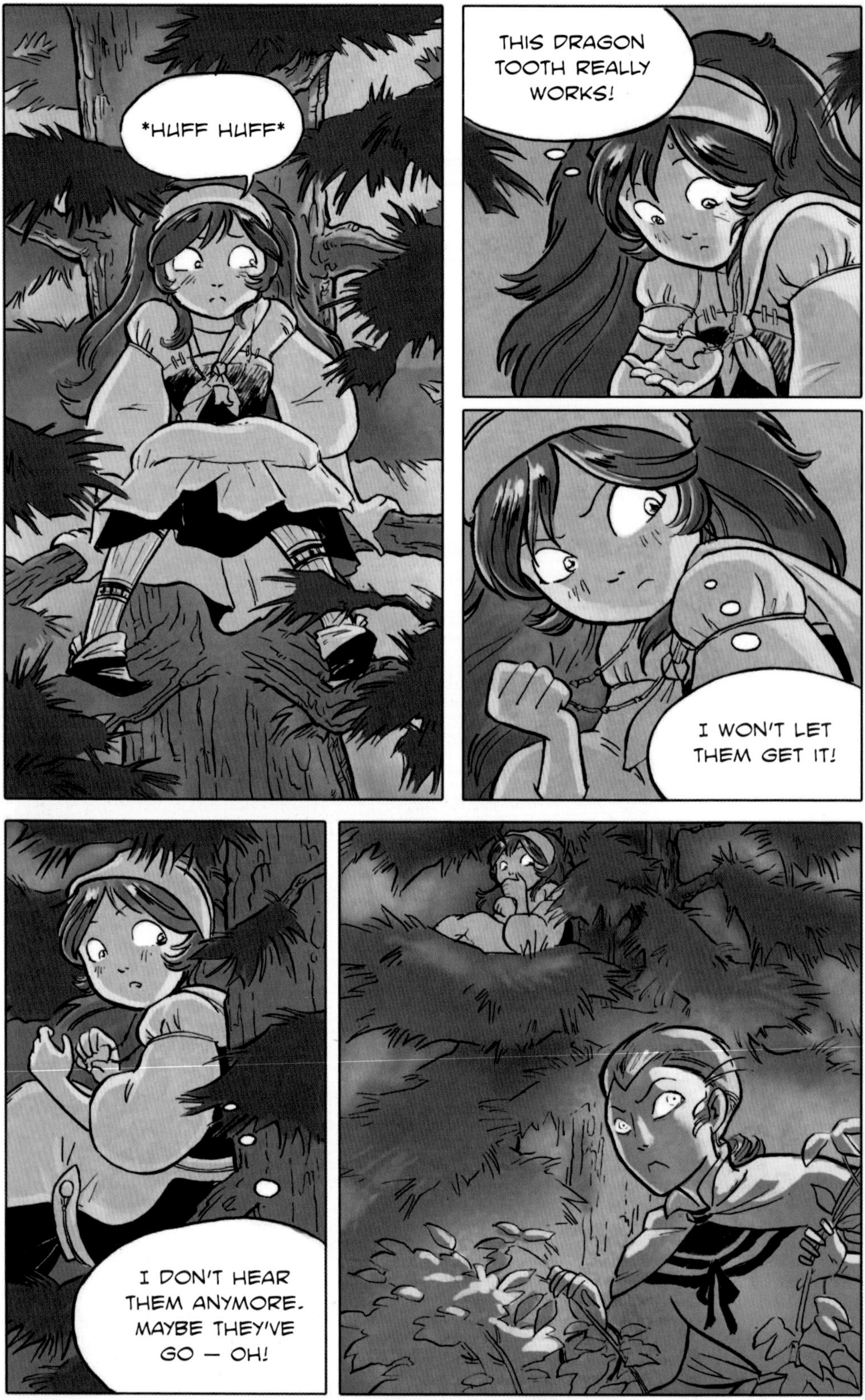
HUFF HUFF
THIS DRAGON TOOTH REALLY WORKS!
I WON'T LET THEM GET IT!
I DON'T HEAR THEM ANYMORE. MAYBE THEY'VE GO — OH!

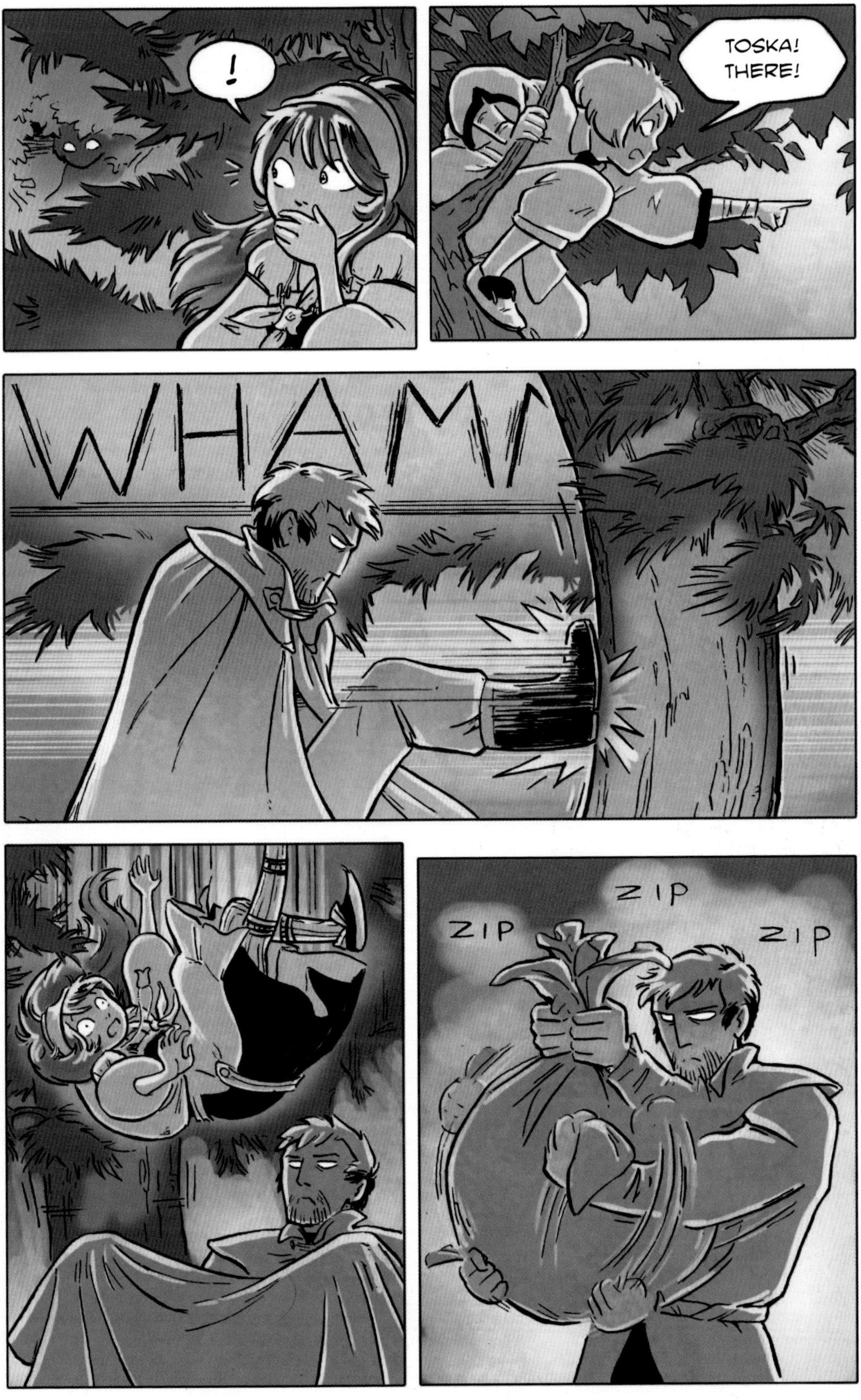
!
TOSKA! THERE!
WHAM
ZIP
ZIP
ZIP

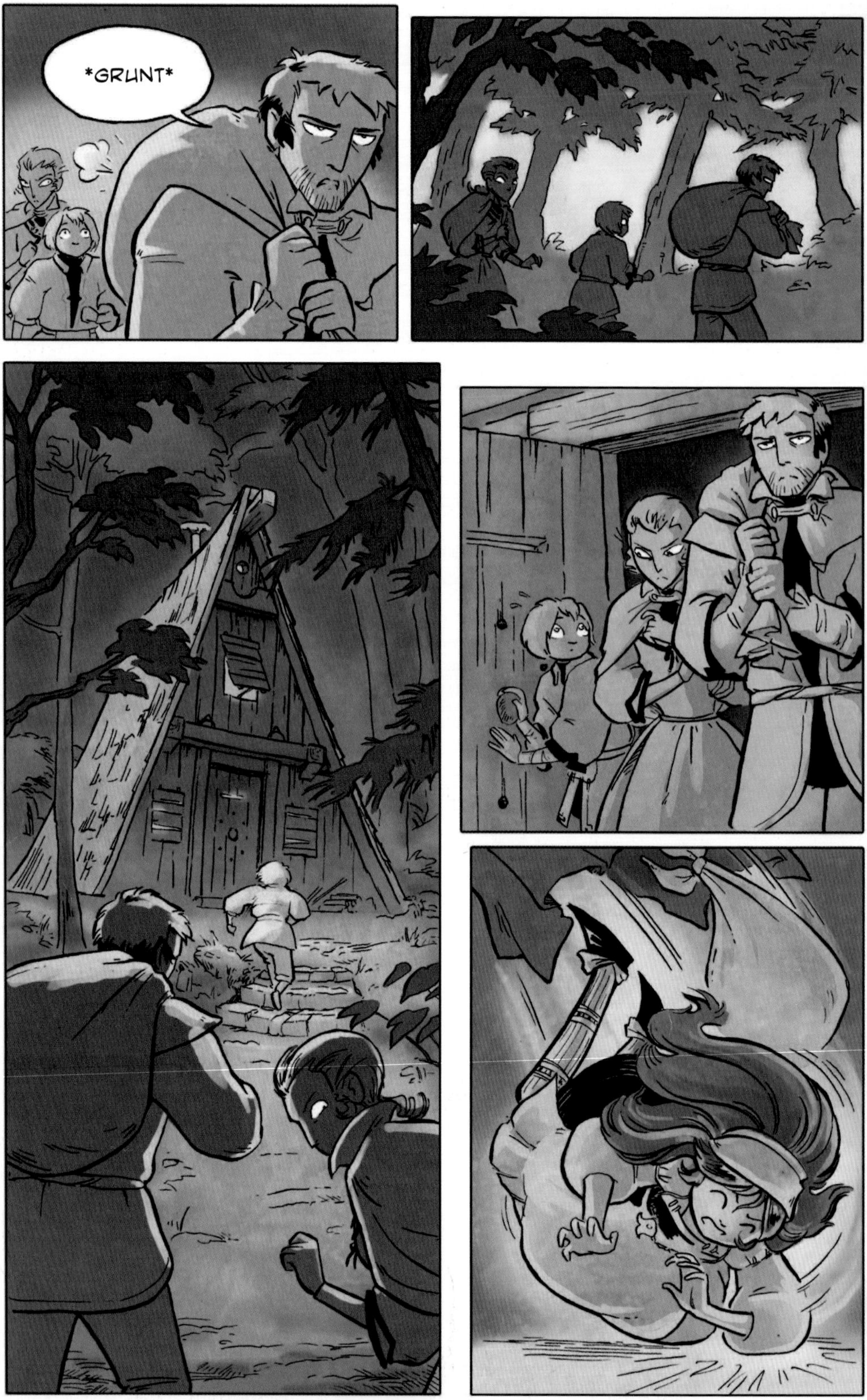
GRUNT

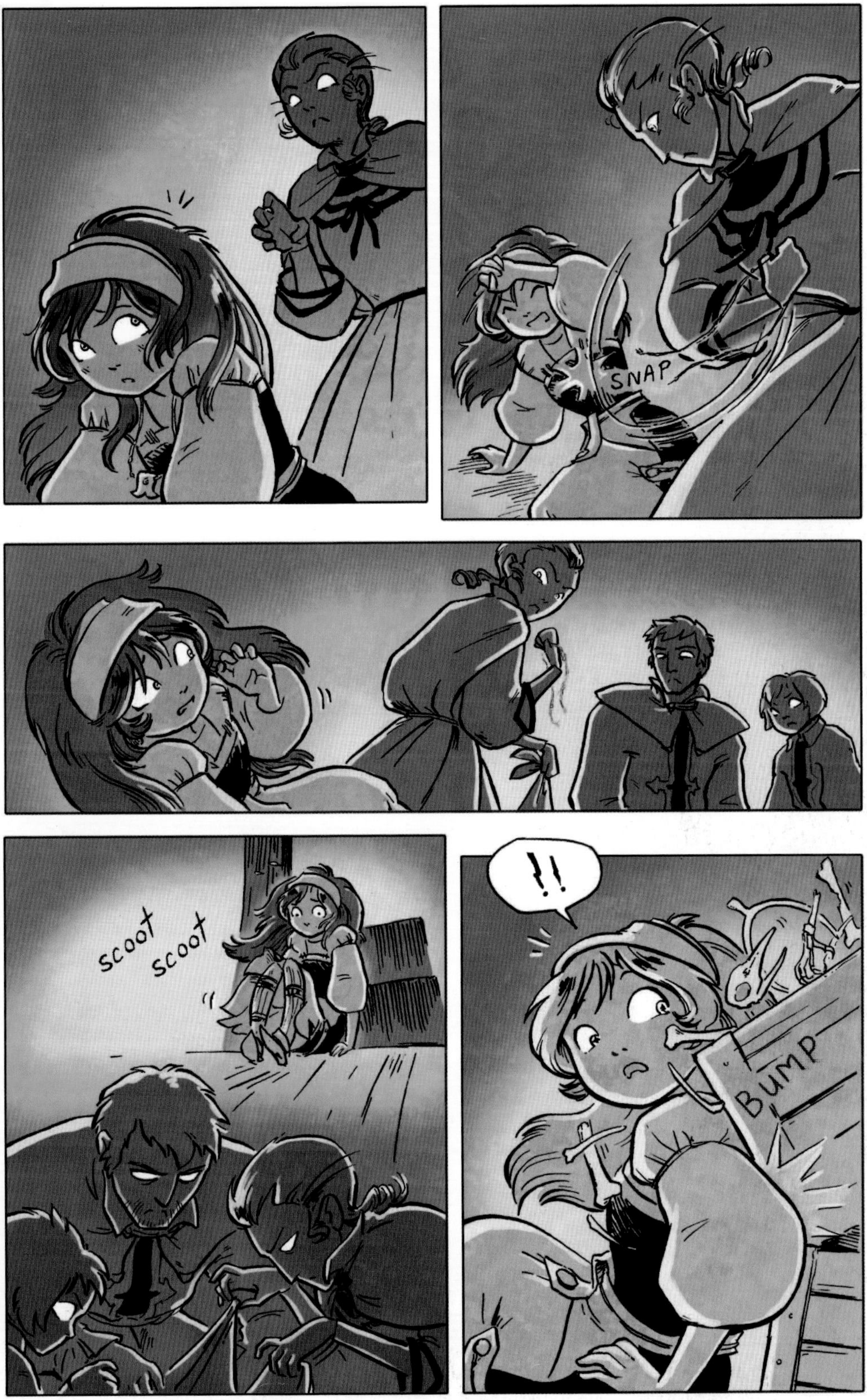
SNAP
scoot scoot
!!
BUMP

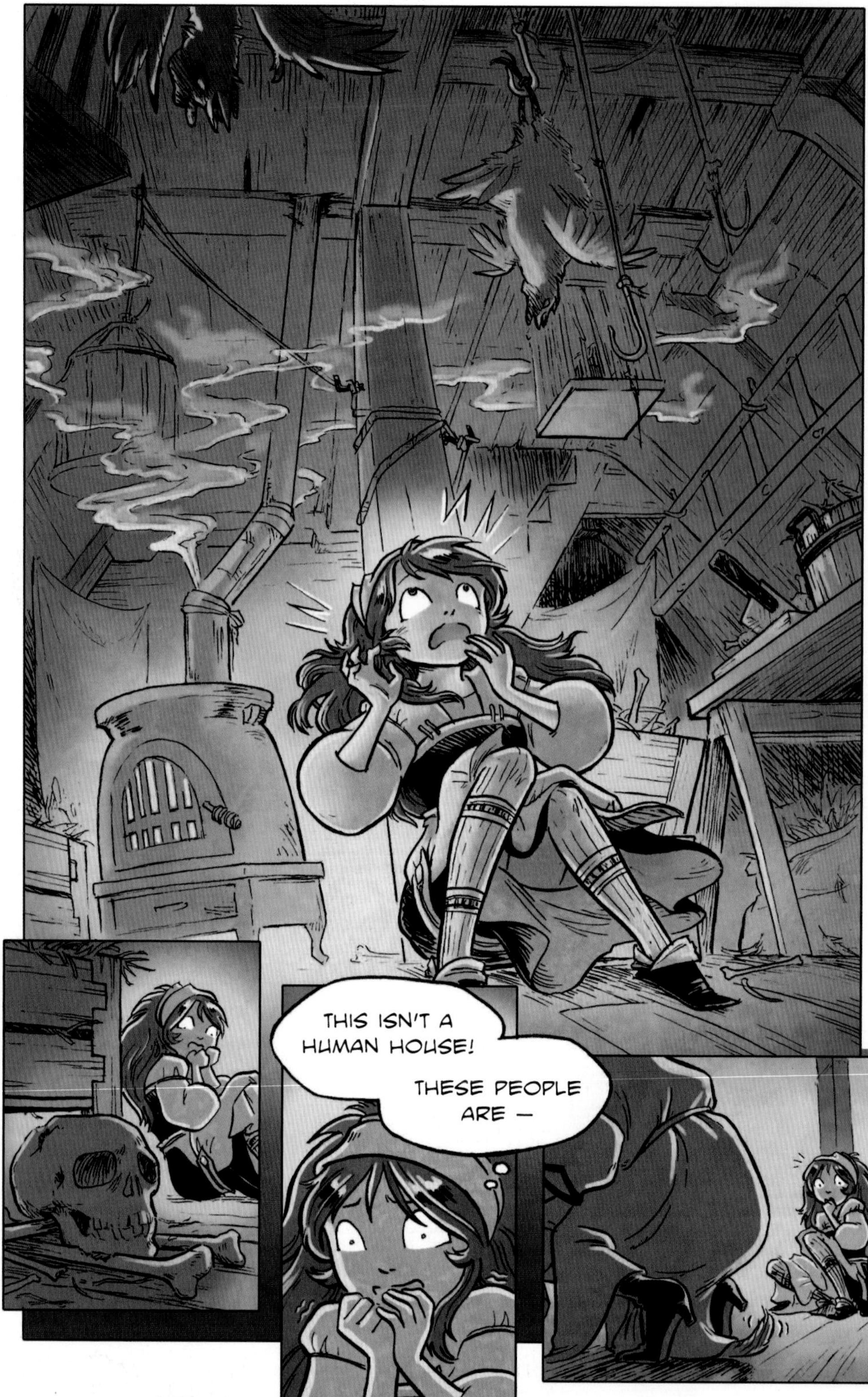
THIS ISN'T A HUMAN HOUSE!
THESE PEOPLE ARE –

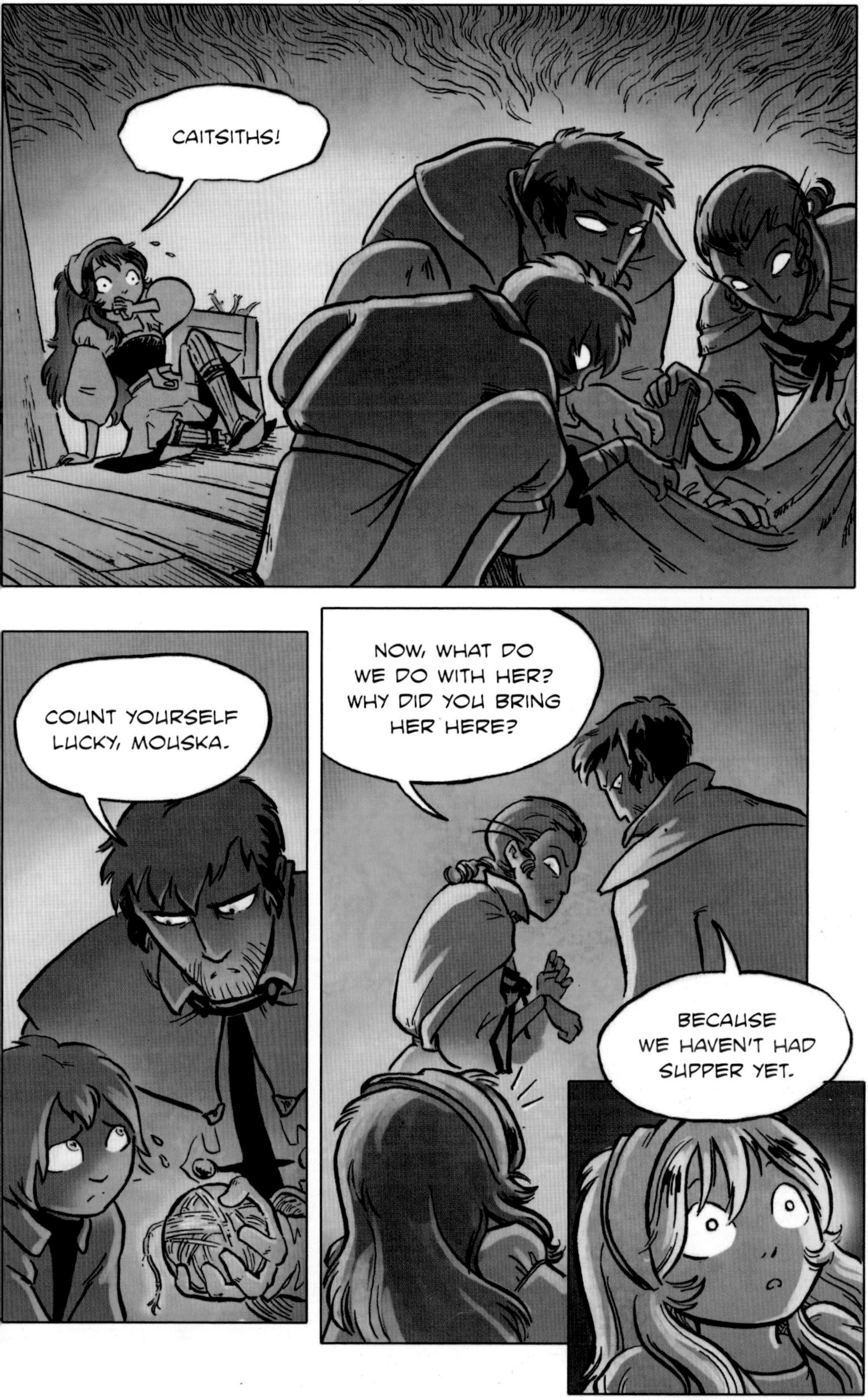
CAITSITHS!
COUNT YOURSELF LUCKY, MOUSKA.
NOW, WHAT DO WE DO WITH HER? WHY DID YOU BRING HER HERE?
BECAUSE WE HAVEN'T HAD SUPPER YET.

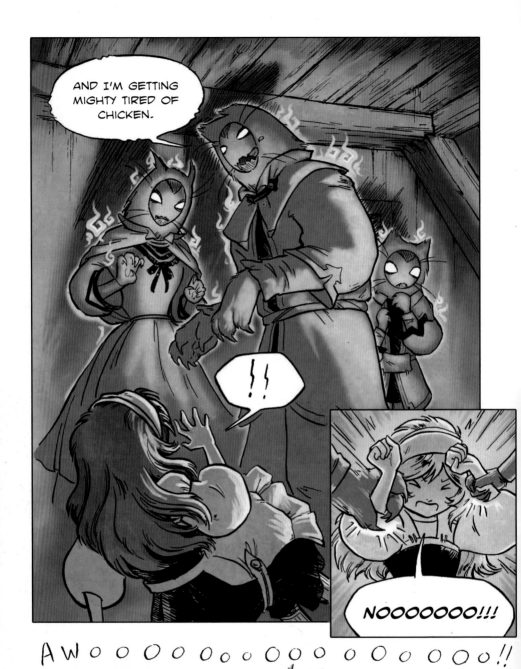

AND I'M GETTING MIGHTY TIRED OF CHICKEN.

!!

NOOOOOOOO!!!

AWOOOOOOooOOOO OOOOOO!!

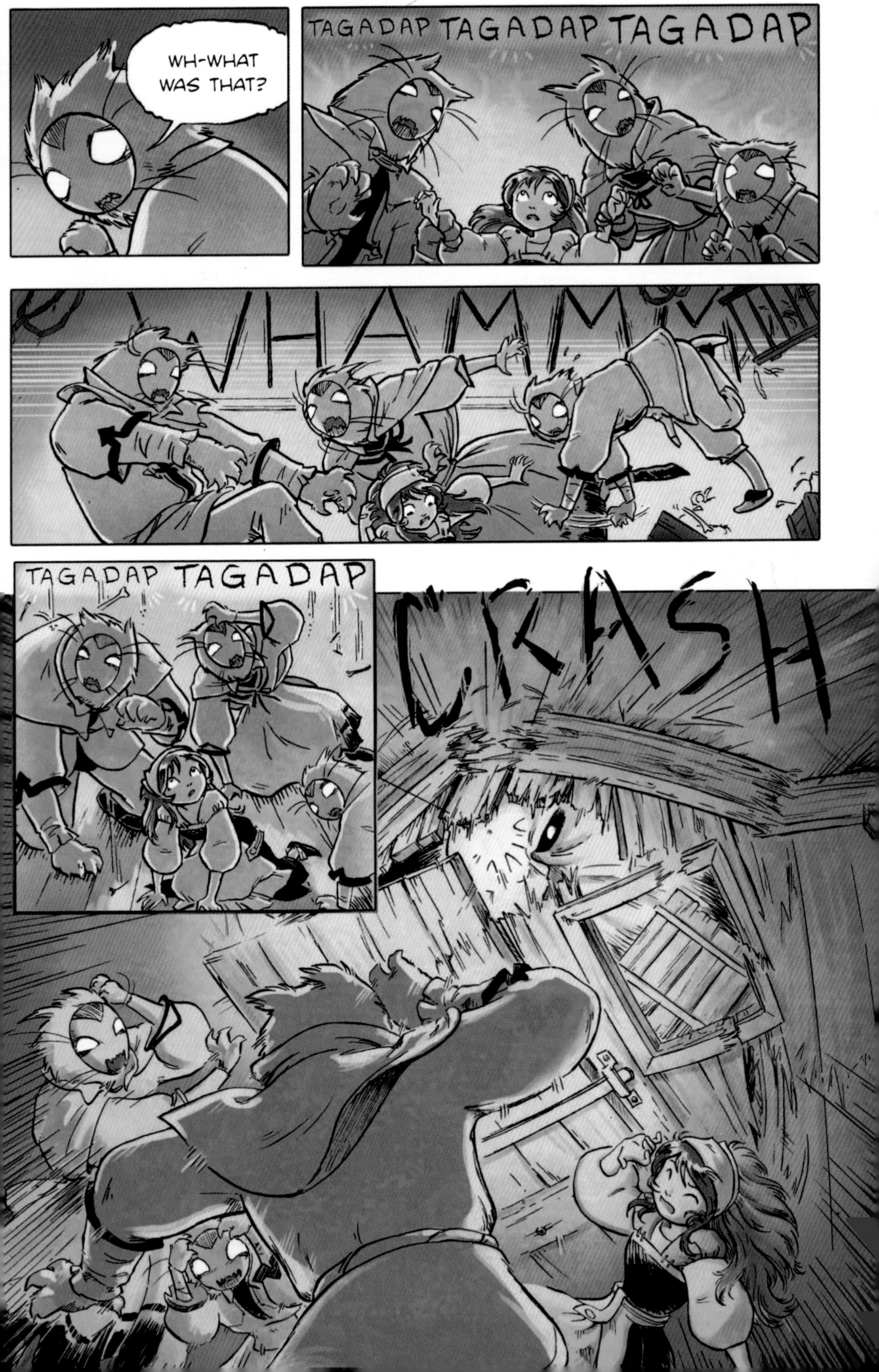
WH-WHAT WAS THAT?
TAGADAP TAGADAP TAGADAP
WHAMM
TAGADAP TAGADAP
CRASH

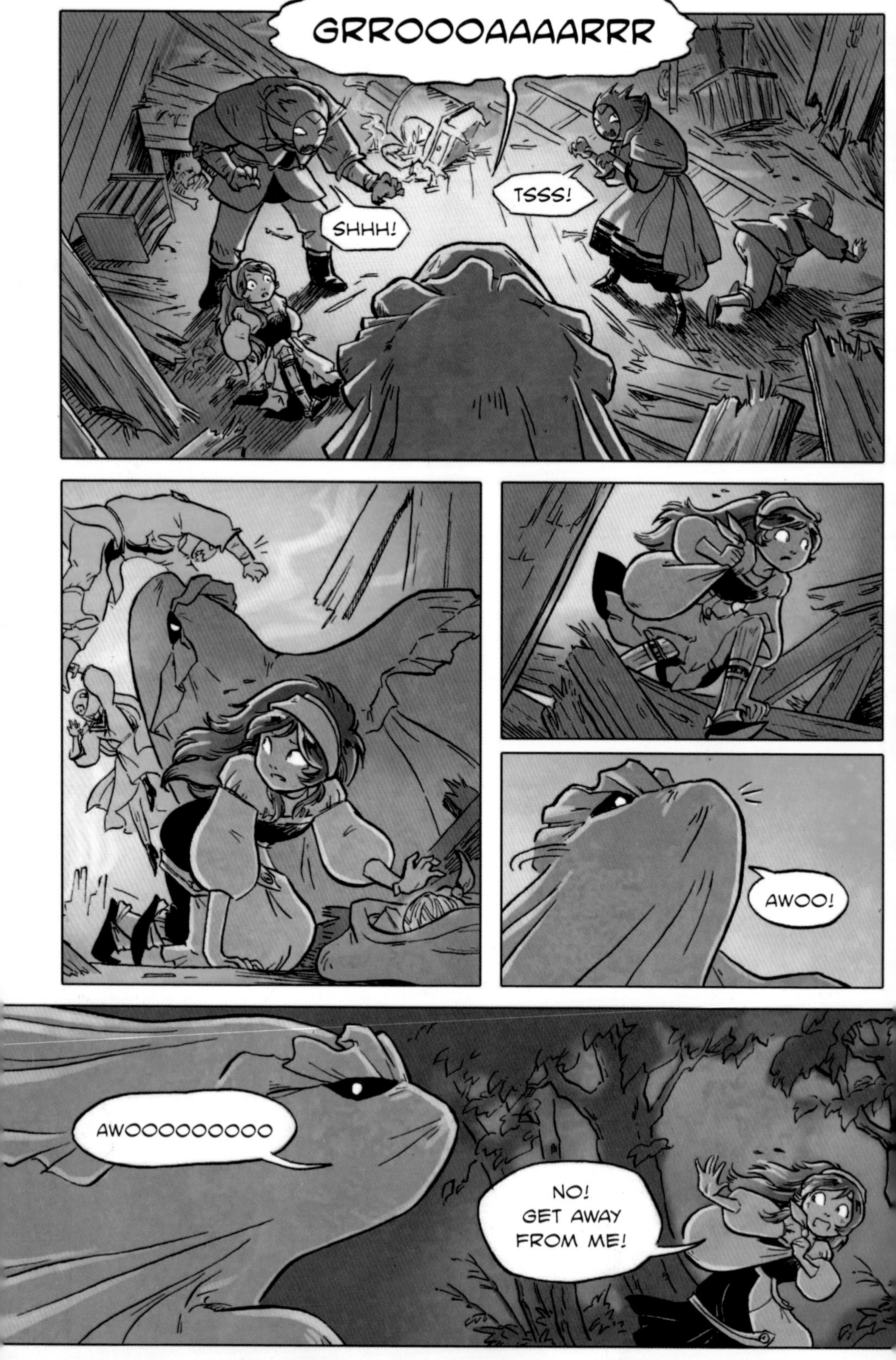
GRROOOAAAARRR
SHHH!
TSSS!
AWOO!
AWOOOOOOOOO
NO! GET AWAY FROM ME!

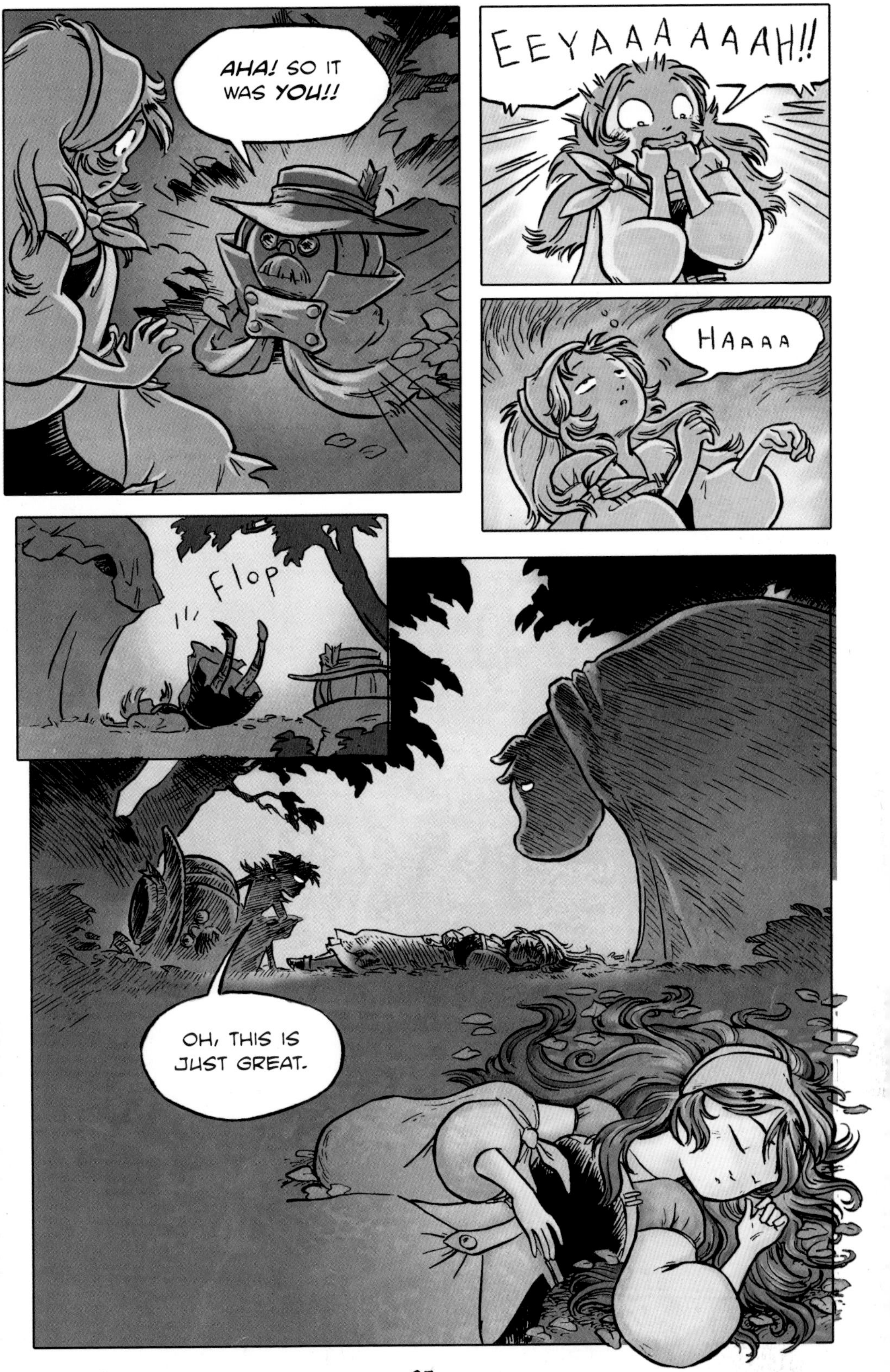
AHA! SO IT WAS YOU!!
EEYAAAAAAH!!
HAaaa
Flop
OH, THIS IS JUST GREAT.

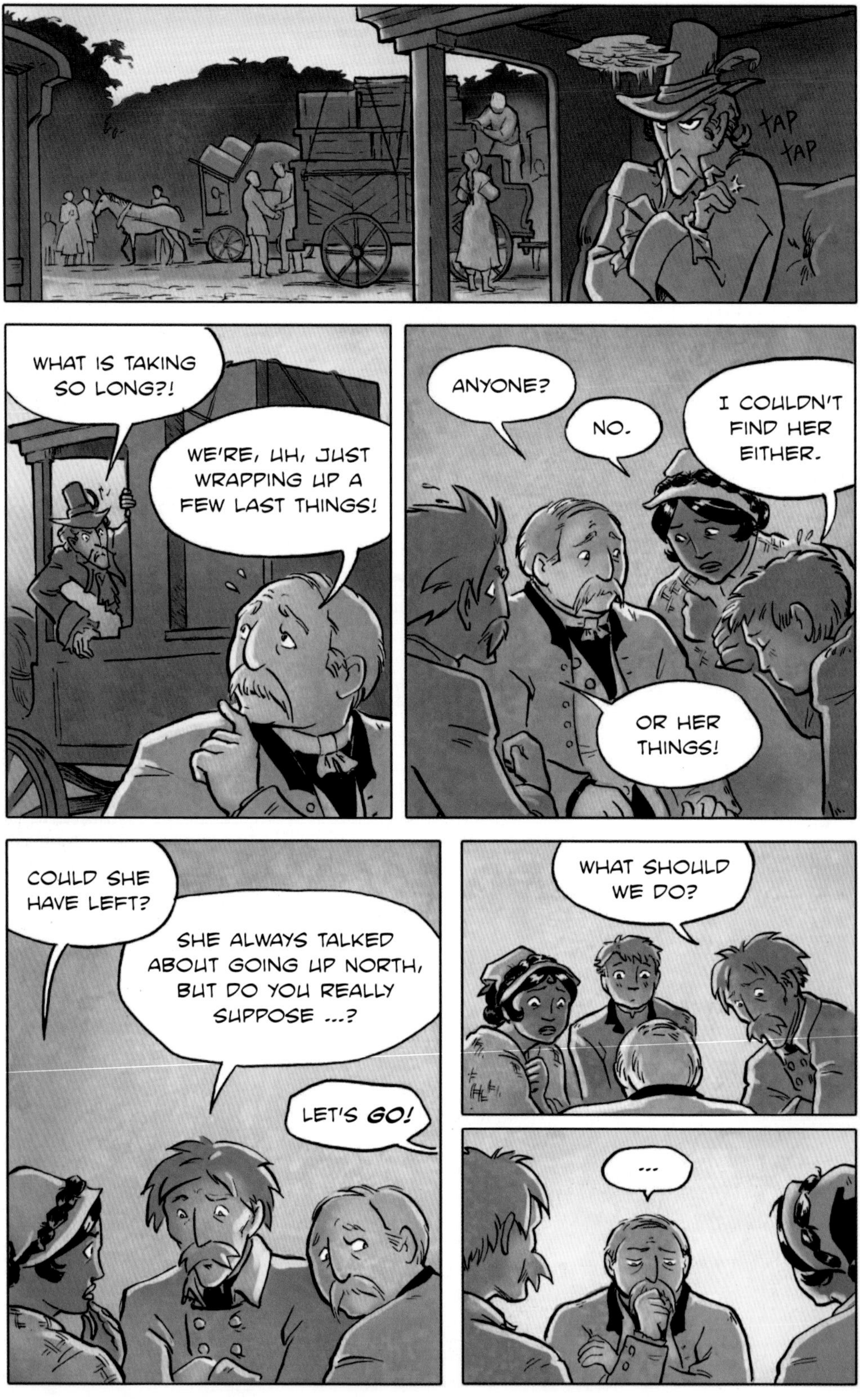
TAP TAP
WHAT IS TAKING SO LONG?!
WE'RE, UH, JUST WRAPPING UP A FEW LAST THINGS!
ANYONE?
NO.
I COULDN'T FIND HER EITHER.
OR HER THINGS!
COULD SHE HAVE LEFT?
SHE ALWAYS TALKED ABOUT GOING UP NORTH, BUT DO YOU REALLY SUPPOSE ...?
LET'S GO!
WHAT SHOULD WE DO?
...

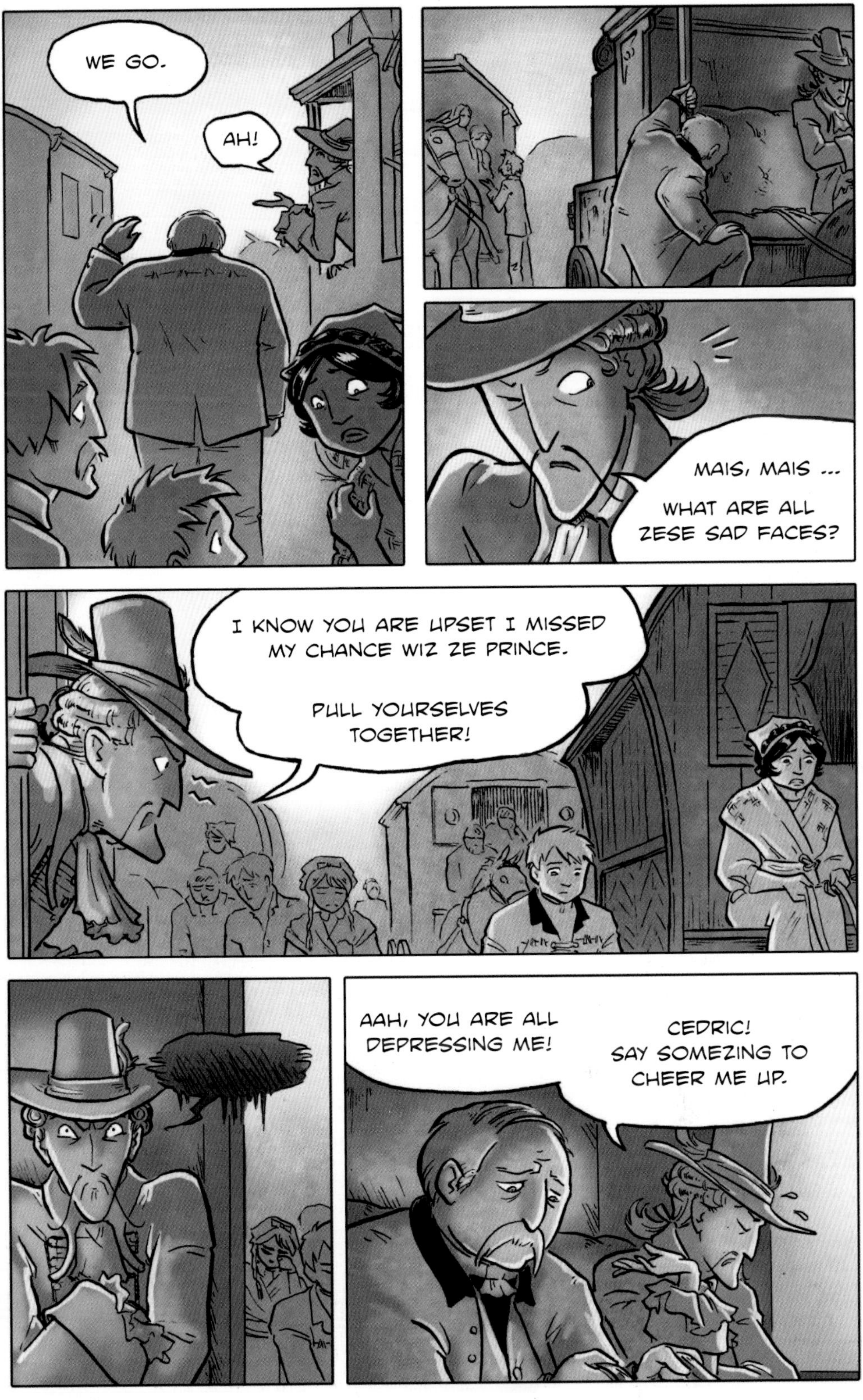
WE GO.
AH!
MAIS, MAIS ...
WHAT ARE ALL ZESE SAD FACES?
I KNOW YOU ARE UPSET I MISSED MY CHANCE WIZ ZE PRINCE.
PULL YOURSELVES TOGETHER!
AAH, YOU ARE ALL DEPRESSING ME!
CEDRIC! SAY SOMEZING TO CHEER ME UP.

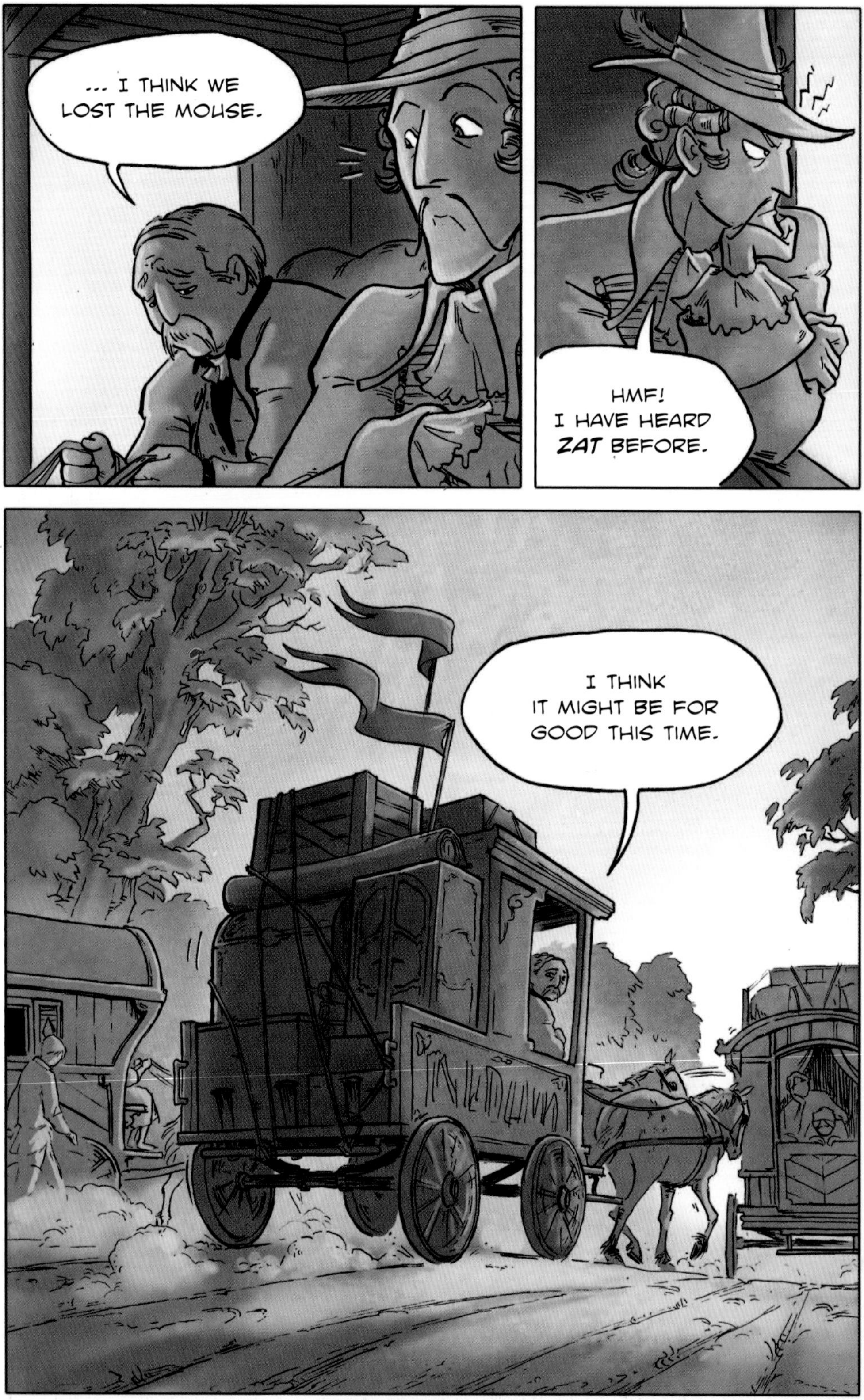
... I THINK WE
LOST THE MOUSE.
HMF!
I HAVE HEARD
ZAT BEFORE.
I THINK
IT MIGHT BE FOR
GOOD THIS TIME.

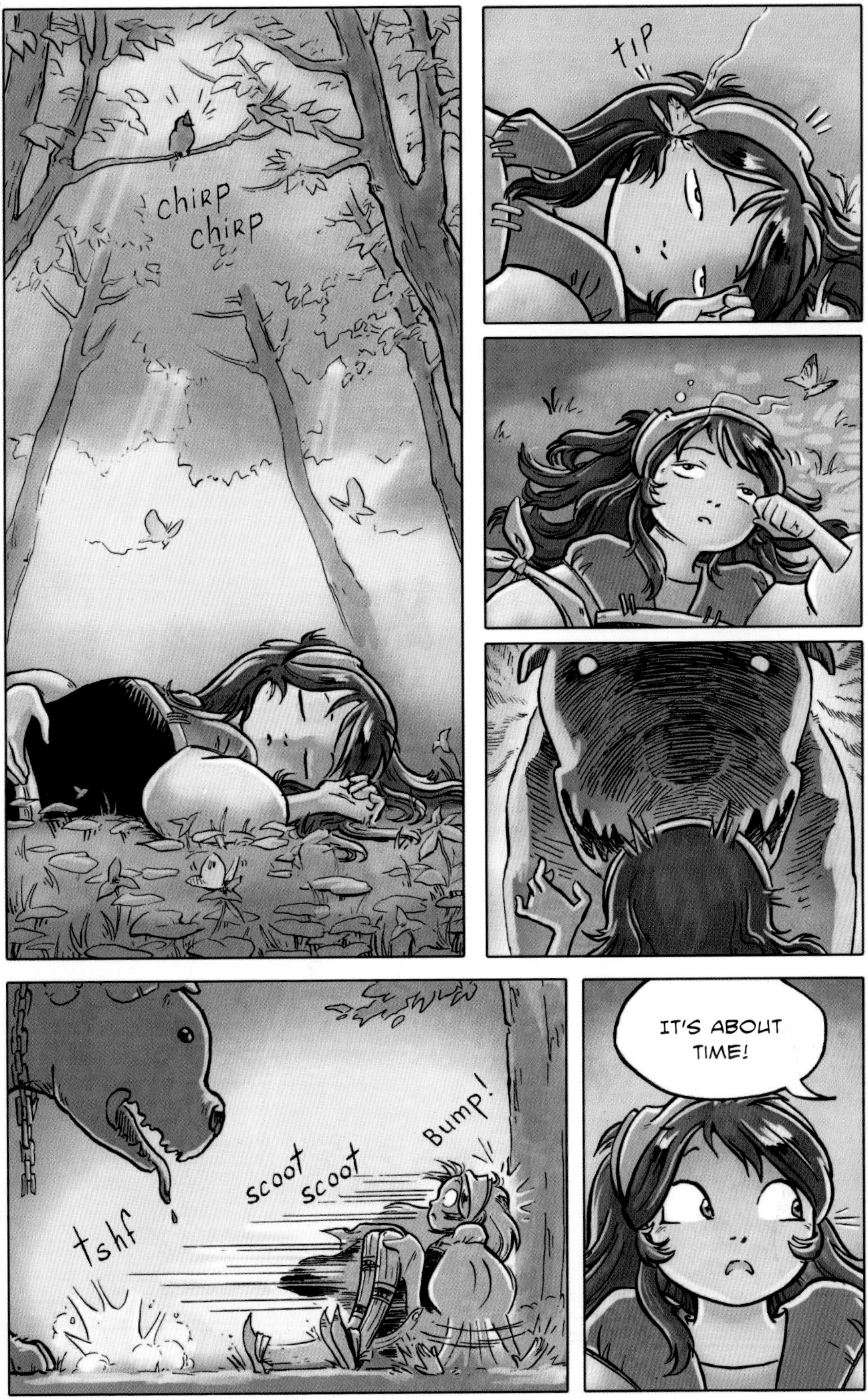
chirp
chirp
tip
Bump!
scoot
scoot
tshf
IT'S ABOUT TIME!

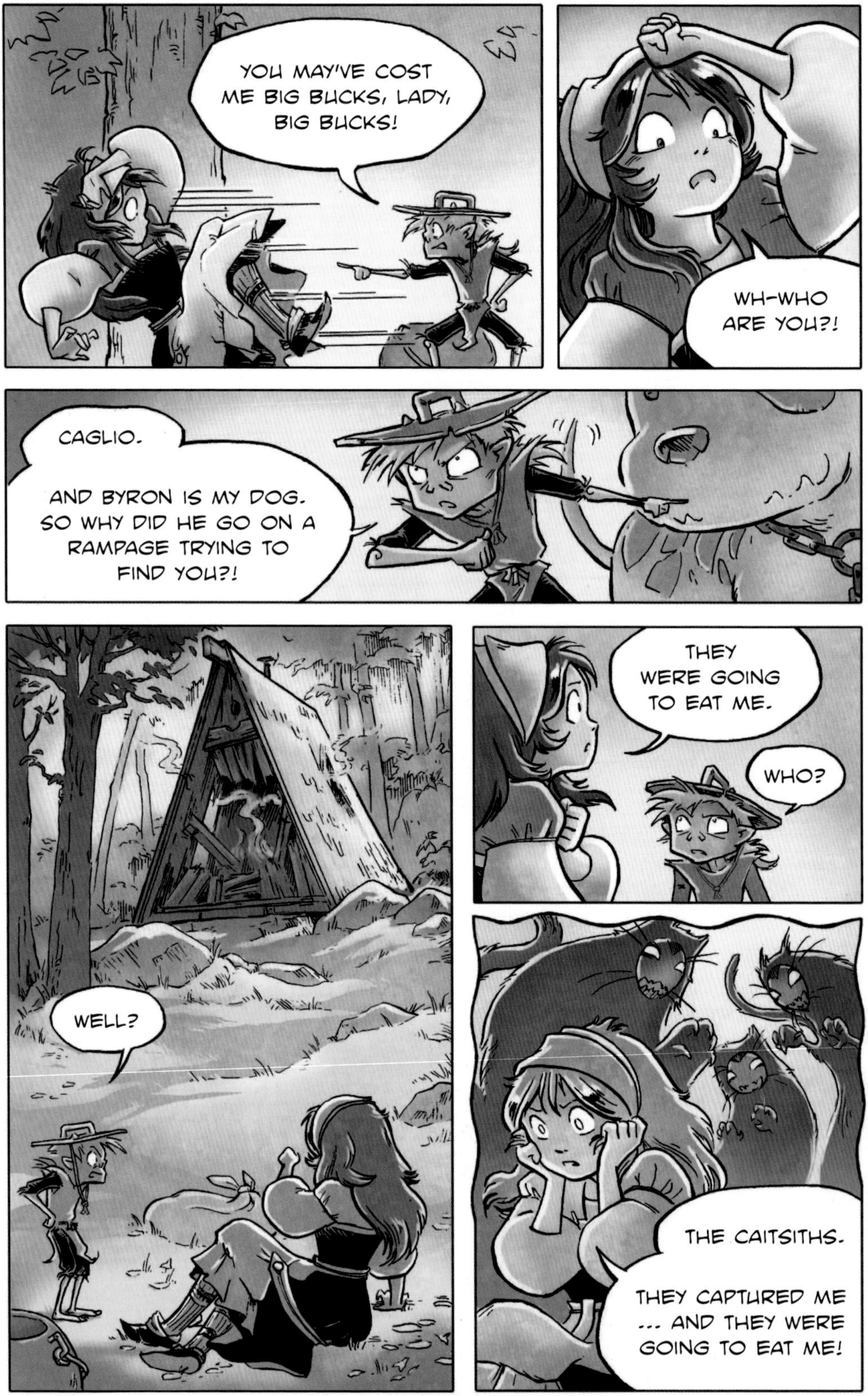
YOU MAY'VE COST ME BIG BUCKS, LADY, BIG BUCKS!
WH-WHO ARE YOU?!
CAGLIO.
AND BYRON IS MY DOG. SO WHY DID HE GO ON A RAMPAGE TRYING TO FIND YOU?!
WELL?
THEY WERE GOING TO EAT ME.
WHO?
THE CAITSITHS.
THEY CAPTURED ME ... AND THEY WERE GOING TO EAT ME!

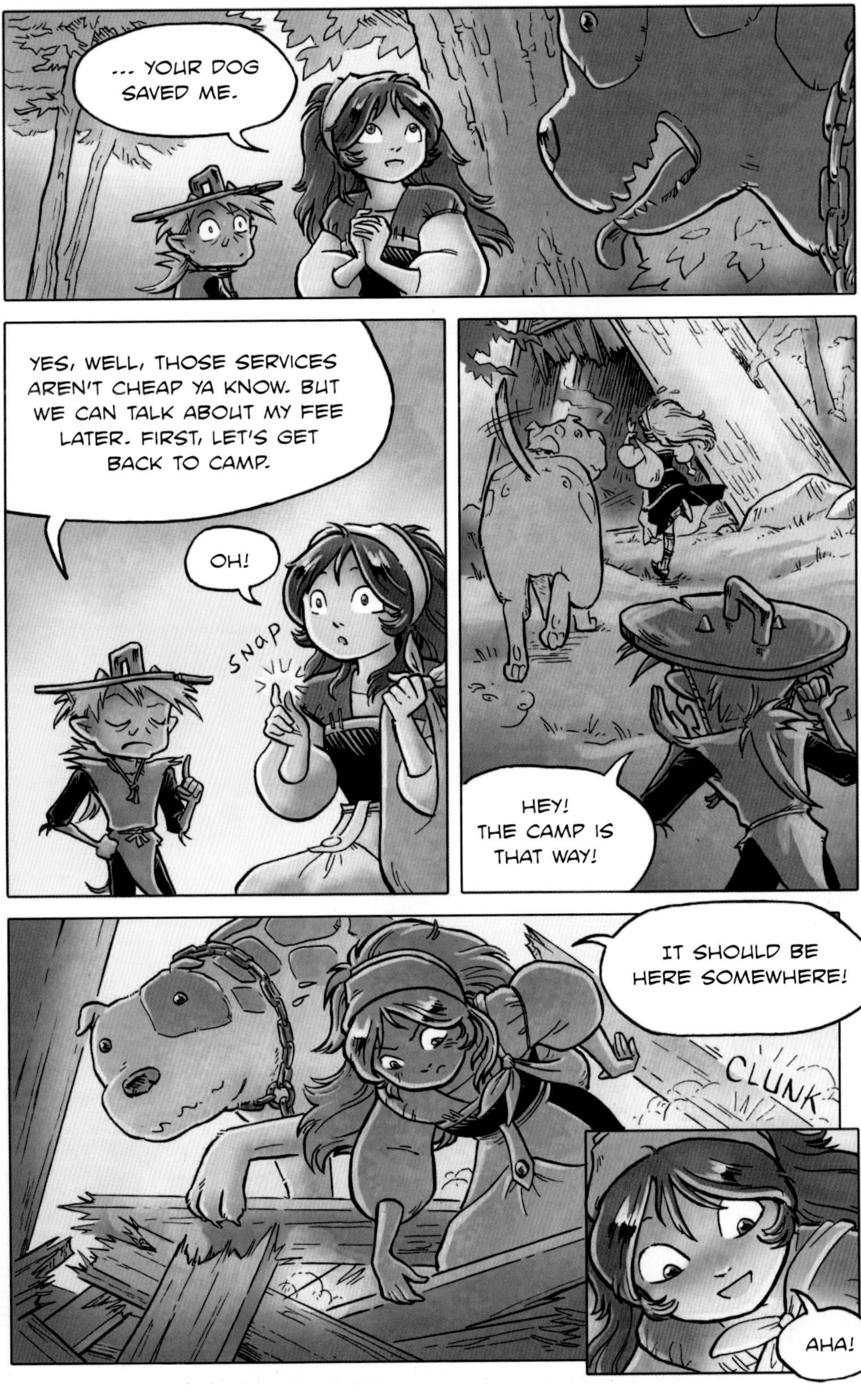
... YOUR DOG SAVED ME.
YES, WELL, THOSE SERVICES AREN'T CHEAP YA KNOW. BUT WE CAN TALK ABOUT MY FEE LATER. FIRST, LET'S GET BACK TO CAMP.
OH!
SNAP
HEY! THE CAMP IS THAT WAY!
IT SHOULD BE HERE SOMEWHERE!
CLUNK
AHA!

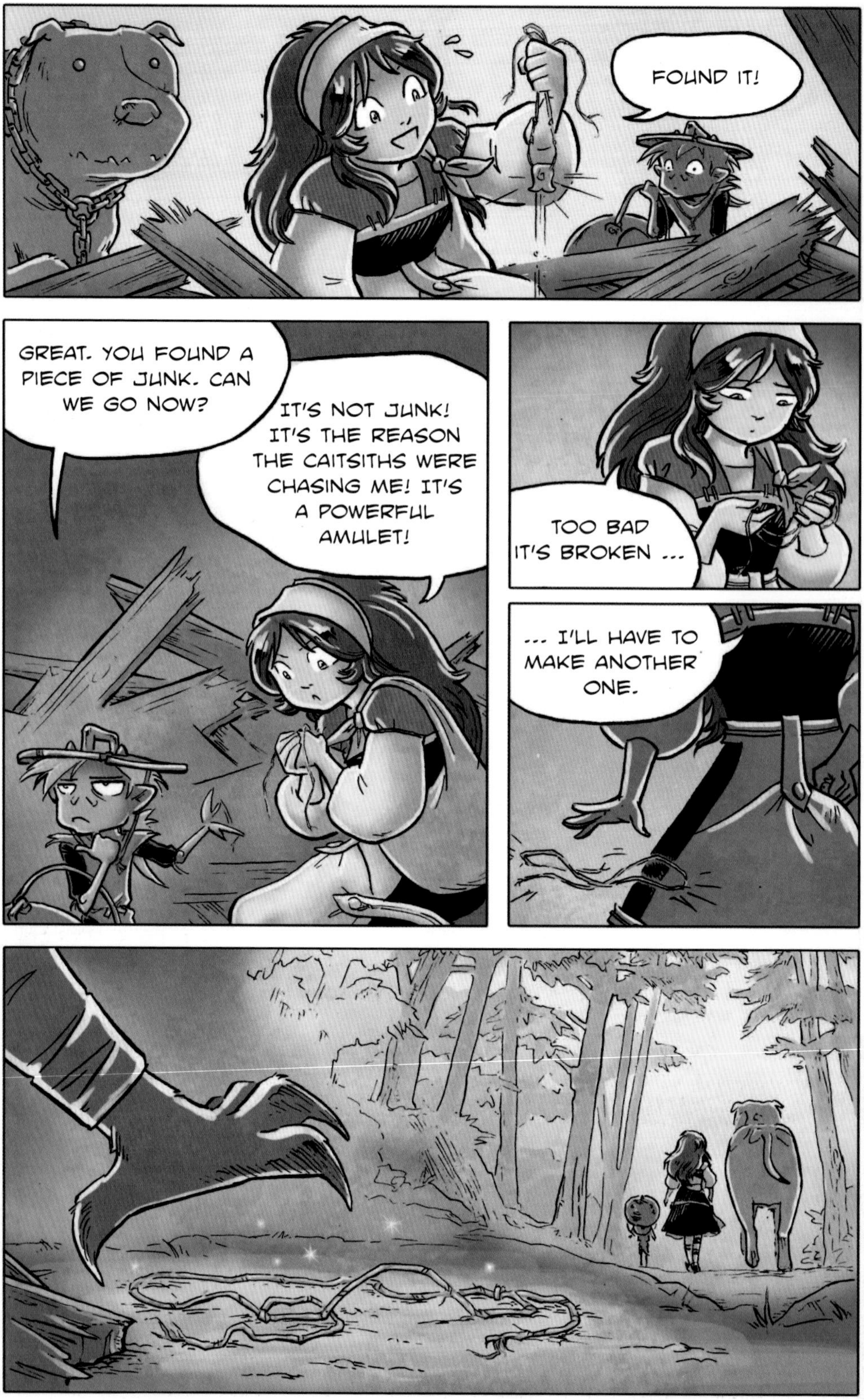
FOUND IT!
GREAT. YOU FOUND A PIECE OF JUNK. CAN WE GO NOW?
IT'S NOT JUNK! IT'S THE REASON THE CAITSITHS WERE CHASING ME! IT'S A POWERFUL AMULET!
TOO BAD IT'S BROKEN ...
... I'LL HAVE TO MAKE ANOTHER ONE.

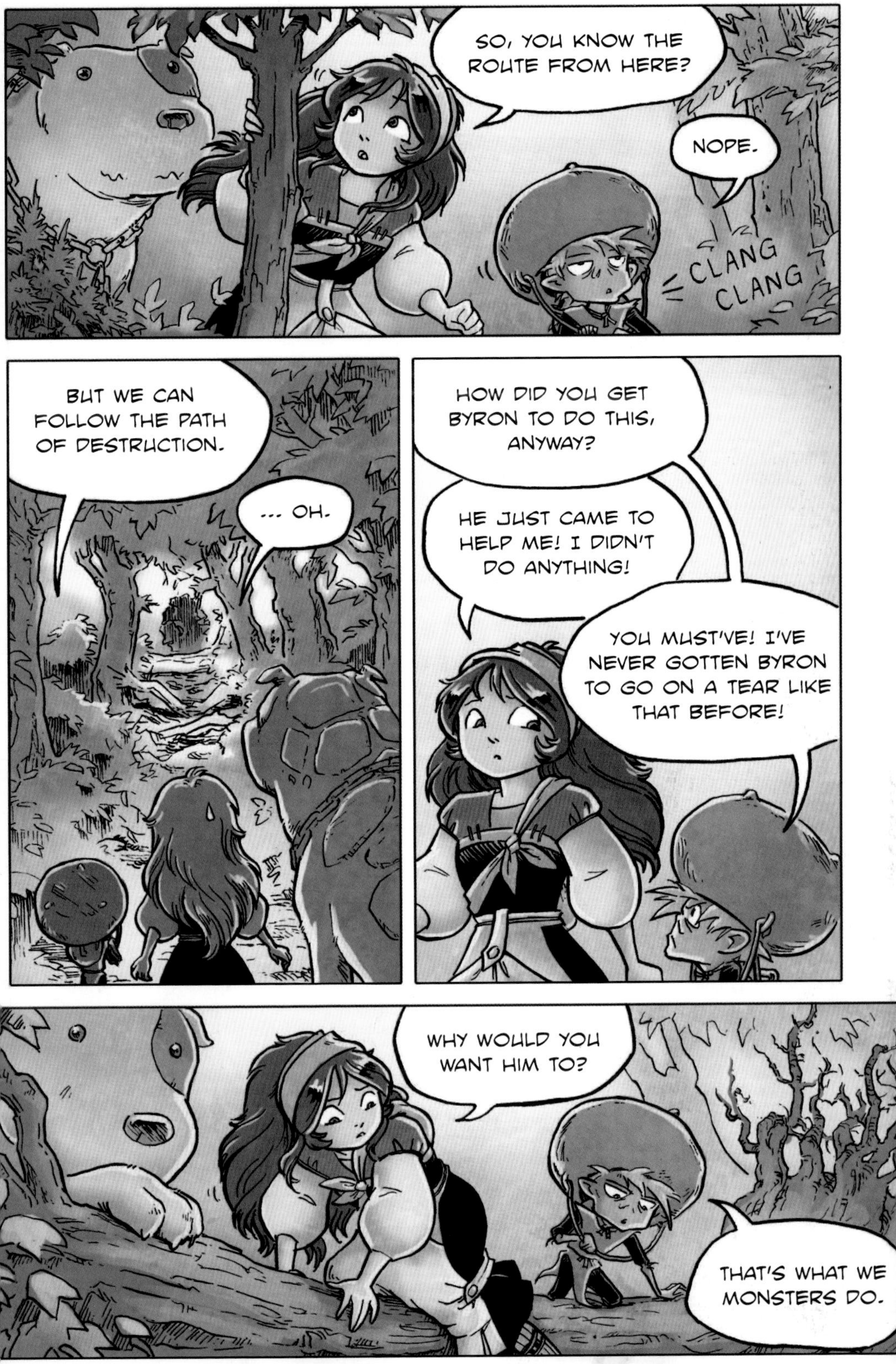
SO, YOU KNOW THE ROUTE FROM HERE?
NOPE.
CLANG CLANG
BUT WE CAN FOLLOW THE PATH OF DESTRUCTION.
... OH.
HOW DID YOU GET BYRON TO DO THIS, ANYWAY?
HE JUST CAME TO HELP ME! I DIDN'T DO ANYTHING!
YOU MUST'VE! I'VE NEVER GOTTEN BYRON TO GO ON A TEAR LIKE THAT BEFORE!
WHY WOULD YOU WANT HIM TO?
THAT'S WHAT WE MONSTERS DO.

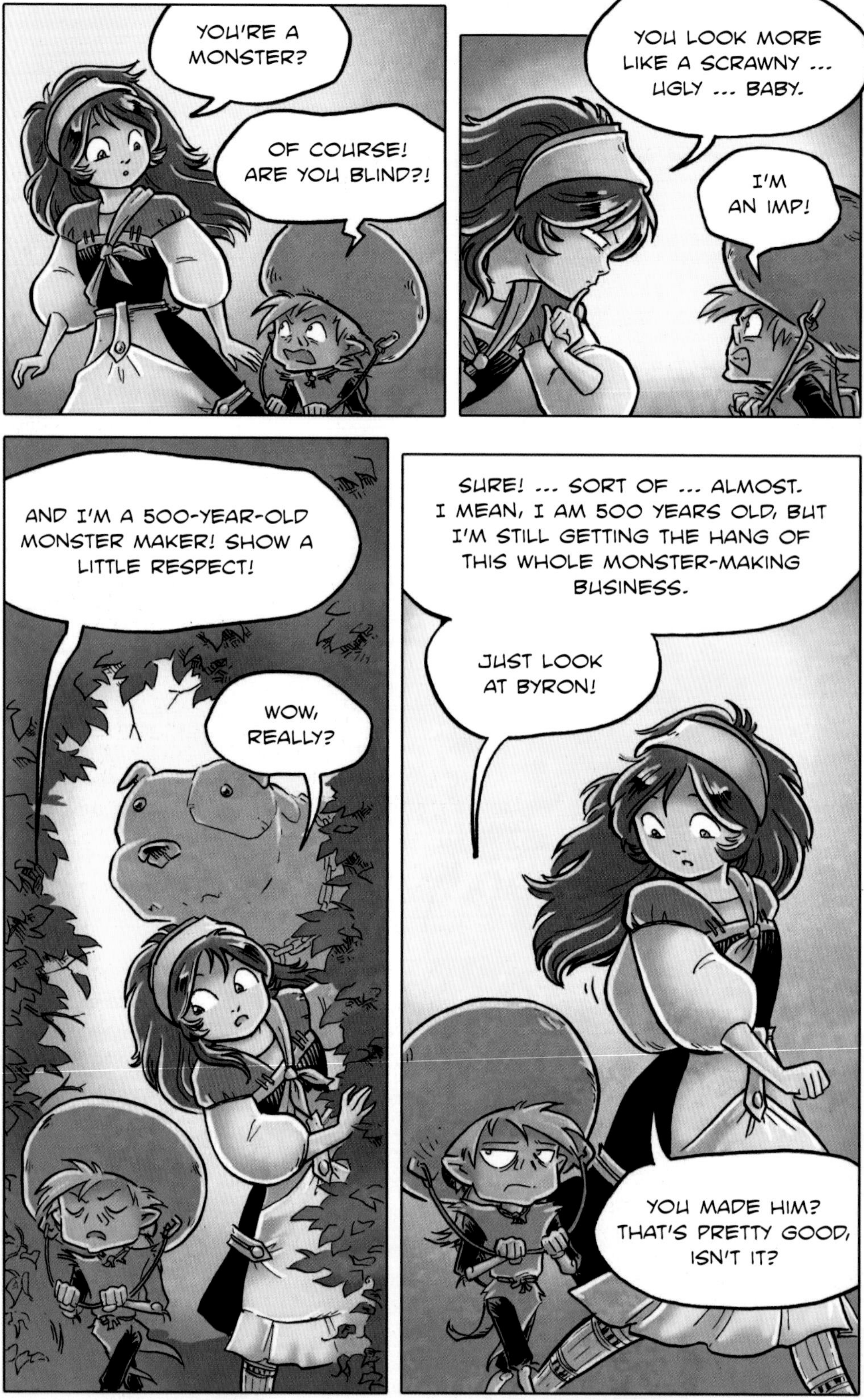
YOU'RE A MONSTER?
OF COURSE! ARE YOU BLIND?!
YOU LOOK MORE LIKE A SCRAWNY ... UGLY ... BABY.
I'M AN IMP!
AND I'M A 500-YEAR-OLD MONSTER MAKER! SHOW A LITTLE RESPECT!
WOW, REALLY?
SURE! ... SORT OF ... ALMOST. I MEAN, I AM 500 YEARS OLD, BUT I'M STILL GETTING THE HANG OF THIS WHOLE MONSTER-MAKING BUSINESS.
JUST LOOK AT BYRON!
YOU MADE HIM? THAT'S PRETTY GOOD, ISN'T IT?

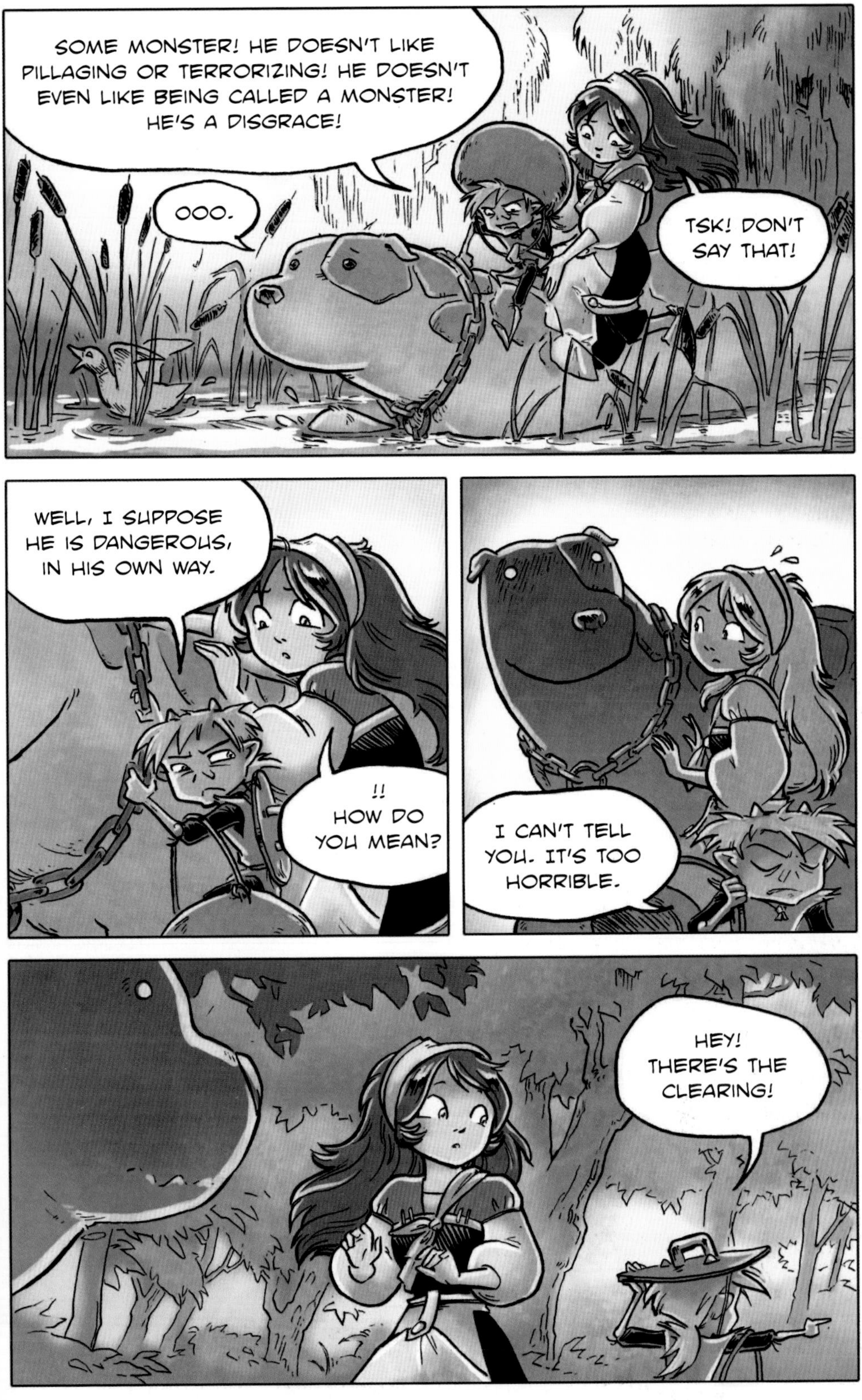
SOME MONSTER! HE DOESN'T LIKE PILLAGING OR TERRORIZING! HE DOESN'T EVEN LIKE BEING CALLED A MONSTER! HE'S A DISGRACE!
OOO.
TSK! DON'T SAY THAT!
WELL, I SUPPOSE HE IS DANGEROUS, IN HIS OWN WAY.
!! HOW DO YOU MEAN?
I CAN'T TELL YOU. IT'S TOO HORRIBLE.
HEY! THERE'S THE CLEARING!

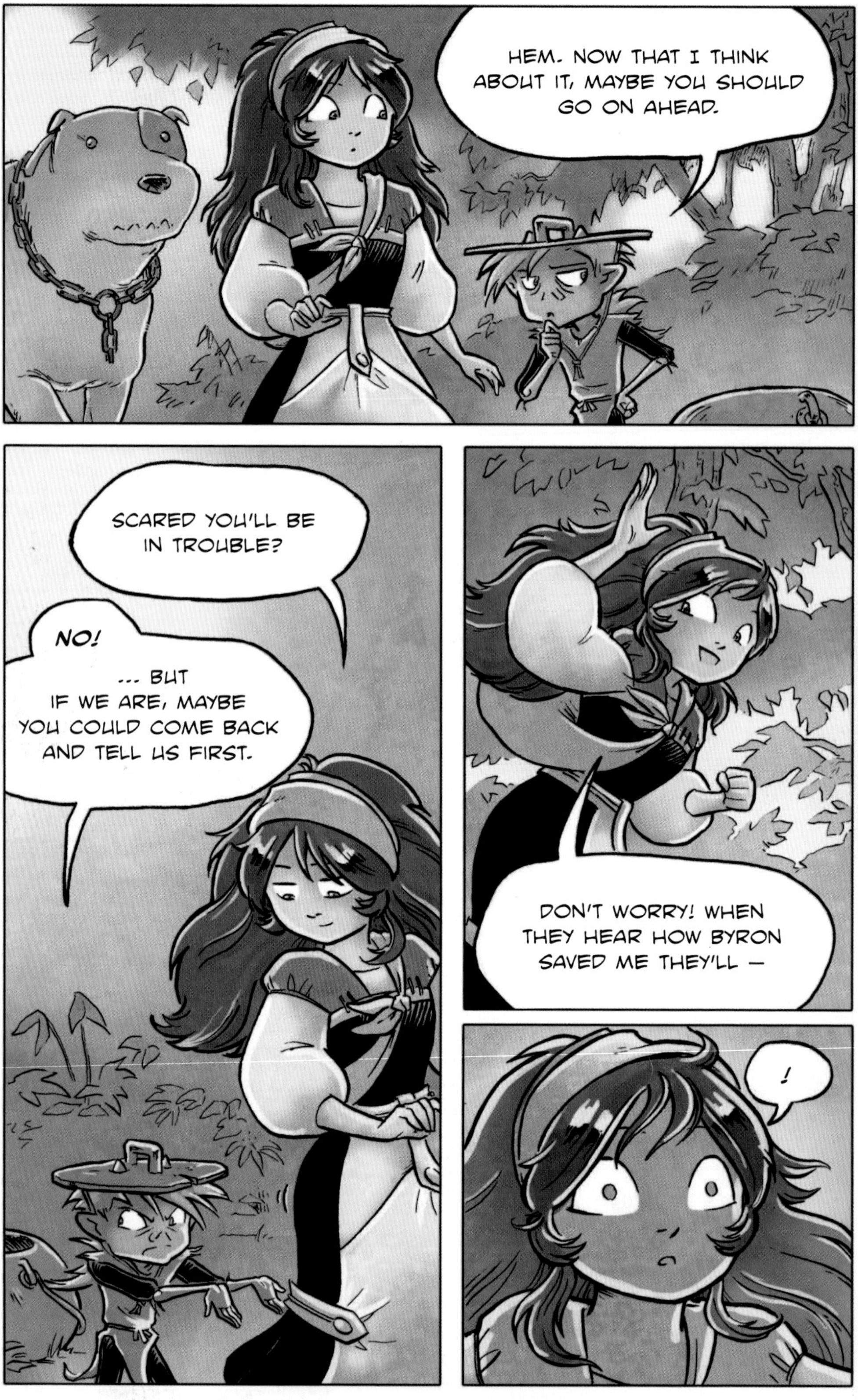
HEM. NOW THAT I THINK ABOUT IT, MAYBE YOU SHOULD GO ON AHEAD.
SCARED YOU'LL BE IN TROUBLE?
NO!
... BUT IF WE ARE, MAYBE YOU COULD COME BACK AND TELL US FIRST.
DON'T WORRY! WHEN THEY HEAR HOW BYRON SAVED ME THEY'LL —
!

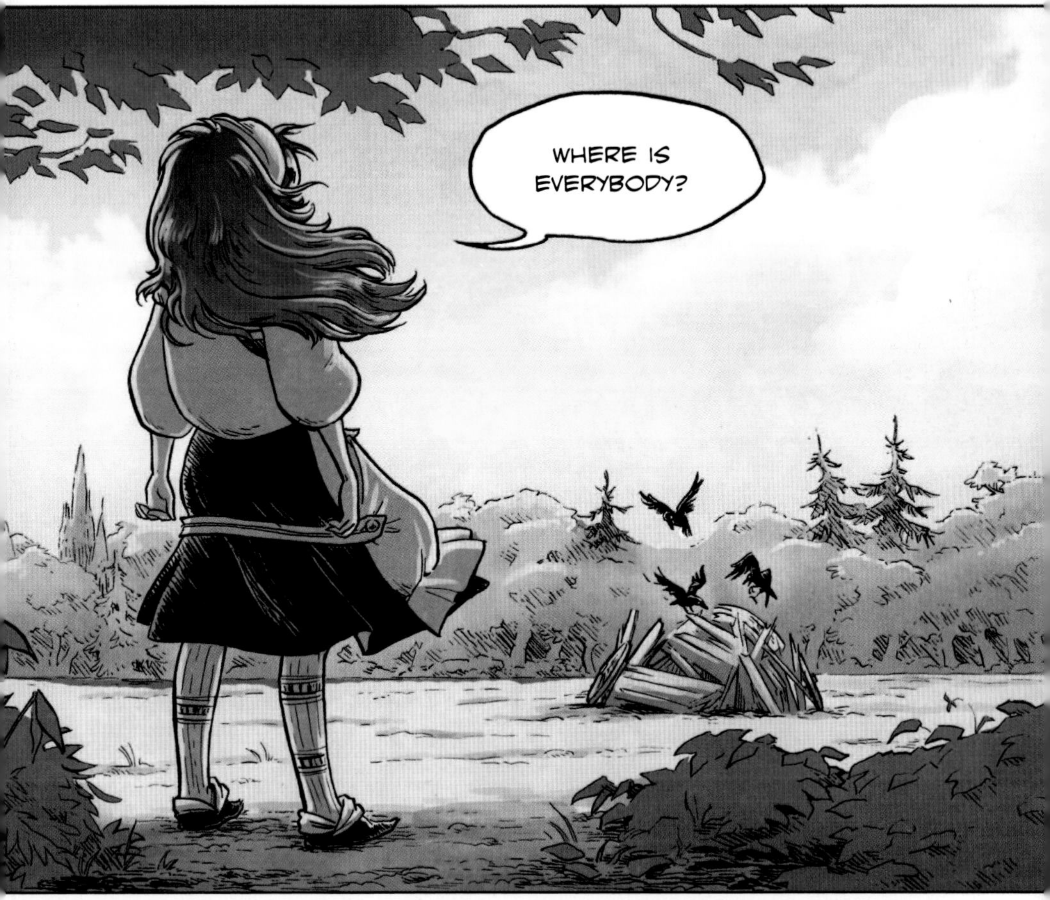
WHERE IS EVERYBODY?

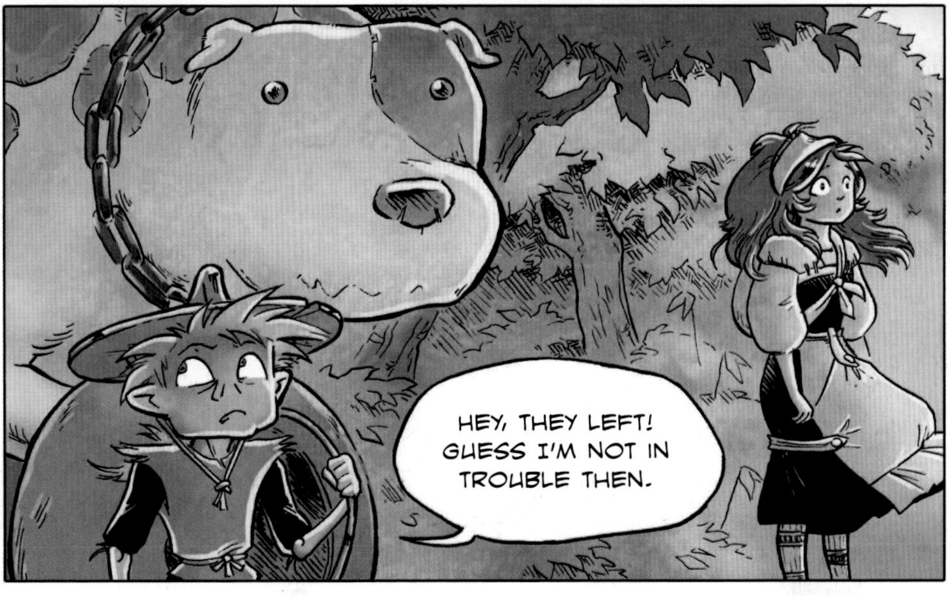
HEY, THEY LEFT! GUESS I'M NOT IN TROUBLE THEN.

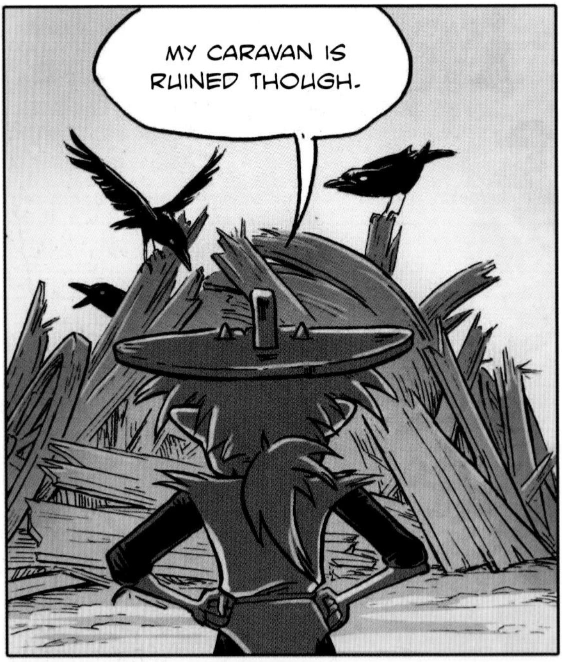
MY CARAVAN IS RUINED THOUGH.

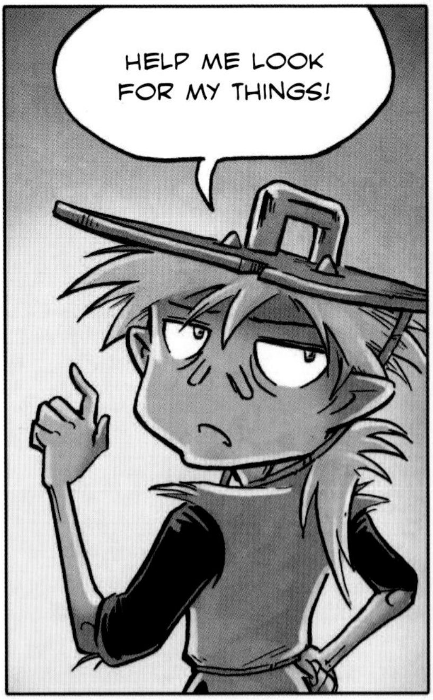
HELP ME LOOK FOR MY THINGS!

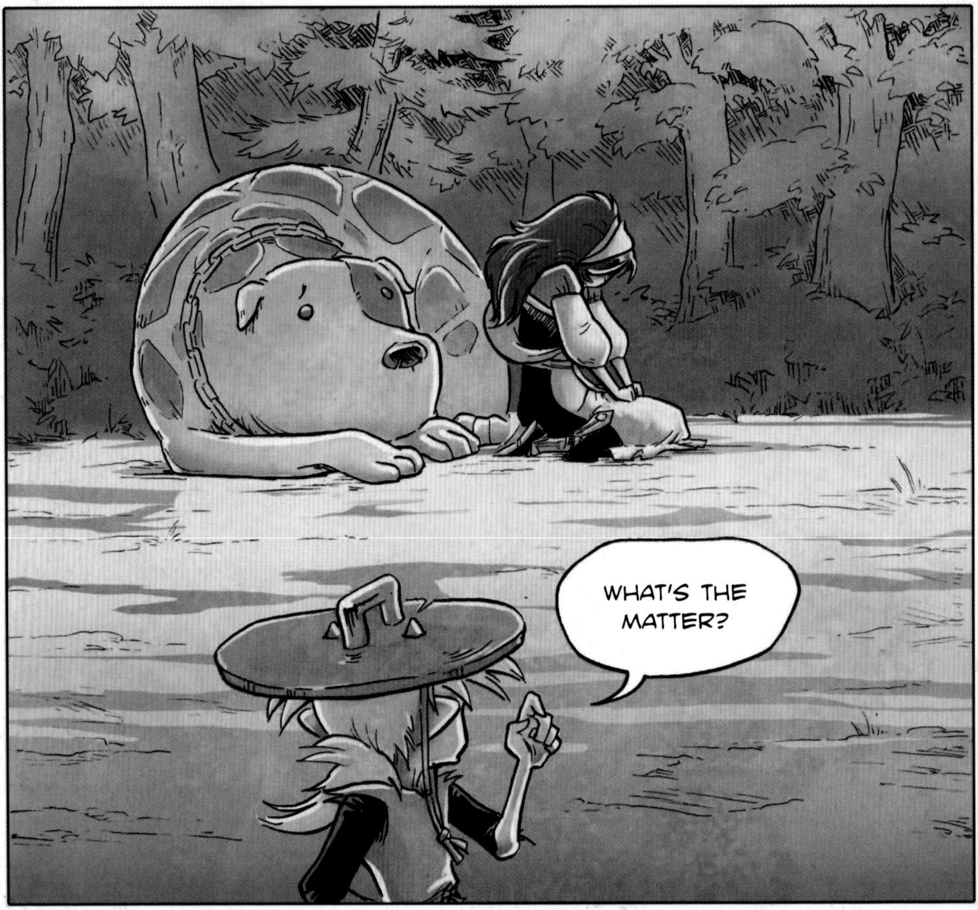
WHAT'S THE MATTER?

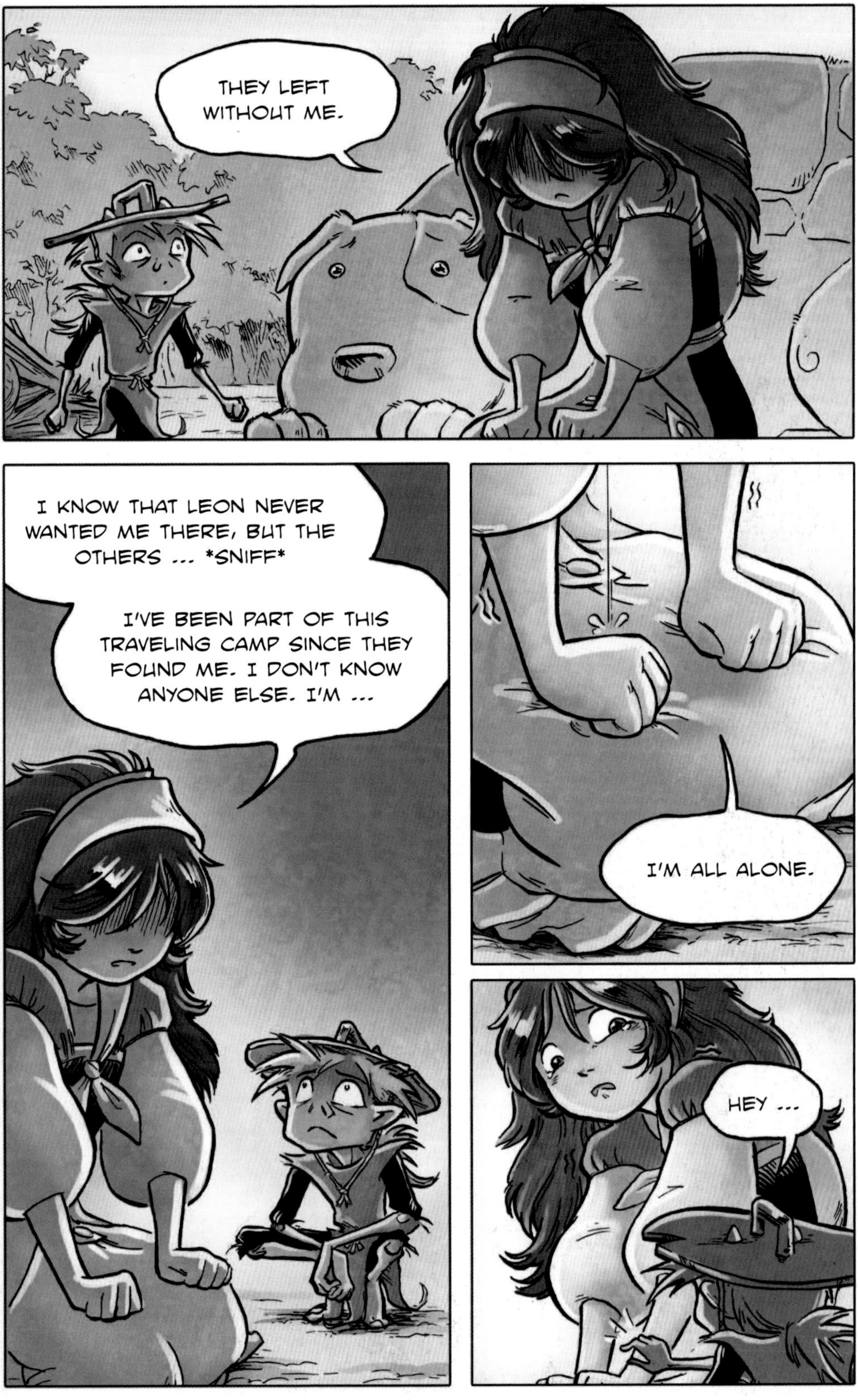
THEY LEFT WITHOUT ME.
I KNOW THAT LEON NEVER WANTED ME THERE, BUT THE OTHERS ... *SNIFF*
I'VE BEEN PART OF THIS TRAVELING CAMP SINCE THEY FOUND ME. I DON'T KNOW ANYONE ELSE. I'M ...
I'M ALL ALONE.
HEY ...

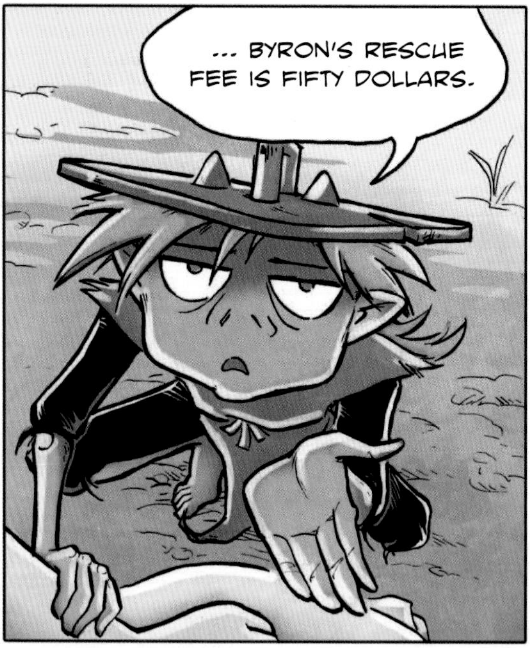
... BYRON'S RESCUE FEE IS FIFTY DOLLARS.
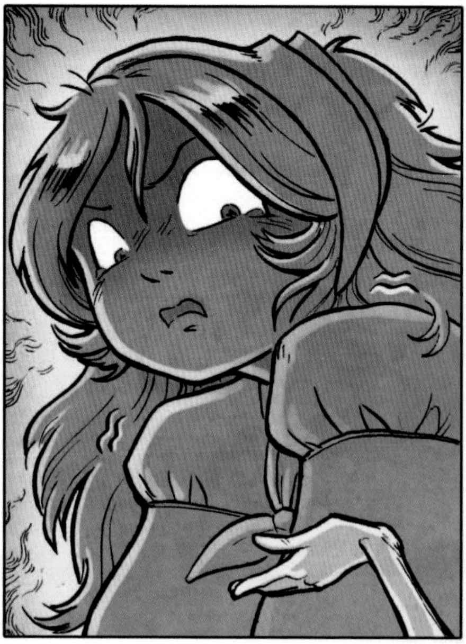
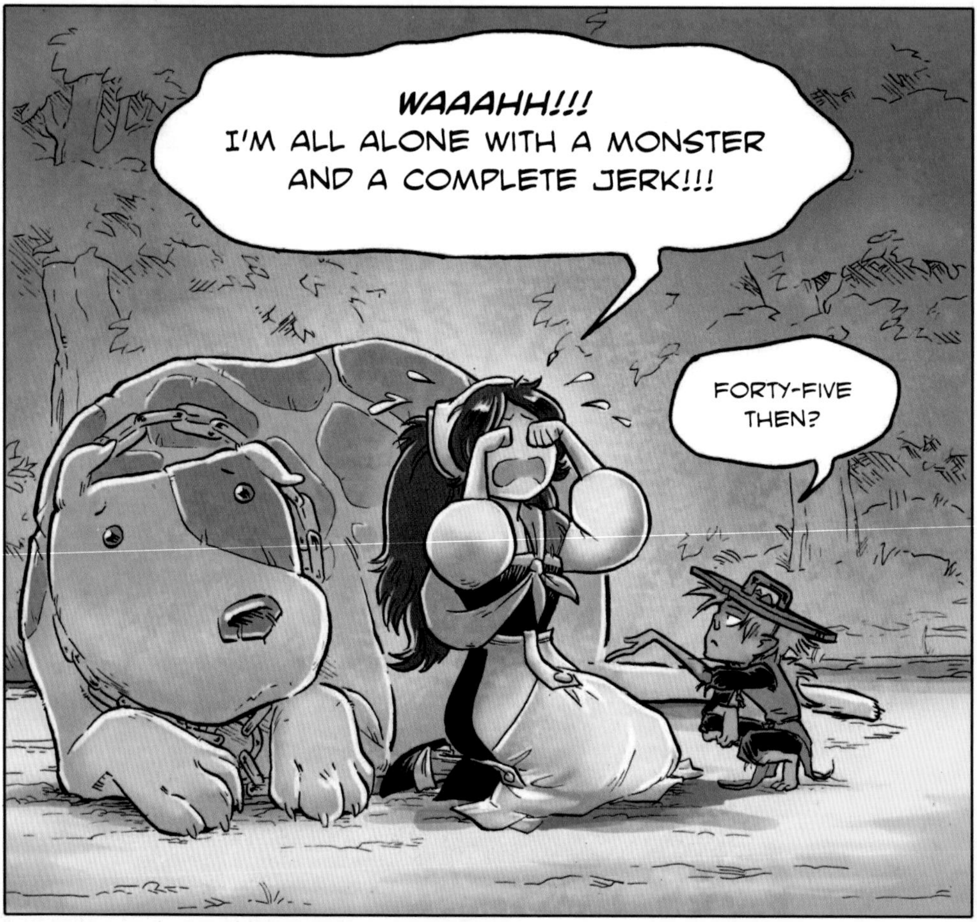
WAAAHH!!!
I'M ALL ALONE WITH A MONSTER AND A COMPLETE JERK!!!
FORTY-FIVE THEN?

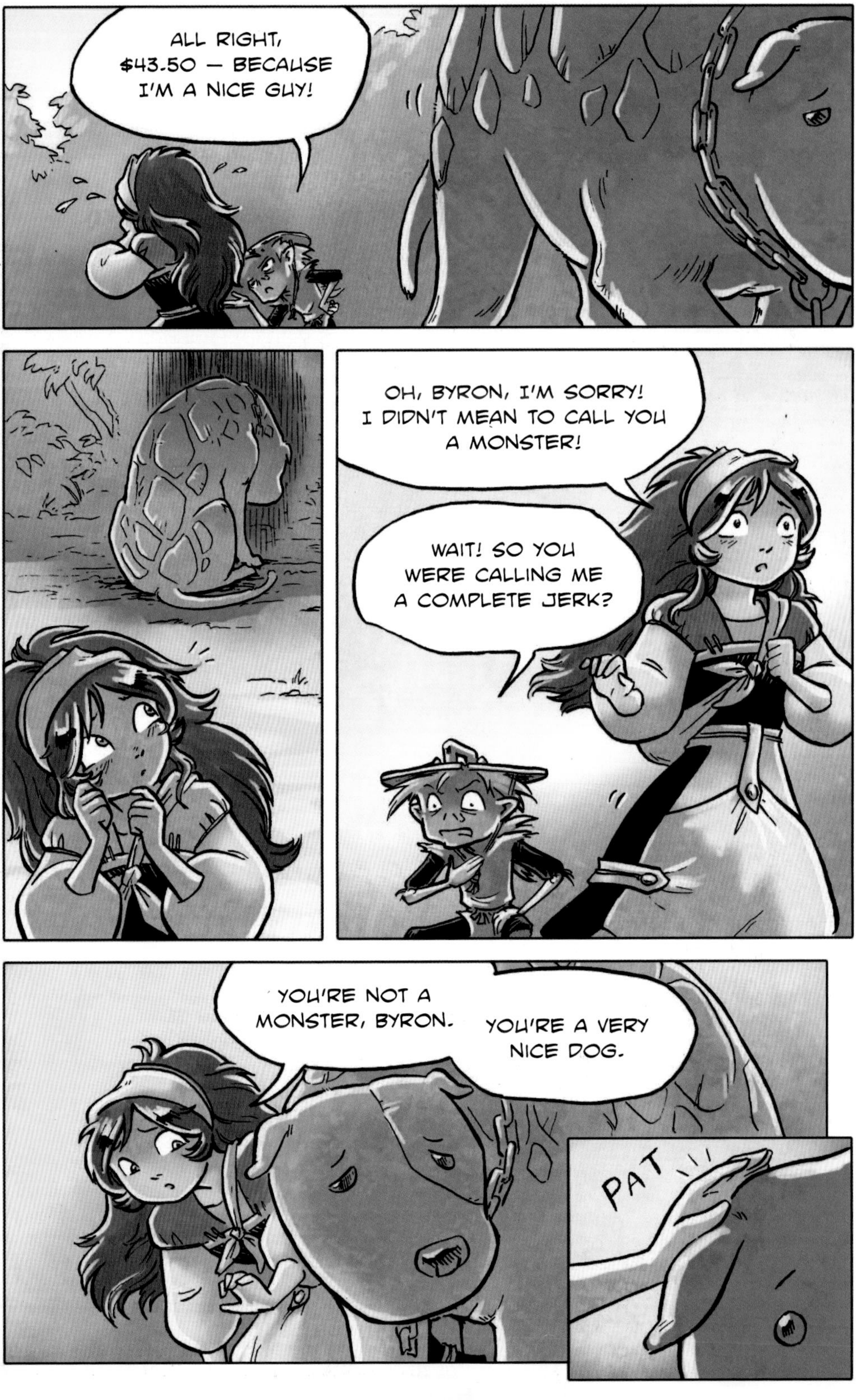
ALL RIGHT, $43.50 — BECAUSE I'M A NICE GUY!
OH, BYRON, I'M SORRY! I DIDN'T MEAN TO CALL YOU A MONSTER!
WAIT! SO YOU WERE CALLING ME A COMPLETE JERK?
YOU'RE NOT A MONSTER, BYRON.
YOU'RE A VERY NICE DOG.
PAT

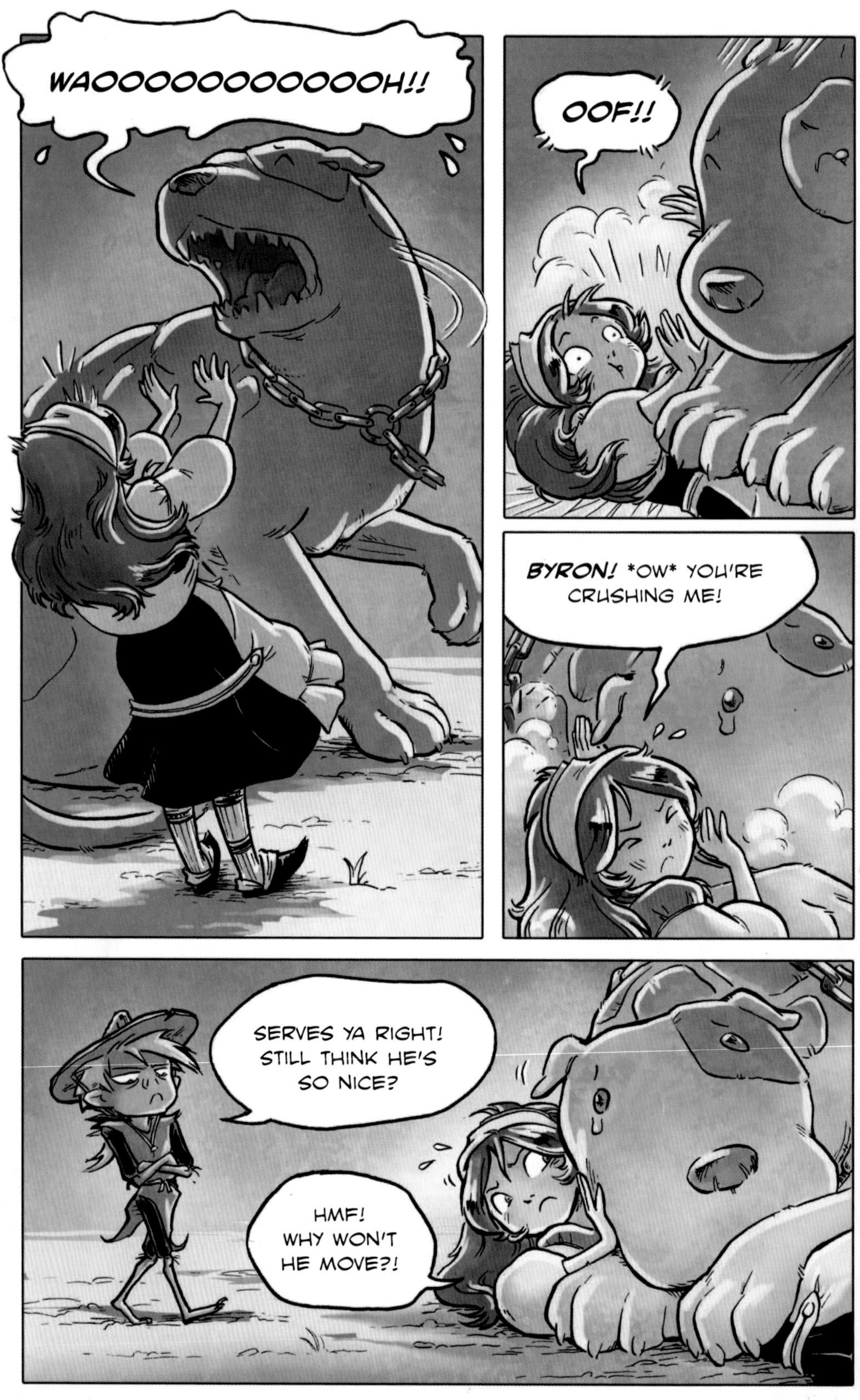
WAOOOOOOOOOOOH!!
OOF!!
BYRON! *OW* YOU'RE CRUSHING ME!
SERVES YA RIGHT! STILL THINK HE'S SO NICE?
HMF! WHY WON'T HE MOVE?!

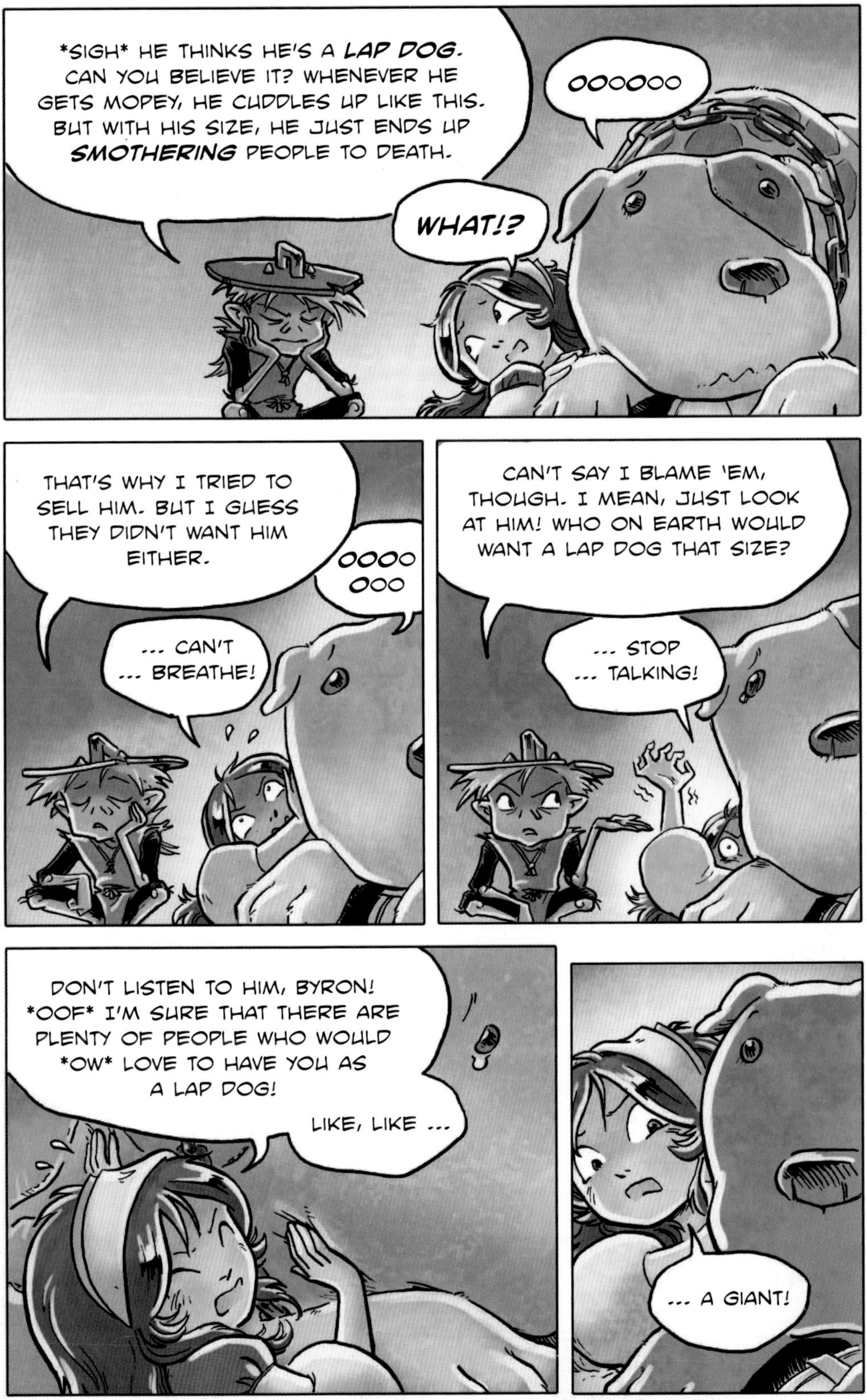
SIGH HE THINKS HE'S A LAP DOG. CAN YOU BELIEVE IT? WHENEVER HE GETS MOPEY, HE CUDDLES UP LIKE THIS. BUT WITH HIS SIZE, HE JUST ENDS UP SMOTHERING PEOPLE TO DEATH.
OOOOOO
WHAT!?
THAT'S WHY I TRIED TO SELL HIM. BUT I GUESS THEY DIDN'T WANT HIM EITHER.
OOOOOOO
... CAN'T ... BREATHE!
CAN'T SAY I BLAME 'EM, THOUGH. I MEAN, JUST LOOK AT HIM! WHO ON EARTH WOULD WANT A LAP DOG THAT SIZE?
... STOP ... TALKING!
DON'T LISTEN TO HIM, BYRON! *OOF* I'M SURE THAT THERE ARE PLENTY OF PEOPLE WHO WOULD *OW* LOVE TO HAVE YOU AS A LAP DOG!
LIKE, LIKE ...
... A GIANT!

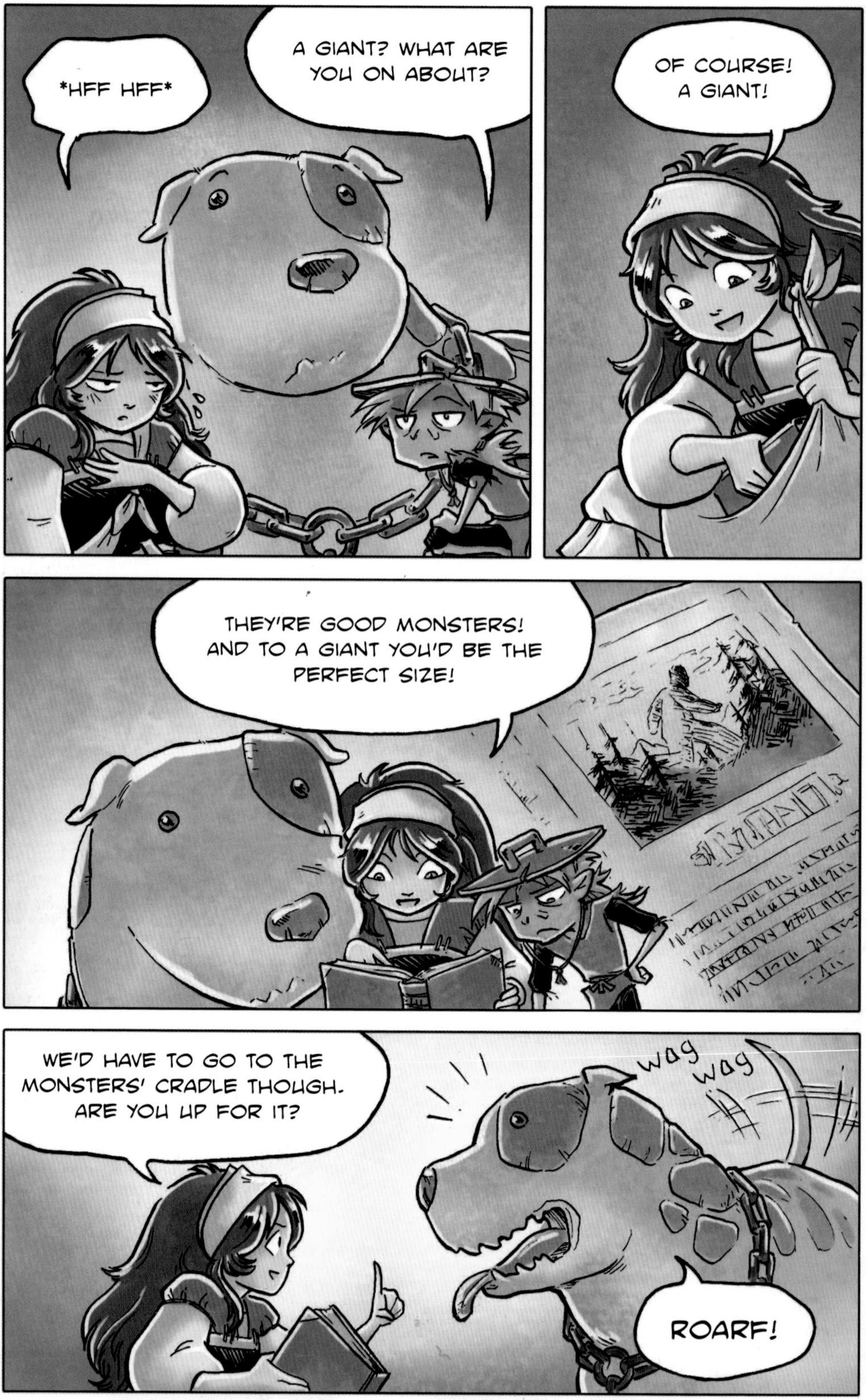
HFF HFF
A GIANT? WHAT ARE YOU ON ABOUT?
OF COURSE! A GIANT!
THEY'RE GOOD MONSTERS! AND TO A GIANT YOU'D BE THE PERFECT SIZE!
WE'D HAVE TO GO TO THE MONSTERS' CRADLE THOUGH. ARE YOU UP FOR IT?
wag wag
ROARF!

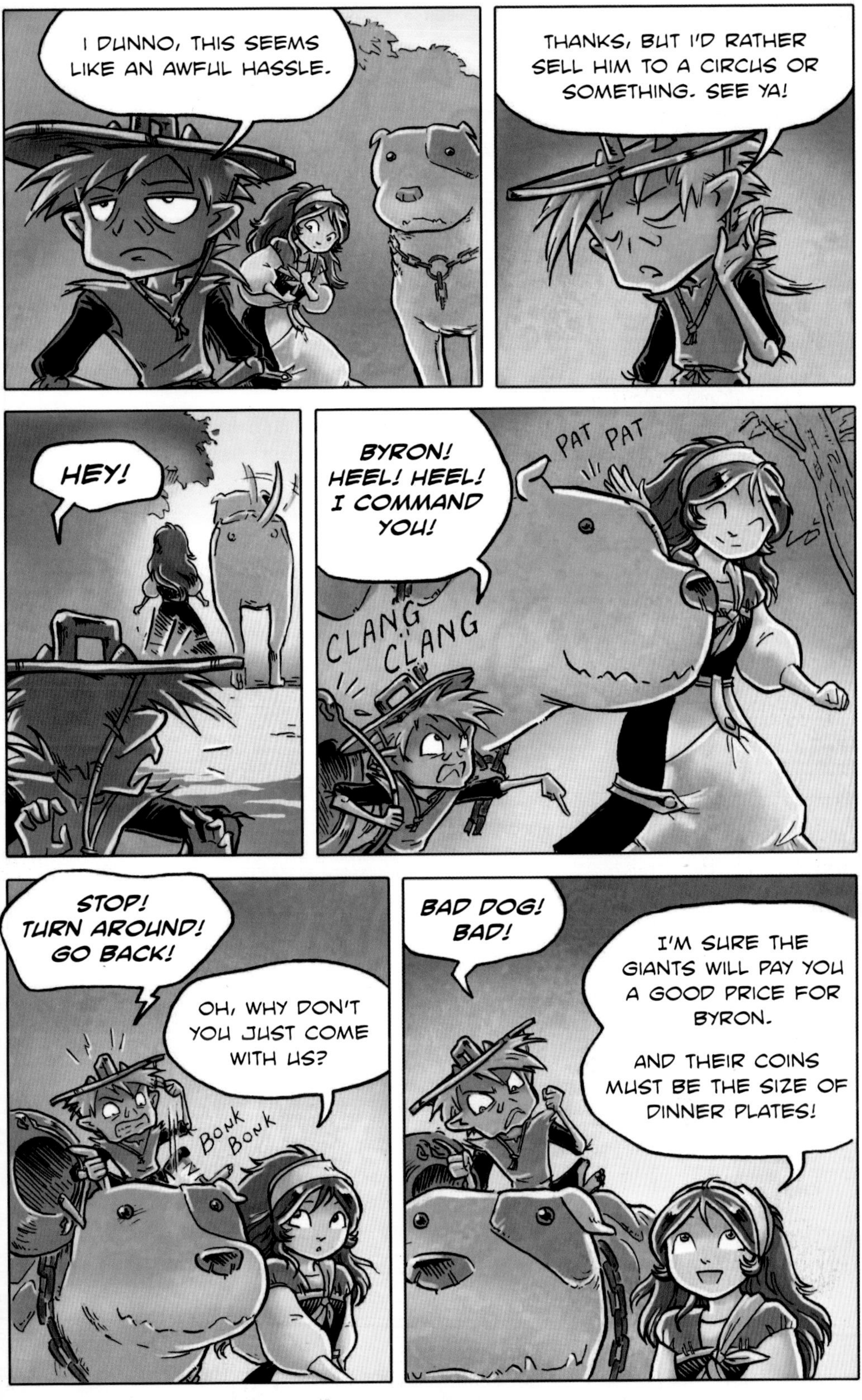
I DUNNO, THIS SEEMS LIKE AN AWFUL HASSLE.
THANKS, BUT I'D RATHER SELL HIM TO A CIRCUS OR SOMETHING. SEE YA!
HEY!
BYRON! HEEL! HEEL! I COMMAND YOU!
PAT PAT
CLANG CLANG
STOP! TURN AROUND! GO BACK!
OH, WHY DON'T YOU JUST COME WITH US?
BONK BONK
BAD DOG! BAD!
I'M SURE THE GIANTS WILL PAY YOU A GOOD PRICE FOR BYRON.
AND THEIR COINS MUST BE THE SIZE OF DINNER PLATES!

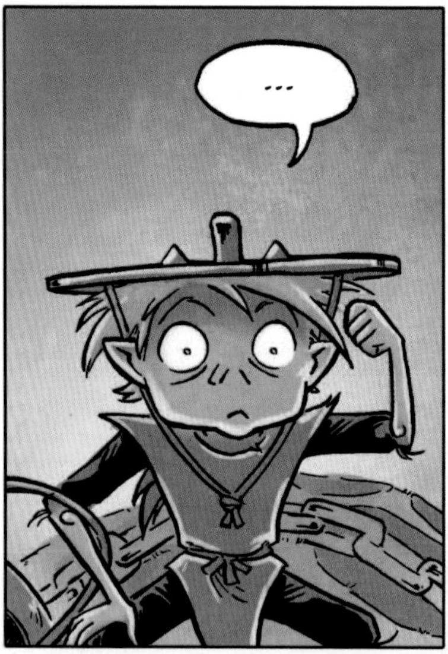
...

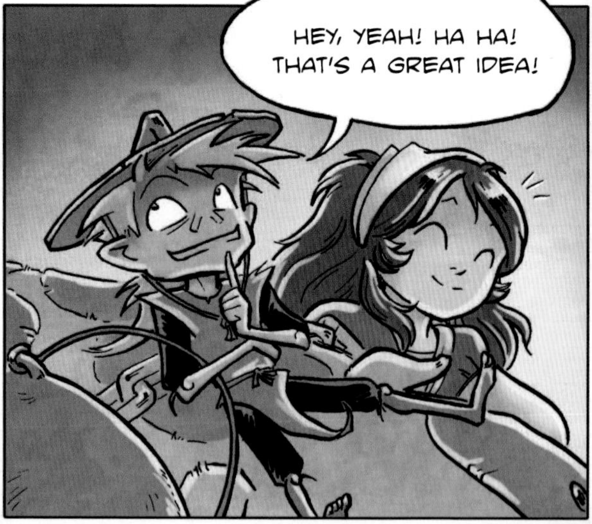
HEY, YEAH! HA HA!
THAT'S A GREAT IDEA!

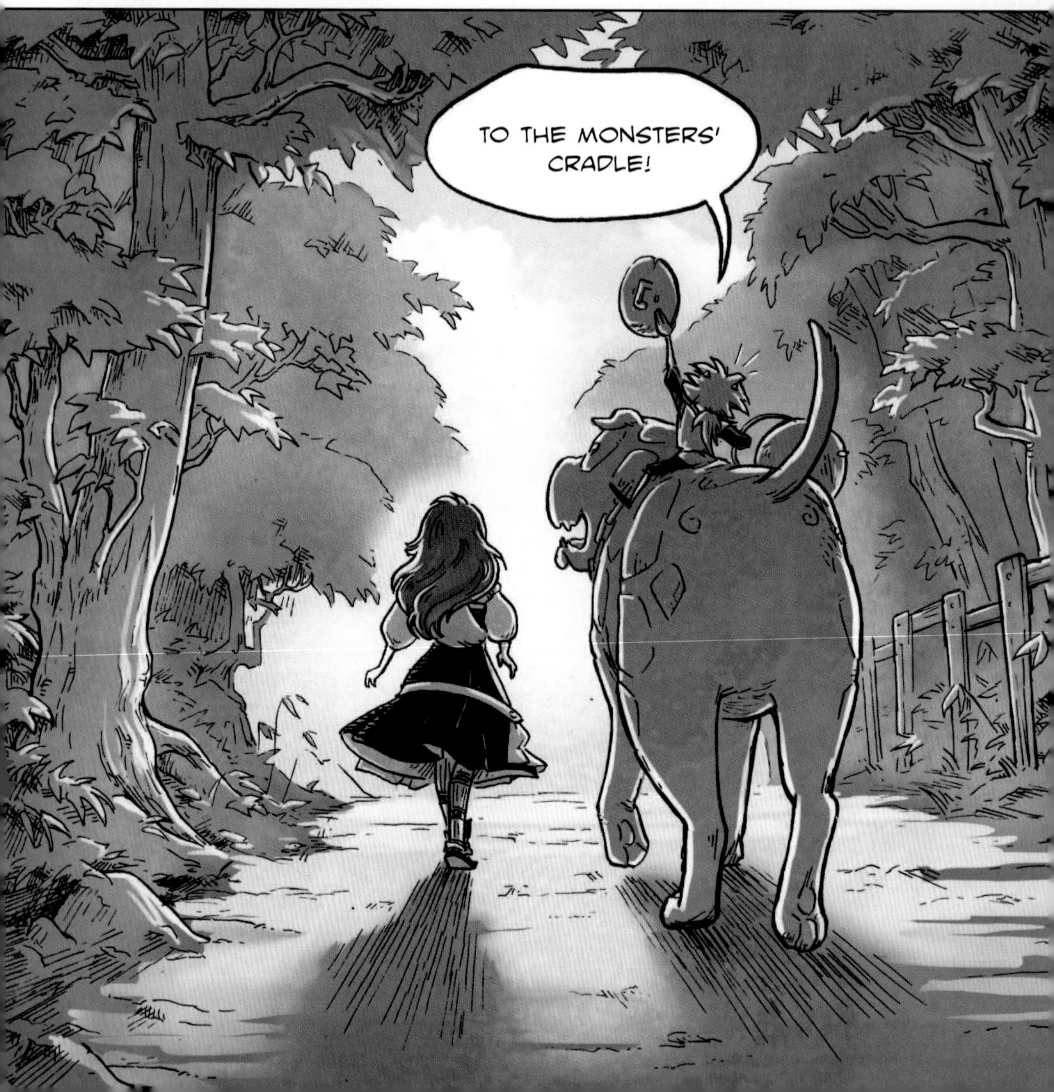
TO THE MONSTERS'
CRADLE!

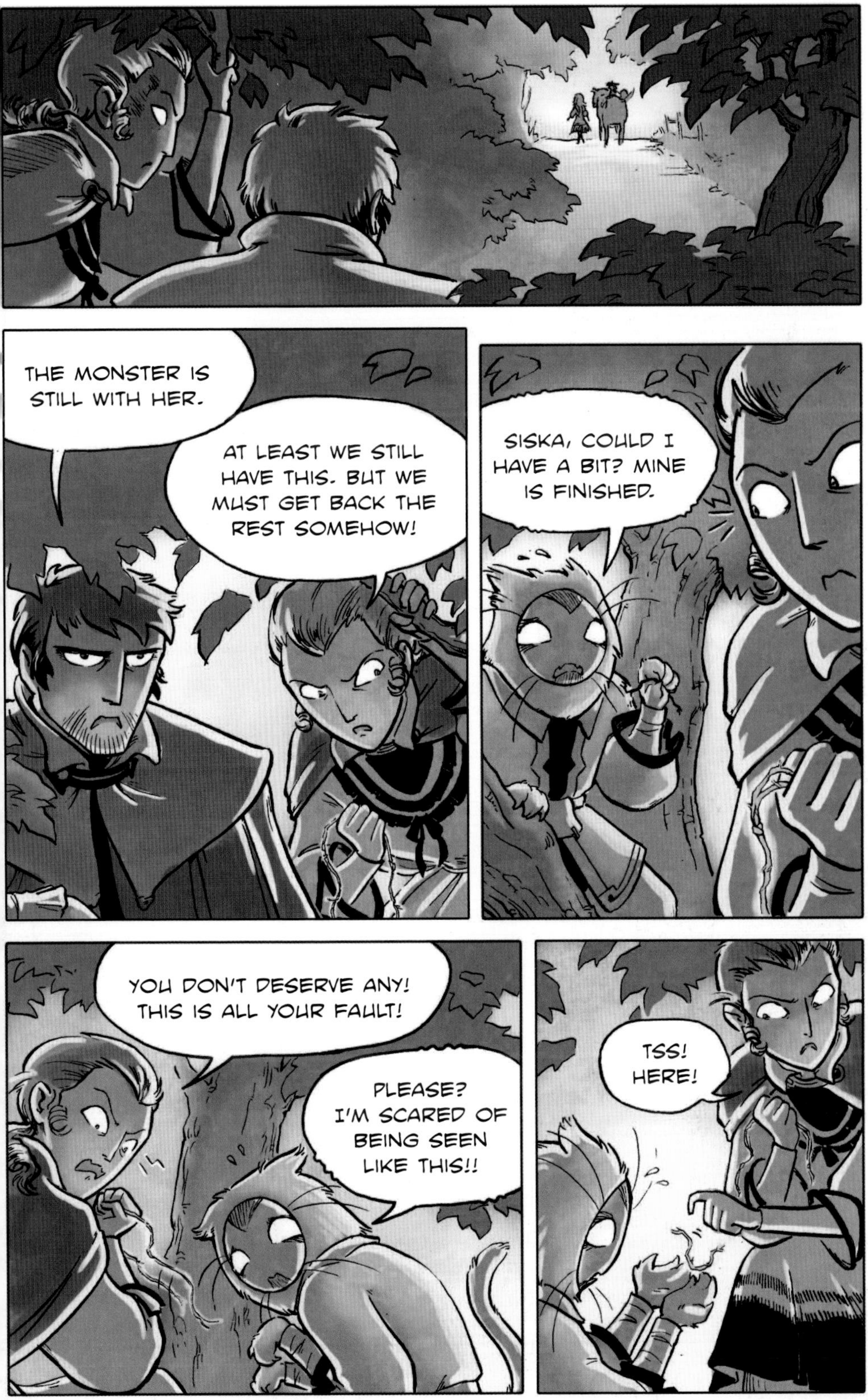
THE MONSTER IS STILL WITH HER.
AT LEAST WE STILL HAVE THIS. BUT WE MUST GET BACK THE REST SOMEHOW!
SISKA, COULD I HAVE A BIT? MINE IS FINISHED.
YOU DON'T DESERVE ANY! THIS IS ALL YOUR FAULT!
PLEASE? I'M SCARED OF BEING SEEN LIKE THIS!!
TSS! HERE!

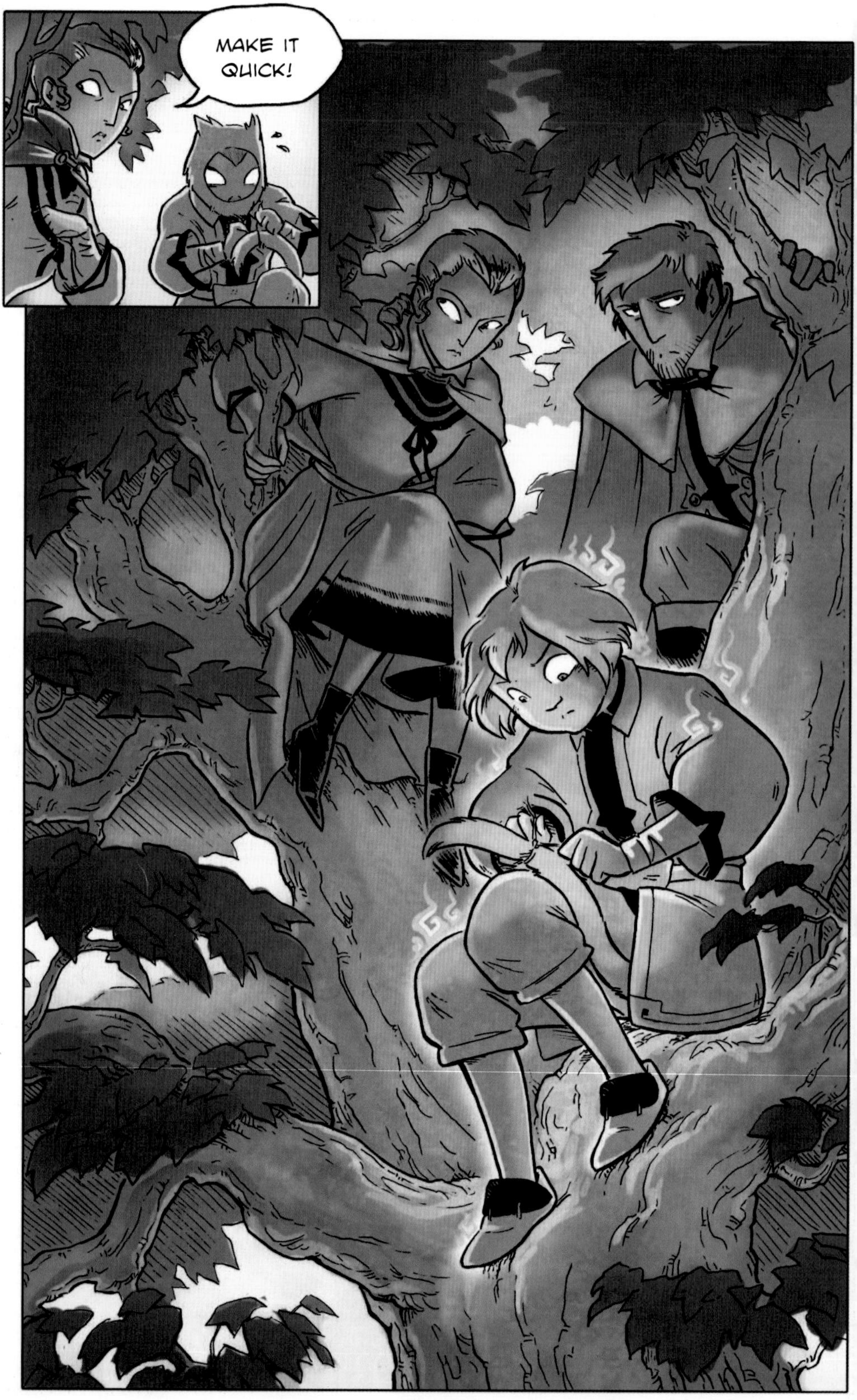
MAKE IT QUICK!

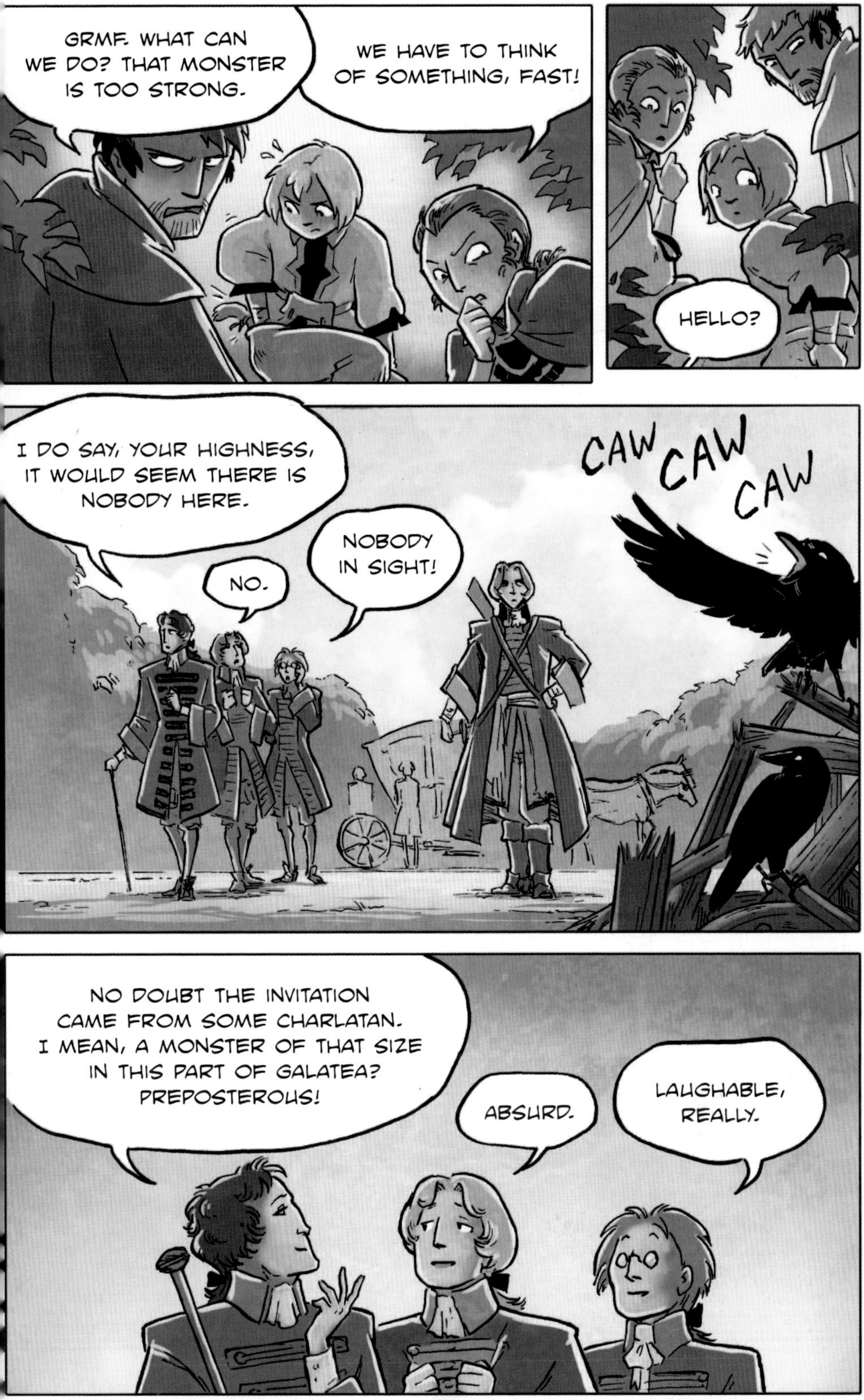
GRMF. WHAT CAN WE DO? THAT MONSTER IS TOO STRONG.
WE HAVE TO THINK OF SOMETHING, FAST!
HELLO?
I DO SAY, YOUR HIGHNESS, IT WOULD SEEM THERE IS NOBODY HERE.
NO.
NOBODY IN SIGHT!
CAW CAW CAW
NO DOUBT THE INVITATION CAME FROM SOME CHARLATAN. I MEAN, A MONSTER OF THAT SIZE IN THIS PART OF GALATEA? PREPOSTEROUS!
ABSURD.
LAUGHABLE, REALLY.

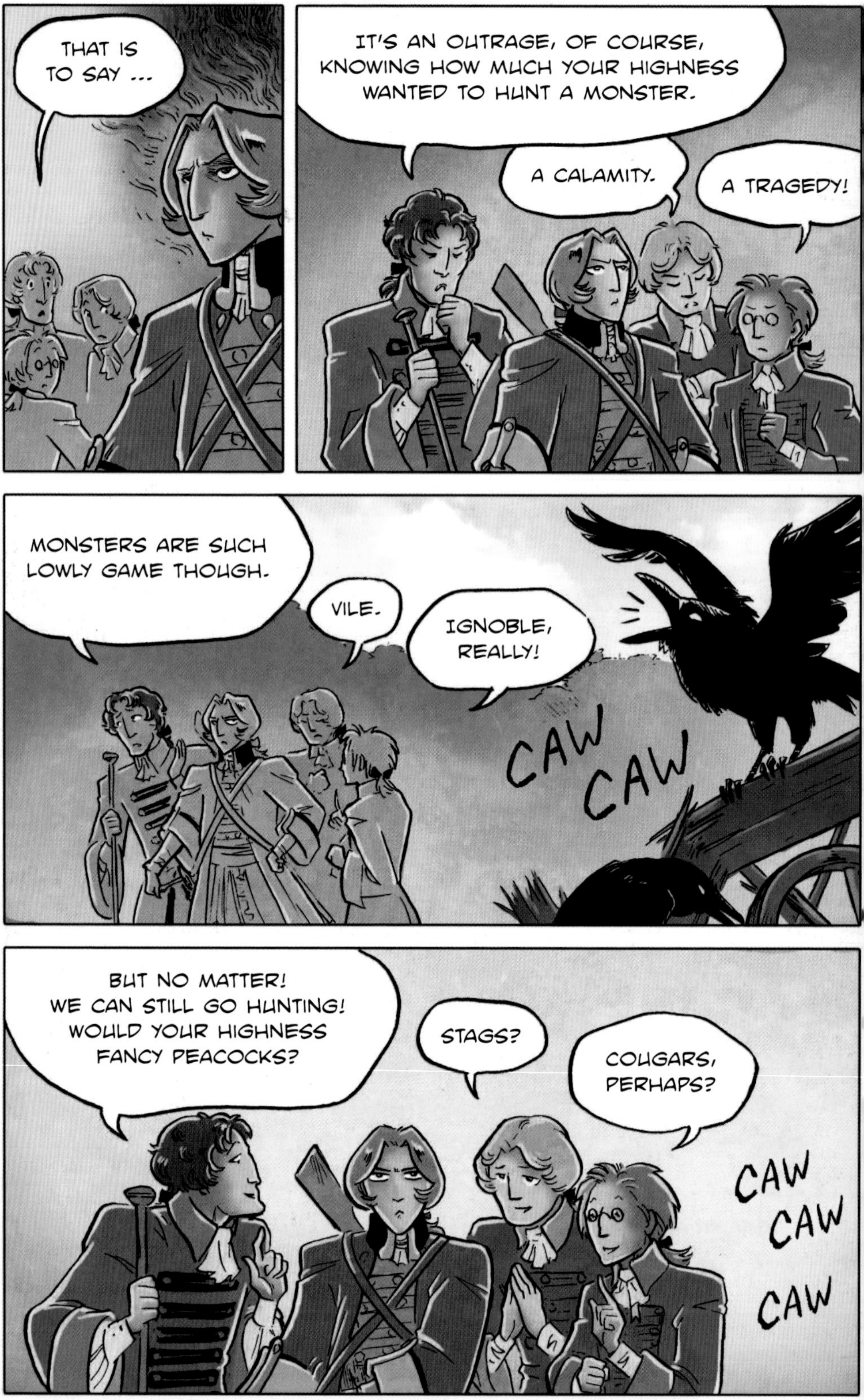
THAT IS TO SAY ...
IT'S AN OUTRAGE, OF COURSE, KNOWING HOW MUCH YOUR HIGHNESS WANTED TO HUNT A MONSTER.
A CALAMITY.
A TRAGEDY!
MONSTERS ARE SUCH LOWLY GAME THOUGH.
VILE.
IGNOBLE, REALLY!
CAW
CAW
BUT NO MATTER! WE CAN STILL GO HUNTING! WOULD YOUR HIGHNESS FANCY PEACOCKS?
STAGS?
COUGARS, PERHAPS?
CAW
CAW
CAW

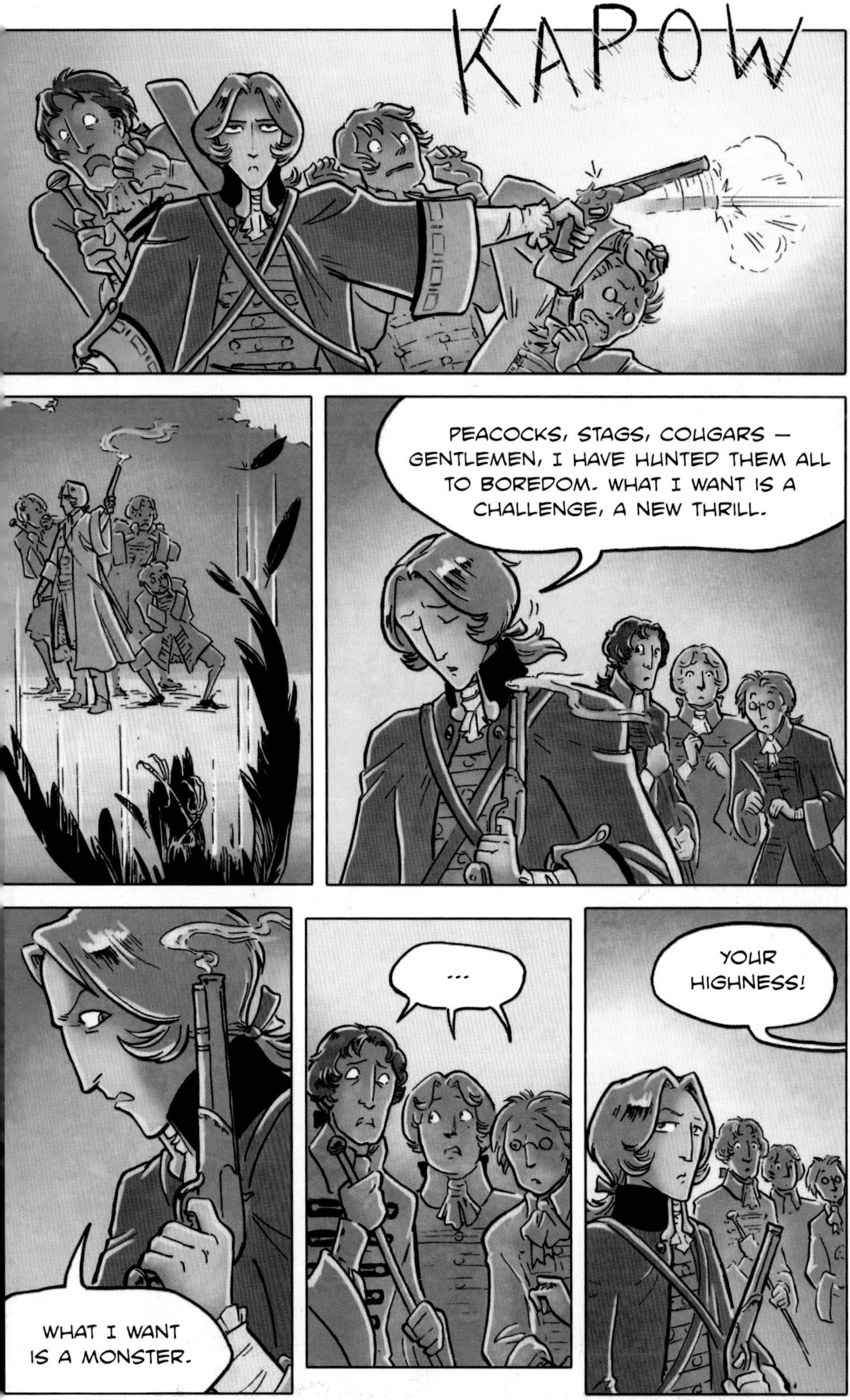
KAPOW
PEACOCKS, STAGS, COUGARS — GENTLEMEN, I HAVE HUNTED THEM ALL TO BOREDOM. WHAT I WANT IS A CHALLENGE, A NEW THRILL.
WHAT I WANT IS A MONSTER.
...
YOUR HIGHNESS!

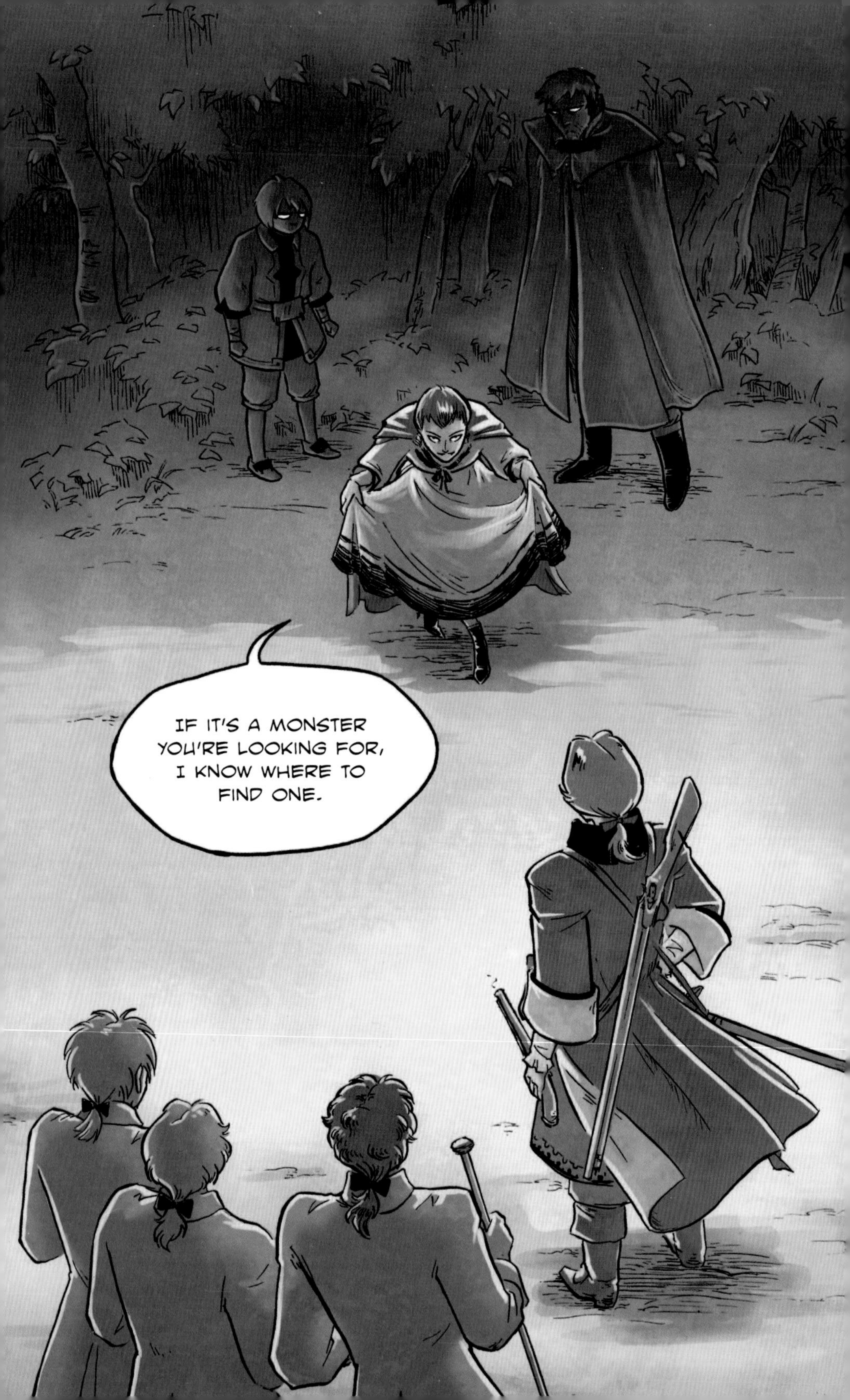
IF IT'S A MONSTER YOU'RE LOOKING FOR, I KNOW WHERE TO FIND ONE.